MURDER

at the Mardi Gras

ELISABET M. STONE

M. EVANS
Lanham • New York • Boulder • Toronto • Plymouth, UK

Contents

Maggie's latest escapade is for Joan Belmont, erstwhile roommate and permanent friend; from whom I have borrowed liberally (both strength and cash) and who stood by me through two wars— shooting and domestic. For this and a sight more, my love and my thanks— "Stoney"

MURDER AT THE MARDI GRAS

1. Ash Wednesday Sackcloth

THE day was Ash Wednesday—and I felt just like it. Sunk in gloom, I sat in front of my desk in the city room of New Orleans' leading afternoon daily and wished fervently I'd never met up with Mardi Gras.

In my typewriter was a sheet of copy paper which I'd stuck there almost an hour before. In the upper left corner were the words, "Slone, city desk, police rewrites." Except for them the paper was a blank. My brain was a blank too, unless you call a trio of fiendish hammers occupants. They were busy enough, all right. All banging away at once and off key.

I was in no mood to do police rewrites.

Unless you have celebrated a Mardi Gras in New Orleans you cannot know what Ash Wednesday really means. Mardi Gras takes place on the day before Ash Wednesday; the day preceding the Lenten season. After it you do penance for your sins—as I was doing. But Carnival day is the signal for everyone, residents and visitors alike, to ditch their inhibitions and go collectively nuts. From dawn of Shrove Tuesday, until the gray of Lent's first day streaks the sky and puts an end to the revelry, New Orleans is ruled by Rex, jovial monarch of frivolity, and anything goes. That is, anything short of murder. And years ago, when general masking lasted from sunup to midnight and the Mafia, with its vicious vendettas, was prevalent in the city, murder often got by too. It was easy to slide a knife into an enemy and slide off amongst the throng of maskers.

But that was many years ago and now, in the year of

11

1934, things had changed. Masking on the streets ended at
sundown and Rex, although he was still the theoretical
ruler of the city until midnight—and later—bowed to the
blue coat and billy rulers who managed to keep things
under fair control, especially as far as murder and mayhem
were concerned. However, even a full complement of the
representatives of law and order couldn't have kept this
Carnival from being the gayest and certainly the noisiest—
not to mention the wettest—Mardi Gras the city had put
on in years. It was the first one since the repeal of the
Eighteenth Amendment. As such, it called for a maximum
in celebration.

It got it.

From the river to the woods, as the city boundaries are
called, bars and cocktail lounges, night clubs and just plain
joints, had sprung up like toadstools. They had all worked
overtime serving thirsty customers who were doing their
patriotic best to help pay the tax on the copious supplies of
unfamiliar good legal whisky. At least that's how it had
seemed to me. Of course, I may have been prejudiced. I'd
been on my feet covering Carnival balls and brawls from
the start of the morning parade at eleven o'clock Tuesday
until Rex dismissed his riotous and somewhat unsteady
court and subjects at five of this, to me, unhappy Ash
Wednesday morning.

I picked up my penance—a stack of clippings to rewrite
—then leaned forward and rested my aching head on the
cool metal front of the typewriter. I closed my eyes and
hoped that whoever had first thought of Carnival was getting a justly deserved roasting. I wondered if there was a
drink of liquor left in the city after last night. Not that I
wanted one. Heaven forbid. I never wanted to smell the
nasty stuff again.

I riffled through the clippings and regarded them with
distaste, sighed gustily, and wondered if my city editor
had any of the milk of human kindness in his veins. Then I

wondered how I'd ever get through the rewrites, much less my own post-Carnival stuff which faced me in the form of a sheaf of notes.

I counted the clippings. Twelve—and they all had to be rewritten before I could even start on my own stories. Just how it was to be done was a problem for which I had no immediate answer. I certainly didn't feel like plowing through a lot of stale police news and redoing it. Nor did I feel up to arousing any creative ability to put into type several accounts of how superlatively special this post-prohibition Mardi Gras had been. In plain truth, I just didn't feel like working. I was a very sick woman.

I groaned audibly and laid down the clippings. Then I turned my head and glared at the back of the burly redhaired head of the city desk, one Dennis McCarthy, whom I had to thank for the stack of clips. On a childish impulse I stuck out my tongue at his hunched shoulders and caught the amused eyes of Jesse Carter, a slot man on the copy desk. He grinned, shrugged, and gave me the old thumbs-up signal. Dennis caught the byplay and swiveled around to see what I was up to. His keen gaze swept over the desk, took in the blank sheet of paper in the typewriter and the stack of clippings lying beside it.

He gave out with a yell.

"Slone! F'crissakes haven't you got that stuff up yet?"

The answer was right in front of him. It couldn't have been more obvious. But I shook my head anyhow—then groaned and wished I hadn't.

"Well, dammit, what's wrong with you? You got glue on your fingers or is it just that Carnival pasted up your brain?"

That called for a verbal reply.

"The last time I got glue on my fingers was when you got playful and smeared it on my typewriter keys," I said tartly. "As for my brain being pasted from Mardi Gras, I'd like to know just what you expect from someone who legged it for twenty hours on Carnival assignments. Anyhow, you expect too much and one of these days I'll—" The threat trailed off in a mumble as I turned back to my typewriter, eyes smarting from angry tears.

But Dennis was not in the mood to be mumbled at that morning. Maybe he felt like Ash Wednesday too.

"You'll what?" He asked.

"Walk out of this city room, that's what!" I spat the words like an angry cat. "And walk out for good, too."

"Oh sure. Sure you will." He sounded weary. "But right now, how about getting on those rewrites and getting them done?"

He swiveled back around and I contemplated his burly shoulders and considered rebellion. Walking out just before deadline would surely be rebellion in a big way. Then I reconsidered and remained in my chair. For ten years Dennis and I had been having periodic squabbles which usually occurred when I'd been working long hours on special assignment and was dead-beat and touchy. None had ever wound up in a really serious quarrel, meaning that he'd never fired me permanently and my angry threats to quit always proved empty. I liked my job. Most of the time I liked Dennis and I knew he felt the same about me. Twice during my ten years with the Phipps combine of morning and afternoon papers, I'd been transferred to the morning paper. Once it had been on my own request and once as a loan to do some special features. Both times I'd only been gone a short time when Dennis discovered a great and overwhelming need for my reportorial services and back to the afternoon sheet I went. So he seemed to have a certain fondness for me. I regarded the husky back with something almost approaching affection, got a glimpse of the big old-fashioned Seth Thomas pendulum job and got to work in a hurry. It was half-an-hour to deadline.

The clippings were strictly routine stuff and we should have had the stories right from the police press room over at headquarters. The rival morning paper had taken us beautifully on seven of the twelve stories, which indicated that our men had been out celebrating Carnival instead of covering their beats. I consigned them mentally to the hot place, felt a slight stirring of pity for them when Dennis caught up with 'em, and went to beating the typewriter keys. Five of twelve stories were finished when Dennis began heckling me.

"Maggie, haven't you finished those rewrites yet?"

"I haven't," I said icily. "And my name is *Margaret*. Don't call me Maggie."

He slanted a lop-sided grin around the room. I knew a rib was coming and braced myself for it. When he spoke, his voice was cheerfully informative.

"Slone once had a boy friend who called her 'Maggie darlin' " he said. "But they busted up and ever since she's had a peeve against a good old Irish name." He turned toward me. "What happened to that guy, Maggie? Did he marry another dame?"

I gritted my teeth and counted to ten. Then I smiled sweetly.

"Why yes, he did. As a matter of fact, he married an economy expert. Tell me, Denny, has your wife raised your allowance lately or does she still allow you two bucks a week for lunch money?"

Hastily swallowed laughs sounded around the room. Everyone in there knew how Dennis' wife rode him about economy. He half rose from his chair, an angry scowl on his reddened face. Then he settled calmly back again, a grin replacing the scowl.

"*Touché!*" He admitted. Then, "But you really shouldn't have given that away, Maggie. For your sake I've always kept quiet about your having had a crush on me and how I gave you the air."

I jumped from my chair, livid with fury. There was just enough truth in that statement for it to hurt. Dennis and I had gone around together, fairly regularly too. And it was true about his being the only person to ever call me Maggie and get away with it. I'd even begun to entertain rather serious thoughts about him when the paper hired an efficiency expert. Her name was Eileen Ryan. It was now Eileen McCarthy. I hadn't been hurt very much, not even in my pride. But his bringing that up made me wild.

"Dennis McCarthy! You know damned well that if you were the last man on earth and I was—"

"The last woman and so forth." He finished it for me. "Yeah, I know, kid. You made that plain enough in the old days. Now—"

He had led with his chin and I threw my best punch.

"Why Denny! I had no idea you really cared. If I had, I'd never have played fast and loose with you and driven you to another woman."

His jaw dropped, then he made a fast recovery.

"All I care about you, now or at anytime, is the work you do. And right now I want those rewrites. I won't need 'em tomorrow."

I remained standing, gripping the back of my chair and shaking—half from rage, unwarranted, and half from fatigue, warranted.

"Let someone else do them," I snapped. "I'm going home. If you'd hire an adequate staff there wouldn't always be a mess of stale news to rewrite from the other papers. Well, I'm not doing it. I'm leaving. Right now."

Dennis spoke gently and quietly. That was a danger signal which even I, in my present state of nerves and fury, recognized.

"You wouldn't quit on me right at deadline the day after Mardi Gras, would you kid? Go ahead and get those stories done, then, if you still want to walk out, I'll sign the chit for the cashier."

He turned back to his desk, only the rigidity of his back betraying his irritation.

I stood there another moment, then plumped angrily into

my seat and began working furiously, thinking: Very well, my fine feathered friend. I'll do these rewrites and then I'm through. Finished. Done.

I cleared away the seven remaining stories in a little better than five minutes. I did them the easy way. A brief phone talk with the desk sergeant on duty at headquarters provided new leads. I typed them, pasted the balance of the clippings under the new leads and began to wonder what I'd been so riled about. I handed them into the copy desk, being careful to avoid catching Dennis' eye, then I went back and settled down to my own Carnival stories.

I found that during the day and night, I'd collected material for one feature, three shorts, and an elegant hangover.

It lacked two minutes to deadline when I finished the four stories and handed them in, this time to Dennis. He merely grunted. There was no mention of a cashier's chit by either of us.

I plodded back to my chair, sat down, and yawned wearily. I wished the deadline coming up had been for the last edition rather than the first and wondered what Dennis would dream up for me to do next. When several minutes passed with no assignments in sight, I picked up the carbon dupes of the feature story and began glancing over the pages.

It was a good yarn—far too good for just a by-line. By-lines and a quarter will buy you a hot dog and a coke. Something of the sort had occurred to me in the early bloom of the evening before, an idea to do a story on what repeal meant to the New Orleans' cafés and try to sell it to a national magazine or a syndicate service. With that in mind, I'd collected far more material than I needed for my feature and while I waited for Dennis to call me, I began to scan the notes I'd taken down when I'd interviewed Gaston Villiere, owner of Le Coq d'Or.

2. "A Cold Hotness of Beauty"

GASTON'S café was famous for its food in a city where the best in food is the rule. This Carnival was very special to Villiere. He had been one of the few café owners who had observed the dry laws to the very letter. He had struggled through the lean, arid years of their enforcement, consistently refusing to serve or handle bootleg alcohol in any form and depending wholly on the reputation of his kitchen to see him through until, as he vividly expressed it, "This great countree comes to be sensible again." He held tightly to his belief that the country would get some sense and continued to serve fine cuisine, even though it must have broken his chef's heart to see it prepared without the delicate wine sauces which such dishes demanded for full flavor.

Like so many of the good French cafés, Le Coq d'Or was located in the Vieux Carré—New Orleans' famous Latin Quarter. Gaston had asked me for dinner as his guest and I'd arrived early and enjoyed a meal that had been excellent beyond description. Replete with fine food and in love with the world, particularly the President, I smiled at my host and began asking questions.

Gaston told me he had arrived in America some twenty-odd years before, landing in Boston. In his jeans was a substantial sum of money and in his heart he nourished a burning desire to cook fine French food. He obtained a job as chef of a New England restaurant and after two years of cooking boiled dinners, roast chicken, roast turkey, and codfish cakes, he fled to New Orleans where, he had

18

heard, he would find people who appreciated the subtler shades of his art.

He had added to his original funds by thrifty saving of a portion of his salary as chef in the east and he had enough money to purchase a café of his own. There he ran into a neat bit of luck, for a few days after his arrival Le Coq d'Or was put on the market. It had been one of the city's most popular cafés for many years, having been established in the early 1800's. Gaston bought it from the only surviving member of the Trezante family, a daughter who was not interested in carrying on the tradition of food. Gaston soon proved more than capable of carrying it on and the café became one of the most talked of and patronized French cafés in New Orleans. Soon its reputation spread throughout the country and epicures from all sections praised the fine cuisine served by Gaston.

He had been in his lucrative business about seven years when prohibition fell upon the land and the cafés of the country shuddered under the blow. But unlike most owners, Gaston did not succumb to the temptation of a back entrance. He simply went about revising recipes which called for wine and brandy sauces, using, when possible, flavoring that was non-alcoholic and adding extra spices to pep up the dishes. His place survived the drought without even one visit from "Pussyfoot" Johnson, the most famous federal snooper of the dry spell. That alone was something of a miracle, for few cafés had escaped Johnson's attention. I asked him how he had managed to evade at least one visitation from the fat man. "He visited every other place around," I said.

"I earned for myself the reputation of being the law-abiding man," he said. "I lived up to that reputation. Agents of the revenue offices, they come here, of course. After they come several times they learn that what is said of me is true, so they do not bother their chief when other places will provide them business. Even though I felt the law was all foolish and could not be enforced, I still did not break it—not even once."

"It's likely a good thing everyone wasn't like you about that," I smiled. "If they had been we might still have prohibition."

He gave me a startled look. "You know, I have given not one thought to that! That would have been very bad, eh?"

We laughed and he went on to tell me that business had been considerably larger in volume that day than it had during the preceding dry Carnivals. He had opened much earlier than usual, about seven a.m., and had served an unusually large breakfast crowd. Business had poured in all day and now, at dinner, the tables were filled and the waiters were rushing back and forth with heavily laden platters of food.

"*Mais oui,* it has been the busy time," he said. "I have been on the trot all day and until you came I had not sat myself down for one little minute. But you are my guest, so I must join you. You gave me the excuse to rest the poor feet, M'selle." He laughed and I asked him if he believed the increased business was due to his fresh license to serve liquor.

"In part, yes," he answered. "But I believe it is much more than just the bottled drinks we now dispense with legal sanction. I believe the largest portion of the business is among the real epicures who know that once more the sauces are being made with wine and the desserts trimmed with cognac. Et M'selle! Now we serve the *Café Diable,* which, as you know, is a part of the history of this city."

I agreed with him that it was. New Orleans was famous for *Café Brûle Diable,* a spiced coffee and brandy after-dinner drink, served aflame in a specially shaped silver bowl.

"Speaking of history, I know that the history of good French cuisine is right in this café," I said. "It has been here for over a century. How about telling me something of Le Coq d'Or's famous specialties, both your own and those you inherited with the purchase of the place?"

Talking about food was meat and drink to Gaston and he at once launched into a long description of what should or should not go into and with various dishes. I listened intently for several minutes but after awhile a part of my mind wandered away from his hosannas to food and I glanced idly about the room to see if I could spot anyone who might warrant mention in the story.

I located several familiar faces, not all friendly ones. Amongst the ones most intent on applying the fork to the mouth was the man who at the time was running the political show of the entire state. He was bitterly opposed by my paper and his hatred of our combine had led him to pull some pretty raw stuff. I thought, with some amusement, that regardless of what we thought of him personally, the fellow sure knew how to order food. The waiter was clearing away platters which had contained Oysters Rockefeller and was ready to serve sizzling hot *Pompano Pappillotte,* a real delight in fish dishes. It's made with a thick, highly seasoned sauce, baked and served in parchment bags. I jotted down the names of his guests and went on to scan the other tables.

I don't know to this day why I got so curious about four diners who occupied the table next to mine. They were all strangers. I couldn't have any real reason for my sudden interest. I studied the quartet for several seconds, particularly the two of the group who directly faced me. The woman was a stunning brunette of perhaps twenty-five, maybe thirty. The man was fair and about the same age. He would have been too pretty if it hadn't been for the saving grace of a too generous mouth.

My pointed scrutiny soon brought unpleasant results and I found myself being appraised by a pair of oblique green eyes which asked quite plainly just who did I think I was staring at and why.

I pulled my gaze away with an effort that was almost physical and suddenly it seemed important that I know the identity of this couple. I broke into Gaston's rhapsody on *Poulet au Gratin* to ask a question which was to involve me in a lot of trouble and excitement—but I couldn't know that then and I hadn't even the vaguest premonition.

"Gaston, who is that couple sitting at the table next to us? Your back is to them, so don't look right away. She's dark-haired and has green eyes. He's very fair and blue-eyed. Who are they?"

"Eh? Who is who?" Gaston asked, somewhat startled over being interrupted in his eulogy of chicken and cheese sauce.

I repeated the question and the warning not to look right away. The Frenchman smiled oddly and shrugged his shoulders.

"It is not necessary that I look at all, M'selle. I know the couple you speak about. But why should you inquire about *them?*"

I wondered why he accented the pronoun.

"I really don't know," I confessed, a little abashed. "There's something about them, particularly her, that attracted my attention."

"What, M'selle?"

I had a plausible reply for that one.

"She's terribly unusual looking. Very exotic. And she has the queerest eyes I've ever seen. They're a real bright green."

"Oh? And the man?"

I had a prompt answer for that one too.

"He looks damned unhappy. Even when he smiles his eyes are sad."

"Ah. Unhappy, eh? Well, I expect he has good reason to be unhappy."

"Then you do know them? Who are they, Gaston?"

He shook his head negatively. "No, I don't really know

them. But I do know her kind. She is bad. Bad through and through. She is evil, M'selle. All evil. Like someone fashioned by the devil himself."

I looked my shocked disbelief. And suddenly as I gazed at the strange expression on the usually amiable Gallic face, it seemed as if a cold wind passed through the café, bringing something faintly terrifying with it. I shivered as though I actually felt an icy breeze. When I spoke, my voice was strained and unnatural.

"What a perfectly horrid thing to say, Gaston! Why, she's really lovely."

"Lovely? Not at all, M'selle. To be sure she is of great beauty, but it is a cold hotness of beauty which puts into a man a devil which may drive him mad."

"A cold hotness of beauty." I repeated the phrase, struck by its strangeness. "Now just what do you mean by that remark?"

"Only what I say, M'selle. You are a reporter but your nature is unwise to evil. You see her only from the beautiful outside which she wears like a mask on a Carnival celebrant. Me, my eyes see more. They see inside and under the smooth skin and perfect features they see the evil which is in her. As for the cold hotness of her beauty, surely you know of the cold that is so hot it will burn through anything?"

I felt that the conversation was getting beyond my depth.

"We—ll." I hesitated. "I know about dry ice. I know it will burn the skin if you hold a piece of it long enough and that it also keeps things cold. I suppose it could be said to have a 'cold hotness.' But," I chuckled over the comparison, "I can't see any connection between that woman and refrigeration."

"So? Then I shall try to explain. The ice you speak of burns only the skin, perhaps the bone. But this one, her spell burns through to the soul."

He hunched closer to me, his voice so low it wasn't above

a whisper. He was deadly serious and I bent toward him, fascinated.

"*Oui,* M'selle. Her spell burns its evil way through flesh to the soul!"

"What do you mean?" I was whispering too.

"She is what you call a vampire. Oh, not the vampire of the movies, who lie on couches and make the eyes at a man. This one, she is a real vampire. She takes all and gives in return only enough of herself to keep alive the hunger for more, to keep the desire blazing higher and higher. When no more is left to take, when desire has consumed the heart and destroyed the soul in its unholy fire—pouf! She is *finis* and out you go—like that!" He spread his hands out in a dramatic gesture and sat back in his chair. He was breathing as hard as a runner at the end of a race.

My breathing was a little uneven too; the effect of his words and manner. Covertly, I studied the strange-eyed woman, trying to see what Gaston seemed to see so plainly and which I didn't see at all.

Finally, I shook my head. "You're way off the track if you mean she's after money. That man is not in any upper income tax bracket. And there's a look of the theater about them both. A—well, a *transient* look. It may be racetrack. It could be very easily. His clothes are good, but they weren't tailored on Park Avenue or Bond Street. They're somewhat flashy while still being in fairly good taste and style. Nope. You're wrong, Gaston." I had made up my mind. "There's no gold-digging intent with that woman."

He turned large, expressive black eyes on me. They conveyed a sort of wonderment at my stupidity. I squirmed slightly, feeling I must *be* stupid.

"*Mais non,* M'selle. You have misunderstood me. It is not of money I speak when I say she takes all from a man. As a matter of fact, money means little to her. It is the heart and soul she steals and kills. Like the great vampire bats of Hungary who suck the blood from their victims and cast away the drained body. She does the same—only it is the heart and soul she drains and destroys."

This time the shock left me speechless. Minutes went by while I tried to recover my voice, to protest against his violent words. At last I managed to stammer, "But, but, Gaston! The soul is immortal. As a Catholic you know that perfectly well. You can't destroy the immortal soul. You, well, you just can't do it!"

"You may think not, M'selle. As I said before, you are unwise to evil. But if a man takes his own life or sells himself to the devil, all because of a woman, is not his soul destroyed? If he becomes a criminal and when he can no longer bear the ruin she has brought upon him and he destroys her, does he not, to all intent and purpose, also destroy his soul?"

I sat there feeling damned uncomfortable and not at all sure about the finer points of the destruction of something I'd always been taught was immortal. I wished heartily I'd never asked about the two strangers. Then I laughed shortly. "Well, you could be right about her I guess. I think you're wrong. But it does seem you are very much upset and in a dither over people you said yourself you didn't know. I don't believe she's like that at all. She is plenty conceited, and with good reason, but she's not very destructive looking. Except that just looking at her would destroy almost any other woman's conceit in her own looks."

"She is like I said," he stated flatly. "It is not necessary for me to know them to know that she will ruin that man. But someday there will come the man who will resist her spell, even though he may succumb to it for a short while. That is the man who will destroy her. That man she must meet someday."

"Gaston, you give me the creeps!" I exclaimed with a shudder. "This is a fine conversation for a Carnival night. You know what I think? I think you're just trying to give me an added Mardi Gras thrill. You really can't expect me to believe you arrived at that awful judgment of her just from seeing them dining here tonight. It's ridiculous."

For a long, tense moment his eyes held mine. Then he shook his head and smiled easily.

"Carnival thrill? But *non*, I am not trying to give you the thrill or the creeps. And tonight is not the first time I have seen these two. They have dined here regularly this winter. I recognize her type and I watch and observe. Soon I know I am right about her. What I have said to you is what I believe to be true about her. That is all."

"All!" I retorted. "I think it's plenty. And see here, Gaston. You don't fool me. I know a part of your popularity is based on the personal interest you take in your clients. If they've been here all through the winter, what you've been saying is more than just surmise. Now who are they? Where are they from? What do you really know about them?"

He quirked a quizzical eyebrow at me. "The inquisitive reporter, eh?"

I nodded my head vigorously. "Certainly. That's my job."

"Well, I shall try to gratify your curiosity but I warn you it will not be much more than just suppositions on my part. What the *gendarmes* call the deductions. Very well: She is French but I am not sure just where she came from originally. She speaks a fluent, grammatical French—but her English is also fluent and grammatical and without even so much accent as mine. Her French is certainly not the dialect of Louisiana, nor is it of any of the French *provences* with which I am familiar. Nor is it exactly of Paris. Perhaps Canada, a convent in Canada. There she could have learned such purely accented French and also unaccented English. *Bien?*"

"I suppose so." I nodded agreement.

"Good. Then a convent in Canada is indicated. To continue: She is of the theater, as you astutely placed her. What she does, I don't know. I have heard her refer to being in plays. The man? Well, he may be her husband. Most certainly he is her lover and they are in abode together at this time. Now, M'selle, does that satisfy your curiosity?"

"Ummmm. Only in part. Do you know her name—or his?"

"*Oui*—in part. He calls her Nita, she calls him Don."

"So much for that." I shrugged. "What really intrigued me was your peculiar antipathy toward her—your assertion that she is bad, evil—whatever you want to call it."

"Ah? So that is what interests you? Well, I shall explain that quite easily. Once I knew such a one as she is. *Mon Dieu!* How long ago that was. Over twenty-five years have gone by since then and I am not yet recovered from the spell and the curse she placed on me. She would have destroyed me. Almost she did—but not quite. *Non,* not quite! And that is how I know about this one. Yes, that is—"

His voice trailed off and he sat lost in his unhappy memories, his heavy, white hair falling in curls over his broad forehead, his full, well-shaped mouth drawn into a taut line. For a moment I had the uncanny feeling that something—or someone—had joined us at table. Perhaps the ghost he had invoked had responded and was lingering near us. I caught my breath and shivered as I remembered the old nursery saying: "Someone just trod on my grave."

As I watched him, he brushed his hair back, raised his head and looked full into my eyes. The expression I saw in his caused me to gasp and drop my own gaze to the table. They held pain and hate—naked and terribly alive. I had the feeling of a stranger intruding on a private and violent scene. It was not comfortable.

Then he gave a short, harsh laugh and the spell was broken. When I looked up it was to find his eyes twinkling merrily, lights glinting in their dark depths. The stern tautness of his mouth had dissolved in a pleasant smile. A little taken aback at the complete reversal, I was nevertheless relieved. It had been a peculiarly bad moment.

He clapped his hands together and exclaimed, "Now,

then, I am desolate! I have made for you a bad feeling and that should not happen on such a gay Mardi Gras. To make amends and restore your smile, I shall order for you *Café Diable*. You approve?"

"I should say so! It's just what the doctor ordered."

"*Bien*. Dr. Gaston, he knows what to order for his patients." He smiled and summoned the head waiter, Martin, a suave, smiling, dark-haired Frenchman who looked enough like Gaston to be his brother and who had been working in the café, first as a waiter, then as maître d'hôtel for as long as I'd been going there, which was about ten years.

"Martin, bring at once the *Brûle* for M'selle. It is a special Mardi Gras prescription, which I have ordered." Gaston smiled at both of us and Martin hurried away, collecting a waiter as he went off.

When they returned with the *Brûle* bowl and the ingredients, Gaston prepared the spicy beverage, filled my demitasse cup and then excused himself and strolled off among the tables. I watched him as he stopped, first at one and then another, greeting old friends and meeting new ones.

I sat sipping the fragrant coffee, knowing I should be on my way to other spots which must be covered before the night's work was done. I knew perfectly well that the longer I lingered in Gaston's, the longer and later I'd be working. But I reminded myself that the late parades would not hit Canal street before ten o'clock. Besides, no one working on a New Orleans' paper ever expected to get much sleep on Mardi Gras night. So I sat and sipped—and the specter of Ash Wednesday morning was far away and not at all alarming. Once again my eyes turned to the next table and the diners who had interested me so much.

3. Emerald-Eyed Hell Cat

THE couple sat with two other people, another man and woman. I could see the full features of the green-eyed girl, the fair-haired man, and the other woman. She was a red-gold blonde, younger than the other one, not so exotic in appearance but with much more than a run of the mill prettiness. Her eyes were a soft and very dark blue, almost the color of violets and she had fine-grained, clear pale skin. All I could see of the fourth member of the party was the back of a crisply curled, dark brown head and an occasional glimpse of a turned-up nose and a determined looking chin and jaw line in profile.

It was apparent the older girl was the dominant member of the group. Her appeal was so magnetic it was like a physical touch. Others must have felt it too, as I noticed a number of diners casting glances her way and more than one man hastily recalled his wandering attention at a sharp word from his companion.

Her eyes were what got me. Slightly slanted, they were clear, dark-green. I mean the shade of emeralds; cold, bright, and compelling attention. And they could be challenging. I'd already found that out once and I learned it again when, for the second time, my obvious interest annoyed her.

She summoned Martin and when he was almost beside her she caught my gaze and held it. I couldn't have looked away if I'd wanted. It was an odd, almost uncanny feeling. Without releasing me, she spoke to Martin in rapid French. It was too rapid for my knowledge of the language, so I didn't understand a single word. I caught his answer, however. I think he meant for me to do so as he spoke very slowly and very distinctly and he knew I spoke a little French.

"The mamselle you ask about is a reporter," he said, in effect. "I'm sure she means no offense in staring at you. Madame is unusually beautiful and reporters are curious people who are always curious about other people."

She released my gaze then, much to my relief, and laughed lightly. She answered in English, for my benefit.

"Oh! A reporter. Well, I expect that does account for her rudeness."

I felt like a fool. I also wondered how much Martin had heard when Gaston and I had been talking about her. I recalled he had been hovering about as we talked. I decided to take my eyes and ears out of there and put them to work where they would be less resented. I began to gather my things and was cramming them in my purse when the fair man spoke. I couldn't help overhearing. It seemed he was indirectly apologizing to me for her having embarrassed me.

"Really, Nita," he said, "it seems to me you might be a little less blunt about something like this. Besides, you never seemed to object to being looked at before—on the contrary. And I don't think it is ever anything but rude to speak a language which others in your party can't understand."

"Really, Don!" She mocked his tone. "It seems to me you should know perfectly well that I don't give a damn what you think or don't think. Anyhow, I was merely inquiring about something which intrigued me. That's nothing to get upset about."

Vaguely resentful about being referred to as a "something," I waited to hear his reply. I could see her words had hit him pretty hard. I wondered how he'd take being talked to like that, but the well-formed and slightly weak chin, the gentle, light-blue eyes, marked him as a temporizer in my opinion. When he spoke his voice was low and hurt.

"You never have given a damn about what I think. Yes, I know that well enough. You've never really given much of a damn about what I do, either. I often wonder if you even give a damn about me."

She leaned back in her chair, an amused smile playing about her full, beautifully-shaped mouth.

"Now you're making it personal—and dramatic. A moment ago you accused me of being rude for speaking in my own language. Why bring in the personal business?"

"I don't mean to be dramatic or personal. It was you who said you didn't give a damn what I thought when I said it was rude to use a language others don't understand."

"If others speak nothing but English, it's their fault," she said, a tinge of a sneer in her voice. "The American schools teach other languages but English. And, whether you like it or not, I shall speak French whenever and wherever I wish. The only charm I have found in this filthy city is that there are people who speak a passable French."

A deep, pleasant baritone voice, which belonged to the man with the solid chin, said mildly, "That's just because you close your eyes to the real charm of New Orleans, Nita. And see here, my girl, I don't mind your rattling off in French, or Arabic either, if it pleases you. What I do resent is your calling my town filthy when it's only slightly soiled in spots."

The lighter note relaxed the tension and for a moment it looked as if the bicker would end in a laugh. But the red-haired girl fixed that. In a deceptively sweet voice she said blandly,

"Really, Nita, I don't mind your speaking French. And Mike just told you he doesn't mind. I don't see why Don should have felt it necessary to call you down about it."

The green eyes glinted angrily and I thought: Oh, oh! That's torn it.

"I'd thank you to mind your own business, Bette," she said, her voice tense with anger.

"I am." Bette's voice was still sweetly calm. "It was my party and therefore it is my business. I'm only trying to keep things pleasant."

"Pleasant!" Nita sneered at the smiling girl. "You must take me for a fool if you don't think I see through you. You want to keep the party together so you can sit and drool at Don!"

"Nita!" Don's exclamation held shock and a curious undertone of fear. I thought: Ah ha. So that's how the land lies.

"Yes?" The green eyes were spitting venom.

"How can you say such a thing? Bette's been damn decent to us. Please—"

"You, too, must take me for an imbecile!" She interrupted. "Decent, eh? She knew damned well the only chance she had to see you was to crawl to me. You know it too."

Near-by diners were all showing interest in the scene which threatened to become a brawl. I saw Martin beckon Gaston, urgency in the gesture. Before Gaston got there, Don spoke sternly.

"You're just being nasty and spoiling the evening for all of us. No one forced you to come out tonight. It was you who insisted on our accepting Bette's invitation. You're not acting like a lady and you owe Bette and Mike an apology."

I applauded silently. I hadn't thought he had it in him to tell her off so bluntly. She rose, pushed back her chair with a violent gesture that almost overturned it and lashed out at him, literally hissing her words.

"Apologize! How dare you presume to call me down? What are you? A cheap race track tout or a chorus boy with a common mid-West farm background! And you dare tell me how to behave? You *cochon!*"

"That means pig." Bette translated calmly. "It's one French word I do know. Now let me tell you something, Nita. Ever since I've known you, you have claimed to be of royal French descent. Well, right now you're acting like a royal ass. As for your claim to nobility, right here in New Orleans we have a number of families which began with the natural sons of French noblemen. You knew what Don was when you first met him. He may be a tout and he may be a chorus dancer and he may have been born on a farm. At least, he knows who his father was. Can you say the same?"

I saw the glint of steel as the woman lunged at the redhead. "Watch it! She has a knife!" I screamed the warning.

Gaston's steak knives are very sharp. If that one had found its mark, I'd have been an eye witness to a murder. But Mike reacted swiftly, caught her arm as she struck and the knife clattered harmlessly to the floor. She struggled to break his iron hold on her arm, a stream of mixed French and English invective pouring from her lips. Finally, panting and squirming, she screamed at Bette.

"Red-headed bitch! You can have him and welcome. I wanted him and I took him. But I'm done now and he's all yours. You can—"

Gaston's arrival put a stop to whatever else she was going to say. The Frenchman was sputtering in outraged shock. Things like this just didn't happen in Le Coq d'Or.

"Madame!" He expostulated, stepping in front of her. "This is not the place for such fighting between ladies. If you wish to act in a manner of the fishwife, please to go to places where such action is permit!"

She broke into vehement French, eyes, mouth, hands working like mad. She was beautiful, even in her vicious fury, but I was now quite willing to admit that perhaps Gaston was a better judge of human nature than I. At any rate, she was a first-class hellion.

Gaston listened to her rapid speech for a moment, then broke into it to say firmly, in English, "I am most regretful, but Madame and her party must leave at once."

Don stepped to her side. "I'm very sorry this happened, Mr. Villiere. We shall leave as soon as we settle the bill."

Gaston turned to a hovering group of waiters and singled out one. "Louis, you serve this party?"

The man nodded.

"Then bring at once the check. At once, please."

"*Oui,* M'sieu!" Louis scurried off toward the cashier's desk in the rear of the room.

"Just one moment, all of you." Nita's voice was now even and coldly controlled. Only her eyes betrayed her anger. She turned to Don. "You may leave with your friends—or remain with them. I leave alone and I never want to see any of you again. I'm fed to the teeth with all of you and I'm through. Quite through. Do you understand?"

"Yes dear." His tone was meant to be soothing but it had the sound of a voice speaking to a child in a tantrum. "I understand. Now let me take you home. Come, dear—"

With a violent gesture she pushed him aside. "I said I was through and I meant it," she said through clenched teeth. "Go back to your perch on a race track rail you—you cheap tout!"

I giggled nervously. The term seemed so mild for the scene. She gave me an angry glare, then addressed Gaston.

"I regret that I have disturbed the placidity of your café, M'sieu Villiere, and I will leave now. But I shall return again to eat your fine food. And next time I shall come alone and perhaps you will speak with me in French, *n'est ce pas?*"

Gaston's expression was the blank one of a café owner in a tough spot. He bowed courteously. "The disturbance is ended. I trust Madame will reconsider her intention to return. There must be other cafés in the city where Madame will find a host who speaks French. Good night, Madame."

She laughed lightly. "*Bon soir,* M'sieu Villiere—but not *adieu.*" Without even a glance at the other three, she walked casually to the door, opened it, and stepped out into the crowded street.

4. *Recipe for Tragedy*

DON, Mike, and Bette made no move to stop Nita from leaving nor did they make any move to follow her from the café. The three stood silently, waiting for the check. After a moment or so, Bette placed a hand on Don's arm and spoke to him. Tears were in her voice; they glistened on the long, golden-tipped eyelashes.

"I'm sorry, Don. This was all my fault and I've caused you a lot of trouble. I should have kept my mouth shut, but I guess I just got so full I spilled over. Truly, I'm sorry."

He turned to her almost violently, "Don't apologize to me! You, of all people!"

"But it was my fault," she insisted.

"No it wasn't." He smiled ruefully. "And, if it had been, think of the many bad times I've let you in for—things like tonight. But this was no one's fault. It had to come, sooner or later."

"Do you—well, do you think she'll leave you? I mean leave you for good?"

Unexpectedly Mike answered. "Hell, no, she won't leave him! Why get your hopes up? This isn't the first time you thought she was through when she wasn't. For God's sake, Bette, where's your pride?"

"Mike!" Her voice was icy. "How dare you?"

"How dare I? My God! How can I sit by silently and let you be—"

"That will do, Mike." Bette interrupted curtly. "This is none of your business."

"You're forgetting yourself, O'Leary." Don's voice was

35

cool and slightly edged. "I know Nita behaved badly. She's high-strung and temperamental, like all actresses. She lost her temper but she'll get over it—" There was a note of uncertainty in the last words.

"You'd be a damn sight better off if she didn't get over it and gave you the air!" Mike burst out. "So she's an actress? She's had a couple of bits in musicals and she calls herself an actress and pulls the old temperament gag. If Bette had any sense she'd get herself—"

"Shut up, O'Leary—before you say something you'll be sorry for." Don took a threatening step forward, although the other man topped him by inches and outweighed him by pounds.

"Yes, Mike, shut up." Bette echoed the command in a dull voice. "Here's the check. Let's pay it and get out of this place."

"All right, all right." He handed a bill to the anxious Louis, telling him to keep the change. Then he turned to Bette. "Okay, hon, I'll shut up. But if they can't get along together why the hell doesn't one or the other of them clear out and stay out?"

"I don't clear out, because I couldn't live without her. I know because I tried to before this. However, I can't see that my feelings are any concern of your's. Let's go."

"I don't know about your feelings, but your actions toward Bette *are* of some concern to me. I've stood by for years waiting for her to come to her senses and get—"

"Mike O'Leary!" Bette stamped her foot angrily. "You'd better keep your mouth shut."

"Okay, okay! I'll shut up and go on hoping. I should be used to it by now. Let's beat it."

They turned toward the door but Gaston suddenly blocked the way. He put a hand on Don's arm and, almost apologetically, asked,

"M'sieu, I would speak to you. Could you give me one moment?"

Don looked puzzled but drew back. "You two go ahead," he told the couple. "I think I'll go home and see if I can't —never mind. Just you go ahead and enjoy yourselves."

Bette and Mike looked at him for a second, she with her heart in her eyes, then they turned and left the café.

"Yes, Mr. Villiere?" Don questioned.

"Would you come to my office? I would speak to you about this woman—this Nita."

Instantly the man stiffened. "What you have to say about Nita does not require my going to your office, I'm sure."

They had moved closer to my table and I had no difficulty in hearing every word Gaston said as, in a low, hurried voice, he spoke earnestly. "You will consider this the impertinence, M'sieu, which is why I wished to say it in my office. Please take the advice of one who knows what he speaks about and leave you that woman. Leave her at once. Do not even go back to your rooms for your clothes. M'sieu—" His voice became pleading as he saw the man's face close against him and cold fury dawn in his eyes. "M'sieu, I would not have the temerity to so address you if I did not have it in my heart to help you. But I have watched you and this woman and I know where it is you are headed. So, I beg of you, if you would save yourself, go now and never see her again. You have a chance to escape—you may not have another."

Don stood there, frozen in icy anger. Then he asked coldly, "Are you quite finished with your impertinent and unsolicited advice?"

Gaston's shrug was eloquent of defeat. "*Oui*, I am finished. I only had a hope to help you as someone once tried to help me in a like circumstance. *Adieu*, M'sieu, I ask your—"

The end of the apology was left floating in the air as Don stalked from the room.

Gaston dropped heavily into the chair opposite me. I wondered what the hell and waited for him to speak. I couldn't help feeling Don had reason to think the café owner impertinent.

He spread out his hands. "Well, *c'est fini.* I have done all I could."

"And got properly told off for your efforts," I said tartly. "And I don't know that I blame him for telling you off. It would have been different if you had known them."

"Would it?" He lifted his eyebrows. "I wonder. But you, M'selle, do you now see what I meant about that woman?"

"I'm not sure yet just what you meant. As for what I saw —well, I saw one elegant exhibition of temper. I saw that the girl, Bette, is in love with Don and that Mike, who paid the bill, is in love with Bette, while Don is insanely in love with Nita, who appears to be infernally jealous of him—so she probably loves him. Summed up it looks to me like a fine recipe for scandal."

He shook his head slowly.

"It is a recipe for tragedy, M'selle. A terrible tragedy. The kind that makes for the newspaper headline news."

"Suits me," I said callously.

"Of course," he answered, unsmiling. "For you it would suit. You see in it a story, but you also see other things. You noticed that the golden-haired one loves this Don with a fire which is consuming her from within. Also that the other man loves her."

"Oh, I wouldn't say she was being consumed by her love for Don. If she is, she's crazy to let herself get so mad about a married man."

He turned searching black eyes on me. "What makes you so sure Don and Nita are married?"

I'd had just about enough serious talk for a Mardi Gras night. I grinned impudently at him and gathered my things together again.

"Well," I drawled, "they're either married or they're damned well living in sin. Or, as you so politely phrased it earlier, are 'in residence together at the moment.' In any case, it's none of my business. Nor," I added somewhat pointedly, "is it your business, my friend."

"No, it isn't my affair, M'selle. Though I admit I tried to make it mine." He smiled ruefully. "Well, as you say, I got told off. It was the unwise thing for me to do. I know that now. But, mark me, M'selle. We have not heard the last of those two and when we do—" He shrugged and left the rest up to my imagination.

I imitated his shrug. "You may not have heard the last of her—she said she'd be back to see you. As for me, unless they do something spectacular, like killing each other, they're no interest of mine. I doubt seriously if I'll ever run into them again."

That was what I thought then. In less than twenty-four hours I found I was wrong about that surmise.

"I hope she has the good sense to stay away from here," Gaston said with tart asperity. "I shall refuse to serve her if she returns. I do not wish her patronage. Her visit would be mutually embarrassing."

"You certainly are down on a strange woman just because she belongs to a type you dislike. Well, it's your café and you can keep her out if you don't want her in here. And I wish you'd have tossed me out long ago! I've places to get to and it will take me the rest of the night to make them all."

"Toss you out? Never, M'selle. Your company I enjoy always. Come again, come whenever you wish."

I thanked him for the dinner and unexpected entertainment. Then I left the café and headed for other places. At dawn of Ash Wednesday I finally crawled home, worn out and already aware of the aftereffects of too many "Why thanks, I'd love one."

I'd covered just about everything there was to cover in New Orleans that Carnival night and consequently the scene in the first café had faded in the brighter light of subsequent experiences. I didn't think of it again until that awful morning of Lent and penance. Then the thought was only a passing one which came as I stood under the shower trying to revive myself sufficiently to get back to work. I grinned, remembering how near the conservative café had been to becoming the scene of a downright brawl. Thought of the café brought thoughts of food and the breakfast which awaited me downstairs and which held no interest for me that morning.

I yawned my way out of the shower and got into a soft rose wool suit. I hoped the color would soften my dark-purple feeling. Then I dug out a pack of peanuts and began chewing on the nuts. I'd found them a more efficient chaser for "alkytosis" than cloves and less likely to arouse suspicion. When I had a mouthful going good, I started for the dining room downstairs.

No one was stirring in my wing of the house, where my mother, two sisters, Vangie and Marian, also had their bedrooms. I slipped down the hall to the other wing where my brother Brett, a charter plane pilot, had taken over two rooms and fixed them up as a den-bedroom suite. I opened the den door and heard a loud snore. I grinned at the sound. It had been my complaints about those queer noises which had brought about Brett's move to the other end of the house. He used to sleep in the room next to mine and he'd griped about moving. Now he loved his quarters. I felt a twinge of envy toward the sleeping family, dismissed it, and went on downstairs, turning into the kitchen instead of the dining room.

Bertha, the ebony-colored hellion of the kitchen, gave me a look that boded a lecture. I tried to stall it by asking for coffee. I merely gave her something more to fuss about. She poured the coffee to the tune of a running grumble which went something like this:

"Aint no lady, des whut. Comin' in hyar fum de street at all houahs o' de mawnin. I heered you when you comes in. Den walks in hyar bol' as brass an .axes fo black cawfee. You oughta be 'shame foh yo'se'f."

I heard the same thing every time I stayed out until all hours. I drank the coffee, ate another handful of peanuts, and asked for more coffee. Instead she plumped down a plate of bacon and eggs and two slices of toast.

"You des eat dem aigs. Ain't no nerishin' in cawfee."

I started to open my mouth in protest when a look from Bertha shut me up. I followed the direction she walled her eyes toward and stood up hurriedly to greet my mother who was standing in the doorway.

"Good morning, darling. You're up early," I said inanely.

"I was about to say the same thing to you." She smiled and leaned over for her morning kiss. I hoped the peanuts would not betray my trust in them. "Why are you eating in the kitchen?" she asked.

"It was so early and the dining room wasn't set, so I just thought I'd grab a bite in here and avoid disturbing anyone."

"Ummm? Thoughtful of you. I didn't hear you come in last night. What time did you get through work?"

"Later than I expected or wanted to get through," I told her—telling her exactly nothing.

She gave me a shrewd look out of her keen blue eyes. "Which, being Mardi Gras, must have been around daylight."

"Not quite that bad," I hedged, hoping Bertha would keep her big mouth shut.

"Well—" She hesitated, then apparently decided not to pursue the subject any farther. "It's a lovely bright morning. Let's eat on the sun porch. Have Bertha bring your breakfast out there and I'll have mine with you. Bertha." She turned to our kitchen queen. "I'll have some orange juice, bacon, eggs, toast, and coffee."

"Yessum." Bertha began to gather up my dishes to remove them to the porch. I took her by the arm.

"Never mind, Bertha, those eggs will be cold by the time you set the table on the porch. Besides, I'm not very hungry.

So just bring me some juice and coffee and maybe a piece of toast."

"Too much Mardi Gras?" Mother's eyebrows lifted in stern inquiry.

"Too much *work* on Mardi Gras." I accented the work. "Honestly, the hours I put in on that job yesterday and last night really beat me. And now I have to get to the office and start the grind over again. I'm too tired to be hungry."

Bertha grumbled something and I gave her a glare. All I needed was for her to tell Mother I'd not even been to bed and that even if it wasn't broad daylight when I got in it was well past dawn. But she said nothing distinguishable and ambled out to the sun porch to fix the table. Mother and I followed her and sat down. Mother took up my long complaint about being tired.

"If you're overworked, Margaret, it's your own fault. I'm sure it can't be necessary for you to put in the hours you do, even on a morning paper it wouldn't be. Besides, you know I've never approved of your job."

"Oh for Pete's sake, Mom, let's not go into that again!" I said irritably. "I've been working for the paper for over ten years now and most of the time I love it. And please remember you were the one who gave me permission to take a job there."

"I remember it quite clearly," she said tartly. "I also recall that I consented only because I believed you would be in the society department where you would associate with ladies. Instead of that you went to work in the city room, where you are surrounded by a lot of profane men. I might add that recently you have not been acting like a lady."

I'd listened to this song before, many times. But this morning the last sentence rang a bell. I had a sudden mental picture of the green-eyed woman when she was told she wasn't acting like a lady. My reaction, although not so violent, was similar. I rose from the chair and shoved it away from the table.

"I'm getting a little sick of hearing that tune, Mother. All you know about a city room is what you read in books and see in movies. The people in them are not a damn bit more profane than they are in a hell of a lot of other places. Why, for the love of Mike, must we go through this same silly nonsense at least once a month?"

Her lips tightened angrily. "My knowledge of a city room may be garnered from books and movies, but your profanity sounds in my ears every day at home. I know you didn't learn it here. Lately you can't utter a simple sentence without cursing. It sounds horrible."

Being guilty that hurt.

"Oh nuts!" I said inelegantly. "I don't curse anymore than your other daughters. Your baby, Vangie, can deal me cards and spades in cussing. You certainly can't blame her language on the city room."

"I certainly can—and do!" she retorted. "Evangeline learned her profanity from you and yours comes from the paper. And there's something else I want to speak to you about, Margaret. You had too much to drink last night. Your eyes are bloodshot and I can smell your breath from across the table."

The peanuts had failed me!

"What of it?" I asked, sulkily. "Everyone I saw last night had too much to drink. It was that kind of a Mardi Gras. So all right. I did get tight. I didn't disgrace you, did I?"

"I really don't know," she answered cooly. "Would you remember?"

I couldn't think of an answer to that one, so I grabbed my hat and bag and stalked out of the room and on out the back door to the garage. I got in the car, backed it rapidly out of the garage and into the street, where I headed it for downtown.

The warm March sun was shining down on a very quiet city. All who could afford to stay home and sleep off Carnival were doing so. Those who had to work were either already at their labors or, like me, quietly and sorrowfully taking their hangovers to work. Still upset over the tiff with my lovely mother, I sailed angrily down the avenue and turned into the street where the building which houses our publishing combine is located. I swung into the parking lot in back of the building and looked at my watch. It was just seven-fifteen and I was better than a half-hour early. I got out and went across the street to a small lunch room where, I told myself, I'd get a cup of coffee without having to listen to maternal admonitions. By the time I'd finished the coffee I was beginning to be ashamed of myself. I paid my check and headed for the office, walking into the city room well ahead of time.

Instead of appreciating my early arrival, Dennis had handed me a stack of clippings to rewrite and then had screamed at me for not getting them done in record time.

At this point in my retrospective wanderings I realized that Dennis was screaming at me. Literally and loudly.

5. *Ash Wednesday Assignment*

"MAGGIE! F'crissakes MAGGIE! Dammit, wake up!"

I came back to the present with a start and announced, with what dignity I could muster under the circumstances, "I wasn't asleep and you needn't scream at me. Did you want me for something?"

"Did I want her for something?" Dennis asked in irritated tones. "Ye gods, would I be screaming myself hoarse for nothing? Of course I want you for something. I want you to try, just try, to earn the money this paper pays you."

"What money?" I asked blandly.

"Never mind that routine. I've a job for you to cover."

I groaned loudly. "Okay, give it to me."

"I said to cover—it's outside."

"Oh Dennis, have a heart! I'm just one person and I went to work at eight yesterday morning and from eleven on I was on my feet. I worked right through until—"

"Until five this morning and you came right back without getting any sleep." He finished the complaint for me. "Well, babe, that's your own fault. I didn't assign you to have a drink in every bar in town. After you had covered the Rex ball you could have gone home. That was about midnight."

I gaped at him. "Dennis McCarthy, that's a lie! You know damn well you gave me assignments to cover all the balls. I've the slips to prove it."

"I didn't tell you to work all night on them," he said calmly. "Here." He began writing on the blue assignment slip. I trudged over to the desk and waited until he handed

45

it to me. "A guy bumped himself off at that address," he explained. "The cops are over there and this shouldn't take you very long. I want it in time for the Home."

I looked at the clock. It said eleven-thirty. The Home edition ran at one-thirty. Then it dawned on me where this assignment belonged.

"But this is on the police beat!" I wailed. "You took me off that months ago. Now today you give me a bunch of police rewrites to do and assign me to a headquarters story. What's wrong with Morgan? Playing sick again?"

"Morgan doesn't play sick—or tired either—to get out of work. He's on the job today but he's tied up in court with stuff from last night's blotter."

"Court closes at noon," I reminded him. "He can get the story then and have it here in plenty of time for the Home."

He gave me a look. "So can you. If the man left notes try to get a look at them. All I want to know is why he gassed himself out and who he was. Beat it."

"All I do know is that it was damned inconsiderate of him," I muttered. "I take it he is dead—not just in a coma from Carnival?"

"Joe Shem, who called for Morgan, said he is so stiff his bones may have to be broken to get him flattened out in a coffin."

"Dennis!"

"Well, you asked—didn't you?"

"You didn't have to be so graphic about it," I snapped. "Well, he chose a good day for dying. A day of sackcloth and ashes and penance for your sins. 'And on this day ye shall do—'"

"Will you get going?" Dennis yelled.

"Kindly lower your voice when you speak to me," I said huffily. "Okay, I'm going—and I hope it turns out to be a murder. If I must do another guy's job, I'd like to have something interesting to write about."

"Don't start that stuff," Dennis warned. "This is a suicide, that's all, and don't try to—"

I didn't wait to hear the end of the warning not to try and cook up a homicide out of a suicide. Going down in the elevator, though, I chuckled, knowing I'd planted a seed of worry in Dennis' editorial mind and that it would worry him until the yarn was written and in the composing room.

Outside of the building I blinked at the brilliant sunshine. Then I focussed my tired eyes on the assignment slip I held in my hand. The address was 1010 Baronne street, apartment 303. I brightened. That was only a five- or ten-minute walk. I struck off in the direction of Baronne street.

The address I was heading for was in a cheaper class theatrical section of hotels, apartments, and boarding houses. My relief over its proximity began to vanish as I realized that if it was the building I suspected it of being, the apartment number meant a climb of three steep flights of stairs. A few minutes later, as I labored up those stairs, I decided that if Dennis had ever been possessed of any of the milk of human kindness, it had dried up long ago. He knew where he was sending me.

The apartment house was a rebuilt affair that had once been a cheap office building. It was five stories high and the apartments had been cut up out of the large, barnlike office rooms, with partitions making each office into a one room, kitchen, and bath apartment. They were given the elegant name of "Studio Suites." I'd visited a girl I knew who had lived in one of them, a night club dancer. But she'd had the consideration—or good sense—to get Apt. 2 on the first floor.

The stairs seemed to me to be just one foot lower than the Alps. They about put the finishing touches on my Ash Wednesday health. I stopped to get my breath on the landing of the fourth floor and the odor of escaped cooking gas almost stopped my breathing entirely.

"Whew!" I muttered into the handkerchief I held hastily to my nose. "This would not be a good place to light up a Camel."

I waited a few seconds then followed my nose to the door of 303. Joe Shem, a uniformed sergeant from headquarters, was leaning against the wall outside the apartment. He, too, held a handkerchief to his nose. A wet one. His eyes smiled at me, then he moved the cloth and said "Phew!"

"Phew is right, Joseph. What happened here?"

"Young fellow killed hisself, Margaret. Used gas."

"Not really!"

"Yeah, sure. Can't you smell it?"

I looked into his twinkling eyes and played up to him. "I hab a code in de heb," I said, sniffling into the kerchief.

"That's too bad." He sounded sympathetic. "You oughta get some nose drops. Now, when I get a cold I just—"

"Never mind, doctor. I came here to collect a story on a suicide, not cold cures for a cold I don't have. What's the dope?"

"It's a damn shame, Margaret. This is a young, good-looking kid."

"Was, you mean. How young?"

"Twenty-five or thirty. No more than thirty."

"Sure it's suicide?"

Shem grinned. He had been on a case when I'd made a neat murder out of what had been called a natural death at first and then a suicide.*

"This time it's suicide, Margaret. There's no doubt about it at all. He left notes, three of them. The guys from homicide just took one look and left. No business for them here."

I grinned, too. I'd found out what I wanted to know.

"So he left notes, did he? Well, notes can be faked. A guy could be drugged and the gas turned on to make it look like suicide. As for the homicide bunch, they have to

* *Poison, Poker and Pistols,* Sheridan House.

depend on autopsy anyhow and they never work harder than they have to on a case."

"They didn't have any work to do on this case. We had to bust the door to get in. See?" He pointed to the shattered lock of the closed door.

"The door to Dr. McGowan's room was locked too," I reminded him. "And it was locked from the inside with the burglar latch. But it was murder right on." *

"Yeah, I know it was. But this ain't. Even after we busted in the door we had the hell of a time getting in the room. He had stuck a big chair up against the door, attached the safety chain and calmly sat down to write his good-byes and wait for the gas to put him out."

I shuddered, chilled by the thought of being so deliberate about killing one's self.

"Can I have a look at him, Joe? Who's in there now?"

"Doc Rollins."

"Oh, lovely! My cherub-faced coroner. How is he?"

"He's fine, but you better not ever let him hear you call him what you just did. I don't think he'd like it."

"It's a good description though, isn't it?"

"It is that. Well, as soon as he says he is finished you can go in and have a look."

My nod got caught in a yawn. Another yawn followed the first, then a third almost cracked my jaw.

Joe grinned widely.

"Oh, oh. What you yawning about? Been out celebrating Carnival and got no sleep, I'll bet."

"Kindly do not mention Carnival to me," I said stiffly. "Not if you want to remain a friend of mine. I *worked* all night, that's why I'm tired. How long has Doc been in there?"

"Only about ten minutes. He got here just a step ahead of you."

"You mean just three flights of steps ahead of me."

* *Poison, Poker and Pistols*, Sheridan House, 1946.

"Yeah man! Ain't those stairs brutal?"

"They certainly are!" I agreed heartily. "What time did you get here?"

"About ten-forty-five, but the door took a long time and we didn't get in until after eleven."

I looked at my watch; eleven-fifty-two. I had plenty of time.

Dragging, weary footsteps sounded along the corridor and I looked down it to see Johnny Morrow, police leg man for the opposition afternoon paper, puffing his way toward us.

I laughed. "Here comes another reporter who's so out of condition he can't climb a few stairs without needing oxygen."

"All—right—Slone," he panted. "I'd like to have seen—you—when—when you got to the top." He caught his breath and added, "What you doing here anyhow? I thought Dennis took you off police after that daisy you pulled at Ted Elison's party to celebrate his appointment to chief of police."

I counted to ten. That subject was a very sore one with me. "This is Ash Wednesday and I'm doing penance enough by just working today. Besides, I only spoke the truth. I still think Tommy Gross would make a better chief and I simply told Elison's wife so. That's all."

Shem tried to choke and Morrow looked at me sadly.

"Skip it," I warned. "I've heard enough about that to last me the rest of my life. If either of you want to see fireworks, go ahead and tell me some more about it."

They looked at each other and shrugged eloquent shoulders.

"I wouldn't think of mentioning it," Morrow said. "But you should have told that to Tommy's sidekick instead of Elison's wife. And you shouldn't have had that last—"

"Shut up!" I took a threatening step forward and glared at him.

"Okay." He backed away hastily and turned to Joe. "What gives here and how come Slone beat me to the scene?"

"Your boss said you was tied up at court," Joe said and went on to repeat what he had told me a few minutes earlier. He added that the police were trying to find the suicide's wife. It was the first I'd heard about any wife and I looked at Shem as though he had betrayed me.

"Wife? What wife? You didn't tell *me* anything about a wife."

"You didn't ask me," Shem said calmly.

"Neither did Morrow."

"He read my mind," Johnny said smugly.

"What mind? Never mind, skip it. What wife, Joe?"

"Why his wife, the suicide's wife." He sounded surprised. "She ran out on him, apparently. That's why he bumped hisself."

"Himself," I corrected absently.

"Look here, if I wanta say hisself I'll say it," Joe said truculently.

"I'm sorry. That's what comes of having majored in English with intentions of being a teacher."

"Well, you ain't no major and you ain't no teacher either. You're just a reporter and don't go correcting my English."

"I said I was sorry. Now what about this wife?"

"They had some kind of fight and she left. She ain't been back since and nobody knows where she went."

"Anyone hear the quarrel?"

"Everyone on the floor, to hear them tell it."

"But this is an old building. Aren't the walls pretty thick?"

"Naw. This dump was built cheap to start with and the walls are just frame molds with a little plaster poured between 'em. The partitions in the apartments are wallboard, which is nothing but paper. Besides, most of this fight took place with her on the outside of the apartment and him on the inside with the door locked."

"In heaven's name, how did that happen?"

"Well, she went out once, then came back for her stuff. He wouldn't open the door and let her in to get it. She raised hell."

"Who told you about that part of it?"

"The woman in there." He gestured with his thumb toward 305. "Oh, brother—is she something! She said that about midnight she almost called the cops, that they were raising such hell people couldn't sleep. *Decent* people, she said, and is that a laugh!"

"Why?"

"Because she's a floozy if I ever saw one."

"Oh. Well, did she hear what they were saying?"

"Some of it. The fight was about another woman, as usual."

"Quite." I agreed. "Well, it's too bad she didn't call for the police. She might have stopped him from killing himself if she had called."

"I don't know about that." Morrow shook his head. "When people get the suicide bug they generally wind up by bumping themselves. Remember that screwball woman on Royal Street who tried to make a final meal on mercury tablets?"

I nodded. "Sure, what about her?"

"She finally killed herself in a hotel room in New York. It's on the wire today and we got it because she had registered from here. It's been a year since she tried it by poison. This time she climbed into a tub of warm water and slit her wrists with a razor blade. It's supposed to be a very painless way to die."

"Nyahh!" I exclaimed in disgust. "How can people do such awful things? I'd never get so tired of living I'd want to kill myself."

"It's supposed to take a lot of guts. Me, I'd never have that much—would you?" Morrow asked.

"Not to do anything like that," I said emphatically.

"Like what, Margaret?" A voice spoke behind me. I

swung around to see Dr. Rollins, our short, roly-poly and cherubic-faced coroner.

"Oh! Hello, Doc." I smiled at him. Rollins was one of my pets. "Oh, we just got to talking about people who commit suicide and Morrow said he'd never have the guts to do it and asked if I would. I said I wouldn't. At least, I don't think I would."

He studied me for a moment. Then, in his clipped, precise tones, which always seemed to me to be at variance with his appearance, he said very seriously, "You have something more, my dear. You have the courage to live and enjoy life as it comes to you or to take the sorrow with the rest and carry on."

"You think so?" I was highly pleased. "And a suicide lacks that sort of courage?"

"Yes, to both questions. Living, my child, requires a great deal more courage than dying. A suicide simply admits to the world that he is defeated. That he is a weakling, without the intestinal fortitude, or guts—as you so graphically called them—to face life down and go on with what he was meant to do. To fight back, when the fight went against him and to fulfill his alloted span which, heaven knows, is only too short at best. A suicide, Margaret, is a quitter—one who falters and throws in the towel before the fight is half-fought."

I gazed at the round, serious mien in affectionate admiration. "Honestly, Doc. Everytime I see you, you confound me with some gem on the philosophy of living and dying."

Rollins smiled, looking more like a slightly bald cherub than ever.

"Well, when a man has seen as much of living and dying as I have—and I see more than the usual share of it—he inclines toward becoming an amateur philosopher on the subject. I'm afraid, however, that my philosophy depends on platitudes for expression."

"And a fine means of expression they are, Doc," Morrow said. "I'm in favor of platitudes. For instance, if a girl gets you in a corner, you can say, 'Let's not spoil a beautiful friendship by getting married.'"

"That's no platitude," I laughed. "That's just a lecher's plea to let him have his cake and eat it too."

"Who said anything about food? But now that you mention it, there's the one that goes—'Why buy a cow when milk is—'"

"That will do." I looked at him coldly, knowing Dr. Rollins didn't like talk that bordered on the bawdy. He shut up and I turned back to the doctor, all business.

"Are you through in there, Doc? May we go in?"

"I'm finished, Margaret, and you may go in now. My work here was soon finished. I needed only to determine the cause of death and ascertain how long he had been dead."

I sniffed the air. "The cause was certainly easy to determine. That gas has made me feel dopey."

Morrow grinned and I knew I'd led with my chin.

"So that's what makes you act the way you do today. And could it be the gas that has turned your bright hazel eyes to limpid pools of blood?"

"You might take a look at your own eyes, my friend," I snapped. "If anyone is likely to bleed to death, it's you. I'd appreciate it if you saved your low brand of humor for someone who enjoys it. I don't."

I turned away and started to enter the room.

"You coming in, Doc?"

"Of course," Rollins answered. "I have to finish packing my bag and then I must wait for my boys. They should be here soon."

I repressed a shiver. Doc's "boys" came from the morgue, that in-between resting place for all who die violently—by their own hand or at the hands of others.

6. Suicide to Music

THE apartment we entered was identical to the one I'd visited in on the ground floor. There was an In-A-Dor bed which lifted up and folded back into a large clothes closet-dressing room. The main room was furnished in Grand Rapids tradition, with a three-piece, plum-colored living room suite which was upholstered in brocaded plush. There were two end tables, walnut finished; two lamps, a standing model and a table lamp, both with parchment shades. A gate-legged table was pushed against the wall which separated the room from the kitchen. Two Windsor chairs, a leather hassock and a small, unsteady looking desk completed the furnishings.

In the kitchen there was a small three burner and oven stove, an ice box, just about large enough to hold twenty-five pounds of ice, a lift top garbage can and a white metal cabinet. A row of wooden shelves were fastened to the wall next to the window.

The instruments of death had been the kitchen stove, the gas heater in the living room, and a similar heater in the bathroom. Rollins told me that every jet in each had been wide open and pouring gas into the apartment when the police finally broke in the place.

The suicide's chair had been shoved aside when the police knocked in the door. It was now in such a position that the door panel concealed everything but a pair of neatly shod feet, about size eight or nine, and a few inches of pajama-clad legs. In sight, near the legs, was one of the end tables and on it a portable victrola sat with the top up and a record on the turntable. The other table was by the divan and resting on it was a tiny radio which was decorated with a grinning miniature of Charlie McCarthy.

I looked at the vic again and noticed that the needle was stopped a little more than halfway through the record. I walked over for a closer look and saw that the piece was a favorite of mine, Paul Whiteman's excellent recording of "Among My Souvenirs." Evidently the machine had run down and instinctively I reached for the handle to wind it up. It was completely loose and as I wound I thought: Well, at least he checked out to sweet music. I kept turning the handle and suddenly the turntable began to revolve and the machine to play!

I started back somewhat horrified and that was when Joe yelled at me—but good.

"Crissakes, Margaret! You know better than to touch anything on police cases." He reached over and hastily switched the stop button. It stopped just as the melody reached the notes that accompany the lines "There's nothing left for me—"

"Jesus!" I said, shocked through and through. "He really felt that way, didn't he?"

Joe was still grumbling about not touching things and I got back enough of my poise to snap at him. "Oh, shut up. This is no homicide." Then I turned toward the chair which held the body.

Over ten years of newspaper work, a large part of them spent covering police, hasn't inured me of a sense of horror of death by violence. I can't refrain from flinching and I've been known to weep over the death of a perfect stranger. I've taken plenty of ribbing because of my weakness, particularly from Morrow, who could survey with maddening calm the body of a man who had been carved to bits. But this was one time I didn't flinch even a little bit. I was too surprised to give way to any other emotion.

The suicide was Don, the man who had been in Le Coq d'Or on Mardi Gras night. The first thought that crossed my mind was that he didn't look at all dead, but as if he was merely sleeping in the chair. When I found my voice all I could say was, "Well, I'm damned."

"What's the matter with you?" Morrow asked quickly. "You know this guy?"

I shook my head negatively.

"Then whatinhell are you so surprised about?"

"Why I saw him last night—in Le Coq d'Or. Just last night he had dinner in Gaston's. Migawd! What do you know about that!"

"Nothing," Morrow said succinctly. "What do you know about it?"

"Me? Oh, I just happened to be having dinner with Gaston. I was on assignment for Carnival. He was in a party of four at the table next to mine. His name is Don and his wife's is Nita. They were having a fight in the café and she walked out on the party, but not before she created a hell of a scene and Gaston all but tossed her out on her ear. Gaston was furious."

"What was the fight about?" Shem asked.

"It started when he, Don, called his wife down for speaking French. One word led to another and she finally accused the other girl in the group, a hell of a good looking red-head, of being in love with Don and wanting to be around him so she could drool over him. That was when the fun began, but Gaston soon put an end to it."

"Say, that's swell!" Shem exclaimed. "If you saw her you must know what she looks like and you can describe her. With a good, full description we can do something about finding her."

I looked at him blankly.

"What's the matter with the landlady? You mean to tell me she doesn't know what one of her tenants looks like?"

"She doesn't," Shem said. "It seems this woman only got

in a few days ago, last week sometime. The man rented
the place and said his wife would be here soon. He'd been
living in the place for about a week before she came. The
landlady said after she got here she slept all day and
wouldn't let a maid or anyone in to clean the place. So no
one in the building ever actually saw her."

"What about the woman next door? Didn't she see her
when she was having the argument in the hall?"

"Not clearly enough to be able to describe her. She said
she opened the door and said to shut up or she'd call the
police but all she got was a look at her back. She said she
was tall. That was all she knew about it."

"Well, I can give you a description all right. No one who
ever got a good look at that woman would be likely to
forget her. Her hair is very dark and wavy and she was
wearing it in coronets around her head. Her eyes are
exactly the shade of emeralds and her features are as perfect as those on a cameo. She has skin like fine-grained old
ivory, a full, beautifully-shaped mouth—with a razor sharp
tongue in it—a figure such as you'd read about in a poem
and the very bitch of a temper. She's French and she's in
show business. She's quite tall and very regal in carriage
and she claims she is of noble descent. She's about a size
fourteen dress and wears about a size six shoe. As I said
before, she has a bitch of a temper and is just as likely to
slash out with a knife as not. In fact, she did that very
thing last night—but missed her aim, fortunately."

"Well!" Morrow gasped. "For not knowing her you know
plenty about her."

"That's because I'm a good reporter, dear," I said sweetly.
"I use my eyes and ears and remember what I see and
hear. She's a regular hellion. Gaston had her tagged right."

"What do you mean? On account of her making a scene
there?"

"Not exactly. He didn't like her even before she created
a rumpus. He doesn't like her type, having met up with it

in his youth. He said the oddest thing about her, said she had 'a cold hotness of beauty which puts the devil into a man.' "

"That sounds like a flowery talking Frog," Joe said in disgust.

"Well—her beauty *is* cold. It has no warmth at all." I defended Gaston. "She's exquisite but it's a cold—" Suddenly it dawned on me that something was missing from this room. Something theatrical people are never without and always exhibit prominently.

"There are no pictures of either of them around here. That's very strange for show people. There should be pictures."

Maybe they were on a vacation from business," Shem suggested.

"Show people are never on vacation from business," Morrow said scornfully. "Don't you know that? Hell, they act all the time, on and off stage, and they always have pictures of themselves around. Slone's right."

"Of course if she packed all her stuff and left, she no doubt took them with her." I was thinking out loud. "That must be it."

"No it ain't," Joe said. "I mean she didn't take her duds. That's what she was bellering about when he wouldn't open the door and let her in. She wanted her bag. I told you that before."

"Did you? I don't remember."

"I thought you kept your eyes and ears open," Morrow jeered.

I just looked at him and Joe went on, somewhat hurriedly.

"The blonde next door said this dame went out once and came back in a few minutes and began to holler for her bag. He wouldn't open up, said he would give her until three to think things over and if she still wanted to leave, she could have the bag in the morning. She left and that's the last anyone heard of her."

I glanced around. "In that case the things must still be here."

"They are. The suitcase is in there." Shem pointed to the dressing room.

We moved as a unit to the closet space in back of the bed. It was roomy, with two clothes' rods and a chest of drawers for flat wear. There was a full length mirror on the door which closed it off from the living room. On one clothes' rod were two men's suits; a light gray flannel and a trim blue woolen with a pin stripe, two sports jackets, both of good tweed, a tan camel's hair top coat and a brocaded silk dressing gown. On the floor, near a couple of pairs of men's shoes, was a smart oversized luggage case, initialed with gold letters, "A.M.J." Next to it was a man's Gladstone bag with the initials, "D.E.B." A pair of limp-soled dressing slippers lay over the handle of the man's bag.

"Haul that woman's case out and let's have a look, Joe," I suggested.

He reached down to lift it and drew back, a slightly surprised look on his face. Then he heaved earnestly and brought it from the floor, hauled it out of the closet and dumped it on the bed. The springs sagged with a metallic protest.

"That thing's heavy!" He exclaimed aggrievedly, as I laughed at him. "You oughta try and heft it. It must have lead in it. No woman could lift that weight. She musta gone out to get someone to help her get it downstairs."

"Let's have a look inside of it." I indicated the case. "Open it up Joe."

He tried the latches. "Locked," he said tersely.

"Bet you I can open it." I grinned and pulled out one of the strong wire pins I use to keep up my heavy, unbobbed hair. "Let me have a try at it."

Joe eyed the pin critically. "You can't open it with that thing. This is an expensive bag and the latches are strong. Anyhow, we got no business opening it if it's locked. It's private property. The lieutenant ought to be here in a few minutes. We better wait and see what he says about it."

I had no intention of waiting for the lieutenant who was likely Kerry Phelan and a pal of the new chief's. I'd get no help from any of that crowd.

"It's evidence, isn't it? Evidence isn't private property. You know that as well as I do. Besides, there must be pictures in it and a picture is what you most need to locate her. As soon as we put a picture of her in the paper someone who knows her will be bound to see it. Maybe she'll see it herself and come forward. Poor thing probably has no idea of what's happened." My sympathy was strictly hypocritical. "Come on, at least let me try this hairpin."

Shem hesitated and lost the chance to say no. I was already busy with the catches and it took less than a minute to release them. The bag popped open—literally popped. It was so crammed with stuff it was a wonder the locks had held it at all.

The three of us bent over the bag, Shem still wearing a worried, doubtful look. Before he could object to my searching, I slid both hands between layers of clothing and felt about until I hit a flat solid object. I pulled out a large brown Manila paper envelope, marked with the name and address of a New York photographer. It was addressed to Annette Jeans, 360 W. 48th St., New York City.

Shem got out his pencil and pad. "I better just take down that address. If we don't find her here, maybe someone there can give us a lead on her."

Morrow and I smiled pityingly.

"You might find she once lived at that address, Joe," Morrow said. "She's probably lived in dozens of such places since then. The date on that is 1932. Show people move around a lot in two years."

"Maybe—but I'll take it down anyhow. It might help out. You never can tell." He scribbled the number down in his note pad.

I made use of his preoccupation to unwind the cord which held down the envelope flap and draw out a sheaf of photos. All but three were of her, those three were of the man who sat dead in the chair nearby. One was in the costume of a Mexican caballero. The others were duplicate head shots and excellent likenesses. I handed them to Joe. He looked at them and passed them to Morrow, shaking his head mournfully.

"Poor bastard. Wonder what she wanted with his pictures? Since she was quitting him, looks like she'd have left them behind."

"True female inconsistence," Morrow said brightly. "Or maybe she only wanted to carry them sort of like Indians carried scalps. Women do things like that."

"What do you know about women?" I asked tartly, irritated at the implied slur to my sex.

"Nothing," he admitted promptly. "Woman, from the cradle to the grave, will remain an enigma to me all of my life."

"Then stop cracking wise." I shuffled through the other photos. They were mixed shots, in and out of costume; heads, busts, and full body shots. The back of each print was stamped with the photographer's name and the warning to credit Flambeau's Theatrical Art Studios when using the pictures. Over the stamp was written her name and the name of the Broadway musical hit, *Shutter's Rounders.*

I laid them out fanwise. "There she is boys. Take your pick."

Morrow gave a long drawn out whistle. "Damn! She *is* something! Oh, brother! I'd put my shoes under her—"

"That will do," I shut him off curtly. "Considering the number of beds your shoes have been under, that's no compliment."

"Why, Slone." His tone was hurt. "That's not a bit nice. What do you know about the places where I've parked my shoes? You never let me put them anywhere near your—"

"No fault of your's." I interrupted again. "No one can accuse you of not having tried often enough. Skip it, we both have work to do. I picked the lock, so I'm taking first choice of the pix. I want one of those head shots of him and these two of her." I pointed to a couple of busts in which she wore her hair coronet style and looked as she had in the café.

"These are for me." Morrow flicked a finger at two poses of a barely covered Mexican dancer. "These two and one like you want of him."

"Leg art," I sneered. "You would."

"It sells papers," he replied blandly.

"I don't know about you taking these pictures away." Joe had gone back to worrying. "I don't know would the lieutenant like it. After all, they're private—"

"Property." Morrow finished the sentence. "Now, listen, sweetheart, we went all over that once. We have to find the dame, don't we? And as Maggie pointed out, the way to find her is to print her pix. Like the French say, *serchez la femmy.*"

"Your French stinks," I told him. "And don't call me Maggie. I don't like it."

"Yeah and don't call me sweetheart either. I don't like that." There was a scowl on Joe's ruddy, usually good-humored face. "Anyhow, I don't think I better let you take these pictures without the lieutenant says so. We can trace her through the cab she took when she left here. Now why didn't I think of that before?"

"How do you know she took a cab?" I asked.

"That just figures. She went down and got a cab and made the driver come up to get her bag, being it was so heavy—"

"Oh sure. And she started yelling and the cab driver turned around and got the hell out as fast as he could make it down those stairs. Make some sense, Joe!"

"How do you know so much?" He asked me. "You didn't see her come up here."

"No, but it stands to reason that no hackie would hang around when a domestic squabble threatened."

As unobtrusively as possible, I'd been edging the pictures I wanted out of the spread-out prints on the bed. I picked them up and studied them nonchalantly. Morrow followed my lead and got the ones he had chosen. Joe set his jaw stubbornly.

"Now look, Joe." I tried reasoning with him. "She may have had a cab driver come up with her, but she didn't get the bag so why would she keep him to drive her around? Most likely she walked off wherever she was going and meant to come back later for her things."

"Then why didn't she come back?" Joe asked with unanswerable logic.

"She's probably still asleep," I said brightly. "Show people sleep late. Maybe she just went to some hotel and checked in for the night."

"Just went to some hotel and checked in for the night!" Joe looked ready to explode. "On a Carnival night—and with no luggage. You're the one what needs to make some sense."

"Maybe she went to some friends," Morrow suggested. "Most wives do that when they have a fight with their husbands. They either go home to mama or find a pal who will let them use a shoulder to weep on."

"She isn't the weeping sort," I informed him. "Anyhow, the best way to find her is through using these pix and I'm taking them to the paper right now."

I meant to put a bold face on it and march right past Joe. I didn't think he'd use force to stop me from taking the pictures. Just as I gathered myself together for the try, it dawned on me I hadn't asked the coroner how long the man had been dead or any of the more pertinent facts—such as his full name. Nor had I got even a glimpse of those notes and, with Joe mad, that latter might prove difficult.

I wheeled back to speak to the coroner and Morrow,

struck by the same thought apparently, did the same. We spoke in unison.

"How long has he been dead, Doc? Who was he?"

Johnny and I looked at each other, then linked our fingers and began reciting the little rhyme that fits the occasion. When we had finished and made our wishes, we turned back to the amused coroner who, after packing his kit, had been sitting quietly while the three of us rifled the suitcase and argued over the pictures.

Doc's smile broadened as he jerked his head in Shem's direction. "You had better ask Joe about who he was. He has all the data on that. As for what caused his death— that's fairly obvious. Carbon monoxide poisoning. Self-administered. He had been dead six to nine hours when I examined him. That was about eleven forty-five. It places the death between three and six a.m. I'm also going by the next door neighbor's statement that she had heard him talking after midnight. Otherwise I would have thought he had died even before midnight."

"Why?" I asked curiously.

"He was diabetic, therefore the rigor is fairly well established."

"What has being diabetic got to do with rigor mortis?" Johnny asked.

"It has to do with the sugar content of the body," I answered, glad to show off my medical knowledge. "A diabetic has something wrong with the sugar in his blood so when one dies he gets stiffer faster than a normal person. Isn't that right, Doc?"

Rollins tried to hide a smile. "Well, that's a fairly accurate capsule description, Margaret. Not every layman knows that much about diabetics."

"Thanks, Doc." I turned to Joe. "You said he left notes. You got them on you?"

7. *Notes of Farewell*

"SURE." Automatically, his hand went to the front of his uniform blouse, then he hesitated, a study in dubiety. "I don't know if the lieutenant would want you should see these things—and I ain't said you could take those pictures."

"Oh damn the lieutenant!" I said shortly. "And the pictures too. What the hell has got into you, Joe Shem? You never used to be so persnickety about helping us out on things like this. Is someone at headquarters after your hide?"

"Nobody's after my hide, but I know correct procedure in these sort of cases and I don't intend to get in trouble by not obeying it."

I groaned. "Oh dear Lord! He's been going to those damn classes and studying police law. That this should happen to a good cop! Lookit, Joe, all, positively *all*, we want is to read those notes—not take them with us. As for the pictures, you know we need those and would get them later anyhow."

He thought that one over for a minute. "Well, okay. I don't suppose it is wrong for you to look at them."

"I said we wanted to read them." I was becoming a little irritated with Shem. He'd never been so balky about stretching a simple rule or two.

He fumbled with the brass buttons of his blouse and finally drew out three envelopes. They were unsealed and each had one word written on the front. He held them out fanwise as I stood on tiptoe to look over one broad shoulder and Morrow peered over the other. They were addressed to "Nita," "Bette," "Jim." That was all. Shem held them tightly in his big paw, like a poker player who has drawn three aces and is afraid someone will grab them and call the hand a misdeal.

"For heaven's sake open them up!" I exclaimed impatiently.

Although he must have known we were most interested in the note to Nita, he proceeded to first open the one addressed to the unknown Jim. I opened my mouth to protest, but shut it quickly at a warning look from Morrow. It said quite plainly, "Don't antagonize him."

The note was brief. It read:

Dear Jim: I know this is going to mean grief and expense for you, but it will be the last time I cause you either of these things. Nita is gone, but this time she won't be back. I know that as well as I know I am going to die tonight. I tried living without her once. It didn't work. So I'm checking out and it should be a good riddance for everyone. I've never done anything but create trouble, expense, and grief for my friends. I'm just no good. You know that, Jim. I'm a cheat and a liar and an actor miscast in the play I'm about to drop the curtain on for keeps. I'm asking only for one last favor. I don't know why I should care, but I don't want to be buried in a pauper's grave. You'll see that doesn't happen, won't you? And see that Bette doesn't pay any part of the bills. I've cost her enough in cash and heartaches. I'd like to be cremated, if it isn't too expensive, and sent back to the farm. You know where it is. And Jim, don't be harsh with Nita—she isn't to blame for my loving her. That's all, except thanks for everything and good-bye, Don.

I swallowed a lump that had somehow found its way into my throat. "Are the other two like that?"

Joe sighed mournfully. "Worse."

"Well, let's get them over with." I scribbled hasty notes from the one he had just read.

He replaced the note in its envelop, tucked it away and opened another. It was the one to Bette.

It began:

My dear: Don't grieve for me, I'm not worth your tears. Your life will be much simpler without me to complicate things. There isn't much I can say to you in this last letter which is being written in my last hour. I've treated you rottenly. And I'm sorry. I simply couldn't help doing what I did. I think you know that for, little as I deserved it, you never stopped being my friend. You rated a much better deal than the one I gave you. Taking myself out of your life is the best break I've ever given you, although my motive is not that unselfish. The truth is, I'm taking the gas because I can't live without Nita. I told you that earlier this evening—or last night, rather, for it is now after three a.m. of Ash Wednesday. Nita has gone and I'm going out soon, for good. Perhaps knowing definitely why I am doing this will help you forget and lessen your grief. So long, kid, be as sweet as you've always been— and give Mike a break. He's a good guy and he's waited for you for a long, long time. Don.

"What an odd letter to write the 'other woman' of a tri- angle," I said. "I don't quite get it."

"I do," Morrow said loftily. "This guy had an affair with Bette—maybe they were engaged—then he met glamour girl Nita, gave Bette the air and married the other dame. But Bette, being a sap, kept carrying the torch for him and when he was broke she'd give him dough just so she could see him now and then. It's simple."

"And so are you!" I retorted. "There's more to this than your puny mind could figure."

"Is that so? How much more? And what'll you bet I didn't tag it right?"

"Shut up." I silenced him, as Shem finally opened the last note. It was the longest of the three.

It read:

My darling: How many times have I written those words to you? And now, I write them for the last time. When you left I said I'd give you until three to think things over. I told you what I meant to do if you were not back before then. I've waited until almost four, hoping against hope you would return, but all along I've known you were not coming back. I know there is someone else and I know who he is. You have gone to him tonight and you have done the wisest thing—for yourself. He can do many things for you that I could never do, no matter how much I wanted to do them. He can give you your big break in the theater and he's your kind, even your countryman. You called me a tout, but just as the theater is in your blood the race track is in mine. You tried to blame this break on Bette. That wasn't fair, beloved, for Bette could no more stop loving me than I could stop loving you—as long as I was alive. The quarrel tonight, I know it was just an excuse. The excuse you have wanted to give you a reason for leaving me. Well, without you nothing has any meaning, so I'm leaving—quietly and painlessly, for I'm too much of a coward to give myself physical hurt. The gas is on and I'm growing sleepy. I'm listening to the melody of "Among My Souvenirs." Very soon I shall be amongst your souvenirs. Think of me whenever you hear that song and know I left because without you there was only emptiness. I'm very, very sleepy and I can't hear the music anymore, only a roaring in my ears like you get when swimming under water. I haven't much more time—

The writing trailed off in a scrawl, then picked up again an inch or so below the last line. The penmanship was so shaky it was hard to decipher but I made out the words:

Can't go without saying good-bye. Good-bye, my dearest love, wherever you are I love you, even with my last breath I love you, I'll love you through eternity and beyond it—if there is anything beyond it. Donny.

Joe replaced the last note in its envelope and tucked it with the other inside of his blouse. I folded up my papers and thrust them in my purse.

"It beats me how men can so often manage to fall in love with the wrong women." I mused. "Poor fool. He went and killed himself for someone who isn't worth the powder to blow her to hell." In the light of what had happened I had fully, if unconsciously, accepted Gaston's indictment of the green-eyed woman.

"How come you say that?" Morrow asked.

"Because it's true. It's right there to be read in those notes. She's—she's—" I groped for a descriptive word and seized on one the café owner had used. "She's a vampire."

"Tch, tch." Morrow shook his head chidingly. "And I thought you were too young to remember Theda Bara."

"The kind of vampire I mean was featured in the play called *Dracula,*" I said coldly. "That was last year."

"Oh! *That* kind of vampire. The undead who prowl at night and attack innocent people who are peacefully asleep in their own beds. Why, Slone—what a thing to say about this lovely creature." He flourished the photo, then hurriedly tucked it back under his arm as Shem eyed it and him with a dubious gaze.

Dr. Rollins, whether by accident or intent, distracted Shem just as he was about to speak.

"Perhaps I'd better take those notes along with me, Joe," he said. "I'll need them for the inquest."

"Oh, sure, Doc." Joe opened the brass buttons again, produced the three envelopes and handed them to the coroner. He looked relieved and his next words expressed his appearance.

"I'm glad to get shed of those things. They give me the creeps when I read them and somehow I kept wanting to read 'em again. They're kinda like hearing a voice from the grave, reading that poor kid's last words."

Morrow raised eloquent eyebrows. "Why, our Joe is a blooming sentimentalist," he gibed. "Well, well, who'd have thought it?"

"Aw—shaddup." Joe made a half-hearted pass at him. "You ain't so tough as you make out to be, you know. I could tell a tale on you, my lad. I mind the time you dug in your—"

"Shem! You tell that and I'll never do another good turn for you as long as I live!"

"Spill it, Joe," I urged.

"Well, one time Johnny got tangled up with this little—"

"So help me, Shem—" Morrow doubled his right into a fist and took a step toward the big cop.

"Aw, tell it, Joe! I'll buy you a drink if you tell it. Anything Morrow is so anxious to keep quiet must be good."

"It ain't much of a story. But Johnny met this stranded chorus girl who needed fare to get back to the farm—*she* said. So our little Boy Scout dug in the sock, gave her fare and bought her a new dress so she'd look—hey! Quit it, John!"

Shem covered up laughingly against Morrow's attacking fists. We all knew that if he wanted, he could floor Johnny with a single blow.

"Well, sink me Susie!" I exclaimed. "Why is this the first time I've heard of your charitable disposition? Tell me, Johnny, did she really go back to the farm?"

Morrow wheeled on me.

"Now look here, Slone. If you gab this around, I'll damn well fix your feet. What about the time you paid a jail fine for a vagrant, a bum the cops pulled in off the street? And you gave him more dough to get a room and a feed. How about that, *Girl* Scout?"

"That, my friend, was not only a good deed but a good investment. That lad got a job, paid back every cent I loaned him, and is now in his second year of college. He works days and studies nights. He's going to be a doctor."

"Says you."

"Says me. And I can prove it. Can you say as much for your chorine? Did she ever write you or send you back your dough?"

"Aw, hell. I never expected to get it back."

"Then you weren't disappointed, I take it?"

"Suppose I was? Is it your business?"

Shem moved in between us. "Behave, you two."

A glance at my watch told me I'd better behave and get back to the office.

"What was this fellow's name, Joe? I mean his full name."

Joe consulted his report book.

"Full name of the deceased is Donald Edward Barnett. Age, 31—we got that off his identification card from the jockey club—height—"

"Never mind his height. He isn't an unidentified corpse. Anything else?"

"His landlady said he paid his rent with a check drawn on a New York bank."

"Hmmm. Did the check clear okay?"

"Yep. Why shouldn't it have cleared?"

"No reason, really. It just seemed strange for a man who had money in the bank to ask a friend to keep him from pauper's field."

"Maybe he just had a few bucks in the bank, enough to pay his rent and expenses for a month or so until he made a score. You know how gamblers are. They eat steaks one day and hot dogs the next."

"That's true enough. I remember she made some crack at him about his farm background and he asked this Jim to ship him back to the farm. I wonder where he came from? The name sounds English or Scotch."

"Could be Jewish," Morrow suggested.

"The Barnett could be, but what about the Donald Edward? No, I'm pretty sure he was Anglo. The finely chiseled features look Anglo. And he had blue eyes, a sort of sea-blue. I noticed them last night."

Morrow snorted. "You must have been concentrating on eyes last night. Her eyes were a clear emerald, his eyes were sea-blue. What color eyes did the other dame have?"

"They were blue too, but deeper than his, a sort of pansy-blue." I had answered the gibing question absently, my attention really centered on a small pile of coins and bills heaped on top of the gate-legged table. I walked over to it.

"This his money?" I asked Shem.

"Must be."

I counted it idly. A five, two ones and some change. And a crumpled bit of blue paper. I quietly palmed the paper as I moved the bills and change around on the table.

"Not much dough here. Seven eighty-five. He hasn't been lucky lately, if that's all he had. No one could go far on that money."

"Are you nuts?" Morrow asked. "It looks to me like he went plenty far on much less than that dough. The gas bill won't be more than seven eighty-five."

"Don't be so crude," I said, acidly. "This is hardly the place for your kind of humor." I motioned toward the still figure and once again checked on the details.

He wore light-blue chambray pajamas and still had street shoes on, a pair of well-made, tan low cuts. His hands were delicate and the fingers tapered to freshly manicured tips. Hardly the hands of a farm boy but rather those of an artist or a loafer. I've seen them on both types of men. Whatever his background, it had been a long time since his hands had had contact with the plow or any other hard work. He had been fastidious. The pajamas were freshly laundered and his hair, like his nails, had had recent attention.

Almost involuntarily I sighed. He seemed so young and handsome to have grown tired of living and chucked away his life by the gas pipe. I wondered if, when it was too late to draw back, he had felt any regret for what he was doing to himself; if he had known any desire to struggle out of the enclosing blackness and shut off the gas which was sending him away. He looked peaceful and relaxed. His hands were stretched out along his legs, his head was thrown back and turned slightly to one side, giving him the appearance of a man napping in a chair. Yet on close study I saw—or imagined I saw—the shade of a worried frown, the faintest bit of a crease on his forehead and a slight tensity about the sensitive mouth. I thought: Maybe he did wonder, just at the end, if this was his only solution.

"What in hell are you day dreaming about?" Johnny's annoyed query snapped me abruptly out of my reverie. "Let's get going, babe."

I turned to go and as I did I had the odd feeling that I was saying good-bye to a friend. Yet, I'd not known the man at all. I took a last look at the silent form and my eye caught the glint of something shiny under the small table which held the victrola.

I pointed a finger at the gleam. "What's that, Joe?"

"An emphy Scotch bottle." Joe's answer was laconic.

"Scotch and Paul Whiteman's music." Johnny shrugged his shoulders. "Well, he sure chose pleasant company to speed him on his way. Come on, Slone. Doc, there's your verdict all wrapped up in a gift package. Suicide while temporarily insane and stinkin' on Scotch." He started for the door while I glared at his back.

"So long, Joe." I got ready to leave. "Good-bye, Doc."

"'Bye, Margaret." Joe was apparently not going to make a fuss about the pictures.

"I'll see you at the inquest, my dear," Doc said.

"Not if I can help it, you won't," I retorted. "You'll see Morgan, not me—I hope."

"Well, I'll be there, Doc," Morrow called from the hall.

I joined him and we headed for the stairs. As we neared the landing there was the sound of heavy feet pounding up the steps.

"Doc's boys." I drew back from the landing. "Let them get by first. I'm not superstitious but I don't care about trying to squeeze past that gruesome basket on a stairway."

We waited for the men to bring the wicker basket past us. Just in back of them was a slim, well-groomed man of medium height and medium age. His carefully chosen, hand-tailored, slightly sporty clothes marked him with the label of a well-to-do race track man. He wore a smart green and brown foulard tie, just a shade louder than a banker would wear. The overall ensemble was a symphony in browns and greens. I drew back and took Morrow's arm. I had a feeling this man was connected with the suicide.

8. *Just a Routine Story*

"WAIT a minute," I whispered to Morrow. "I wonder who this man is?"

"How should I know? I never saw him before."

"Maybe he's going to 303. Let's wait and find out."

"And maybe he's going to any of the other nine rat traps on the floor. Come on, let's beat it."

"Go ahead. You don't have to wait for me."

The man gave us an incurious look and then took in the fact that we were blocking the landing passage to the hall.

"Pardon me." His voice requested room to move by us.

"Oh, sorry," I murmured, then was impelled to ask. "Are you looking for someone?"

"Just going to see a friend." He smiled, showing teeth so even and white they looked false but weren't. He could have modeled for a dental ad. Then, with a shade of worry in his eyes, he asked me the question I'd hoped for.

"Is someone on this floor dead? I saw undertaker's attendants bringing in a basket and taking it down this hall."

"Yes, someone is dead," I answered and added, "But those men were not undertaker's assistants. They came from the city morgue. A man has committed suicide in 303."

His reaction, half-expected though it was, startled me. His face turned as white as a sheet and he staggered back, gripping first the stair railing then my arm.

"Hey, leggo my arm!" I yelped.

He gave me a shake. "It was Don! Don Barnett, wasn't it? God! I knew this would happen. I knew it was he when I saw that basket."

I pulled away from him. "Well, you don't have to give me a black and blue mark over it," I said sharply. "I wasn't the one who drove him to suicide."

He looked at me as if he was seeing me for the first time and wondered who I was.

"I gave you a black and blue mark? Oh, of course, you're the young lady who told me he was dead. I'm sorry if I hurt you. I was terribly shocked. Don was my friend. He was almost like a son to me. How—how did he—?"

"Gas. You can still detect the odor. Is your name Jim?"

"Yes, it is. But how did you know?"

"I wasn't sure. That's why I asked. But he left a note for a friend whose name is Jim. I just had a hunch you were the man. The coroner has the note and he's still in the apartment. I'm sure he will let you see it."

"Thank you." He almost choked over the two words and pity rose in me as I saw the stunned, hurt look which had frozen the man's face to a mask-like appearance.

"Don't feel too badly." I comforted clumsily. "He didn't hurt. I mean, it didn't hurt him to die. He just went to sleep."

"Just went to sleep," he repeated softly. "Poor kid. Poor Donny. He must have been very tired and unhappy."

"He must have been," I agreed. "And with his youth and looks it seems a crying shame he had to get so damn tired he bumped himself off."

He straightened his shoulders and settled the well-cut padded coat about them. "Even the young get tired, you know. Tired enough to want to sleep forever. And when they are unhappy as well, life becomes meaningless to them. That's what happened to Donny."

"I suppose so. By the way, what did Don do for a living?"

"Oh, he just worked around the past few years. First at one thing and then another." He was being very vague.

"You mean he had no special field or vocation to follow?"

"Well, he used to ride horses for me. I'd offered him another job and he had said he'd take it. But he didn't show up this morning and I grew worried thinking he might be ill."

I gave Morrow a triumphant look. This was information.

"Then he was a jockey? He seemed a little too heavy to ride."

"He was too heavy but he became a trainer when he quit riding. He was a good one, too. The kid knew horses and he had a way with them. It was a trainer's job I had for him."

"Wasn't he also in show business?"

"Oh *that.*" His tone was scornful. "Donny had a light, pleasant singing voice and a natural talent for picking up dance steps. He was just good enough for the chorus, that's all. And the stage wasn't his world. He belonged to the race track."

He stopped abruptly and gave me a keen, searching look. I realized it had dawned on him that I was a stranger and he wanted to know what the hell business I had asking questions. His ensuing queries confirmed my idea.

"Pardon me, but who are you? What interest do you have in Donny? Did you know him? I knew most of his friends and I've never seen you before."

"No, I didn't know him. That is, not personally. My name is Slone, Margaret Slone. I'm covering the story for my paper."

"A reporter?" The tone of his voice indicated he had a very low opinion of the Fourth Estate. "I might have known. Look, must this be splashed all over the papers? The kid was just a punk trying to get along, to make a dollar and have a few things out of life. Why should his death be news?"

"Because he killed himself," I said quietly. "But don't be upset Mr.—Mr?"

"Dunn." He supplied the last name dully.

"Well, Mr. Dunn, it isn't much of a story. Just a routine piece that will be tucked away in the body of the paper after the first edition it runs in gives it front page. Maybe it won't even get front page in one edition. As you say, he isn't news. Except as a suicide, of course."

He sighed deeply. "I don't suppose it really matters. There are only a few people here who cared about him. Only two, in fact. Myself and Bette."

"What about Nita?" I watched him narrowly but I wasn't prepared for the venomous look that sprang into his eyes upon the mention of that name.

"Nita! Yes, by God, where is Nita? Where was she when he—when this happened? And where is she now?"

"Nobody knows the answer to those questions, Mr. Dunn. She took a runout powder last night and she's still missing from the scene."

The words recalled to mind the pictures I was carrying. They also brought to my attention that deadline was coming up fast. I yanked at Morrow's sleeve.

"What are you waiting for?" I asked, as if it had been his idea to wait for Dunn. "Let's scram out of here. You'll have to excuse us, Mr. Dunn, we gotta beat it—and don't worry, the story won't amount to much, it's just a routine yarn—" I called the last few words from the third floor landing up to the astonished face which was peering down the stairwell.

Morrow and I raced into the main hall under full steam and skidded for the door.

"I'll see you later," I told him, and tore down the street. I'd been far too long on this assignment. The Home ran in forty-five minutes.

When I reached the city room, I slid quietly past Dennis, went to my desk and sat down, trying to look as if I'd been there at least twenty minutes.

I hadn't lied to Dunn—the story was just routine and all race track towns have their quota of just such tragedies. The only thing that gave this a different twist was the missing show girl wife. I knew it was my best lead and I began the story by using it. I was half through the second paragraph when Dennis called to me.

"Well! Where is it, Slone?"

"Where's what?"

"The suicide story, stupid. Didn't you get it?"

"Certainly I got it," I said tartly. "Where do you think I've been and what do you suppose I'm writing now? Poems? And don't call me stupid."

"Don't call her Maggie, don't call her this, don't call her that! Cripes, you're hard to please. Okay, sweetheart, give me the story."

"Don't call me sweetheart, either. I'll give you this in just a minute—if you'll be still and let me finish it."

"How long will it go? I'll dummy it in and you can send it over in takes. Any pix?".

"Yeah, two. The story will go about five hundred, maybe seven-fifty, maybe a thousand."

"Crissakes, Slone! Make up your mind. How much will it go?"

"Seven-fifty," I said hastily.

"That's better. Make it in short takes. Where are the pix?"

"Right here. I took two of her and one of him, but we'll only need one of her."

"Her? Him? Who in hell are you talking about? Don't tell me there's a woman dead too!"

"No, the woman is only missing. She's his wife and he took the gas line out because she left him. That's all."

"Oh? That's all, is it? That's fine. When I think of the years I've wasted trying to make a reporter out of you, I could—but never mind that now. Just hand me the pictures, dammit!"

I brought them to him in a hurry. His eyes brightened at Nita's photos.

"Hmmm. Not bad. Not bad at all."

"She's no good," I snapped, faintly annoyed about his having admired her.

"How do you know that?"

"I'll tell you all about it later," I said. "Right now I have to finish this yarn."

"Okay. First give me cutlines for a three column cut on her and an overline caption. Give me lines for one column on him. And step on it."

"Of course, *he's* only worth one column, he being the one who bumped himself. But green eyes gets a big splash."

"How do you know her eyes are green?" Dennis was regarding me with frank curiosity now. "Do you by any chance number this lovely creature amongst your many friends?"

"I should say not! And I told you I'd give you the details on what I know later." I walked off, pleased with the knowledge I'd given him something to wonder about, went back to my desk and wrote out the cutlines and caption. I took them over to him, then got back to my typewriter and began to beat out the story.

When the last take had been handed in, I settled back in my chair and lit a cigarette. God! I was weary. My eyes felt like they were full of grit and my head weighed one ounce under a ton. The only thought sustaining me was the one that this day, like all days, must end and eventually I'd get to bed.

I was sprawled in the chair, eyes closed and half asleep, when Dennis called me. I pulled myself erect, expecting to be sent to the other end of town. But he got up and lumbered over to my desk, sitting down in the chair alongside of it.

"Tired, kid?" He asked mildly.

I just nodded, hoping I looked as if I was one jump ahead of the undertaker.

"Well, you've had a long stretch of duty. So if you'll tell me what you know about the woman in this suicide case, you can go on home and get some rest."

It was times like this that endeared Dennis to me. I smiled wanly at him and related the tale of the scene in the café and of how upset Gaston had been about the whole business.

"I was pretty shocked at the way he spoke of that woman and told him so. It seemed a strong denunciation of a stranger, but in view of what's happened since then I'm convinced Gaston is a rather shrewd judge of human nature. What do you think?"

"Ummm. Yes, I guess he is. What was that term he used to describe her? Oh, yes, a 'cold hotness of beauty.' Odd choice of words but I can understand what he meant."

"You're pretty good then—I couldn't," I said drily. "Nor am I sure I understand the full meaning of the term even now, after all that has happened. All I could find to compare it with was dry ice, not a very adequate similitude."

"Oh, I don't know. Roughly, it gets at what he was trying to say about her."

"You think so? Well, maybe you're right. At the present moment, however, I don't give a damn about her or where she is or if she burns through the skin, heart, or soul. Or, for that matter, if she is slated to burn in hell. Which she probably is. However, I'm too tired to worry about any part of it." I dropped the last as a not too gentle hint that I was over-ready to accept his offer to let me go home. He got the hint.

"Well, they'll turn her up somewhere. You get on home now. If anything should pop about her, I'll give you a ring."

"You can give Morgan a ring," I informed him. "Police is his beat and I don't want to do him out of a good story."

"Well, well, Miss Slone! How generous you have become of late." There was a decided jeer in his tone. "But it so happens you will have to take the police beat for the next day or two. I've sent Morgan to Hammond—there's been a killing up there—and you win the toss for police until he gets back."

"You mean you're sending me to headquarters?" I asked incredulously.

"That's what I mean, sweetheart. Get in early tomorrow, about seven-fifteen, and you can go right—"

"But, Dennis!" I interrupted. "You know how Ted Elison feels about me. I'm about as welcome at headquarters as a walking case of leprosy!"

"I can't help it if you started a personal feud with the chief of police," he retorted. "Morgan's gone and you know the beat better than anyone else up here—so you cover it until Morgan gets back. Now get out before you pass out— or I change my mind and put you to work."

The last few words changed my mind about any further argument over covering police. He knew perfectly well that I was poison to the new head of the police department. If he wanted me to buck that well-known antagonism, it was okay by me. I'd buck anything, just to get home now.

"I left five minutes ago," I said and proceeded to get out of the danger zone. When I got downstairs, I ran into Miles Hansen, photographer for our paper, and Elliot Sellers, who clicked camera for the morning sheet. They stopped me in the hall.

"Where you going? To lunch?" Hansen asked.

"I'm going home," I said smugly. "Dennis recovered his heart and let me off early. I worked all night." I finished the last word on a wide yawn.

"You look it," Hansen stated bluntly. "We're headed for up the line, Hammond. Some guy caught his wife cheating and blew her brains out with a shotgun."

"Dennis told me there had been a killing up there," I said. "He sent Morgan to cover it."

"Yeah, I know. We are going in style, we are. Haney, upstairs, has chartered your brother's plane to take us to the scene."

"That's fine. I hope Brett sticks him for a good fat flight charge. Me, I am going home to bed. Tomorrow I have to cover for Morgan while the cops look for a woman missing in a suicide case."

"You're covering for who?" Hansen asked unbelievingly.

"Morgan," I answered tersely.

"And after what you said to—"

"Skip it," I warned. "If Dennis is fool enough to send me over there, I can't help it."

"Well, kid, it's been nice knowing you." Sellers shook his head mournfully. "I hope Elison doesn't tear off your pretty hide, strip by strip."

"If he does, I'll tear him apart—word by word," I retorted and went on out to the parking lot where I'd left my car. I got in and headed for home, hoping I'd not fall asleep at the wheel but not caring much if I did. I made it to the house in just half the usual driving time and pulled up to the drive to find the gates closed. Any other time I'd have got out and opened them myself, they weren't locked. But I was too tired to be bothered, so I just sat there and blew the horn. Finally Scotty, our yard and handy man, came shuffling out of the garage and over to the gates. He stood and peered at me through the iron gratings.

"Whuffo you is blowin' dat hohn so long?" He grumbled scoldingly. "Ah isn't deef. Dat hohn beez loud enuff to wake de Angel Gabr'el. Look lak to me you is yong enuff to git on out 'n open dese hyar gates yo'se'f, onstid o' mekkin a ole man lak me do hit fo you."

"I'm tired," I said sulkily, in no mood for a scolding from anyone. "The gates hadn't ought to be closed this time of a day anyhow. If you closed them, you can damn well open them up. What else are you good for? Looks to me like you might try to earn your salt."

He gave me a stricken look.

"Miss Marget! Yo mammy ain't nevah talk lak dat to me and Ah bin hyar sence Ah wuz bohn. You got no call talkin' at me dis way. Ah gwine tole yo mammy. Hit's time you got some mannahs. Ain't none o' you kids gots too many 'n hit's a shame fo sho. De quality folkses you comes fum."

I sighed with exasperation. An apology was expected and until it was received, I'd probably sit there on the wrong side of the gates.

"I'm sorry, Scotty. I've been working since yesterday morning and I didn't mean to snap at you."

But Scotty was not that easily mollified.

"Thet haint no reason fo to snap at me," he scolded. " 'Sides which is you ain't got no call to be wukkin all de night 'n day. Ah heahs you comin' in hyar, so tard you kaint put one foot front de yuther. Gits now to whar you kaint eben open de gates you is so weak. Yo mammy wants you should stay home lak a lady should stay. Whuffo you ain't doin' lak yo mammy wants? You gots a nice home, fine folkses fo a fambly. You got no bizness wukkin fo dem cussin' paper peoples."

My patience, what little I had left of it, went kiting sky high. "Dammit! Open those gates and let me in!" I yelled. "Who the hell do you think you are to be reading me a lecture?"

He flung the gates wide and looked toward the rear door which opened just at that moment. Mother came out and her expression was anything but pleasant.

I put the car away, got out and started up the back walk to the door. As I passed Scotty he said loudly, "Fine langwidge fo a propah raised lady to be a-usin'. Oughta be shame fo yo'se'f."

I glared at him. "Oh, shut up!" I snapped and advanced to my bawling out. The door hadn't closed on us before I got it.

"I'm ashamed of you! Cursing at Scotty and screaming loudly enough for the whole street to hear you."

"I wasn't cursing at Scotty. I just said hell and damn. I didn't say damn you or go to hell. And since this is the only house in the block, I daresay no one but you heard me cursing."

"I heard you—and I heard him call you down for the

language you used. Do you think I enjoy having a servant of mine find it necessary to take my daughter to task about her profanity?"

"If you resented his doing that, why didn't you call him down?"

"Call *him* down? When he was right to resent your cursing him?"

"I didn't curse him!" I wailed. "I told you that before. And I wouldn't have cursed at all if he hadn't stood there arguing with me instead of opening the gates like he should have done. That's all I wanted him to do—just open the gates so I could get in. I didn't want a sermon from him."

"Why didn't you open the gates yourself?"

"Because I was tired, dammit, and I didn't feel like getting out of the car. Then he had to start yapping at me just because I asked him to do a small job of work. What do you pay him for, anyhow? In fact, I often wonder why you pay any of these lazy blacks you employ to loaf around this place. Outside of the possible exception of Bertha, the only one worth keeping is my Ida and that's because I make her stir herself. Bunch of lazy loafers is what they are."

Mother went white to the lips in rare anger. I knew I'd said too much and wished I hadn't.

"Margaret Slone! How dare you call them loafers? Most of them were born right here and my family has always cared for its people. I'll do the same as long as they'll let me."

"Which will be as long as you live," I muttered.

"And why not? They're my friends as well as my servants and—"

"Yes'm, I know." I interrupted her wearily. "And I'm sorry I yelled at Scotty, but I am not in the mood for arguing or being scolded. I'm going to bed."

I turned my back and started for the upstairs, then I paused to ask where Vangie was.

"Your sisters have gone to get their ashes." She looked

right at my forehead. "It doesn't look to me as if you got your's."

I groaned inwardly and decided on evasion of that subject. "I've had enough sackcloth and ashes to last me for a lifetime of Ash Wednesdays." I left her to figure that one out and went on up to my room.

9. *Vangie Provides a Surprise*

I PEELED off my suit and rang for Ida, whom I paid eight bucks a week to look after me and my things. The sight of her wide, white smile brightened life for me at once. I'd been half-afraid she too would be jumping on me about Scotty.

"Whut you want, Miss Marget, honey?"

"A hot tub, and don't spare the bath oil, something to eat, and then I'm going to bed."

She ran the tub, came back, and got me a fresh nightgown, then she stood off and surveyed me critically.

"Honey, you looks powahful bad. Dat job too hahd fo you. You gwine kilt yo'se'f effen dey don't stop mekkin you wuk so hahd."

The sympathetic voice was balm to my ears. I gave her a grateful look.

"Oh, I'll be okay as soon as I get some food and sleep."

"Sho nuff you will, honey. Now whut you wants to eat?"

"Anything. A sandwich or a salad or a bowl of soup. Just get me anything you can wangle out of Bertha."

As soon as she had gone, I went to the bath and stretched out full length in the tub of warm, scented water. I stayed there soaking and relaxing until I heard Ida re-enter my room, then I got out, dried off and powdered my body, put on the gown and a robe and went into the bedroom. Ida had done a noble job of foraging, she had two thick slices of baked red fish, a tomato aspic, bread, butter, cake, and a pint of milk.

"Gee, that looks good!" I applauded. "But how did you

manage to get the aspic and the fish? Isn't that for dinner?"

She grinned widely. "Butha wuz out fum de kitchen when Ah got to scrabblin' aroun' 'n by de time she gits back I had dis hyar tray all fix up. She fuss at me but hit wuz too late den."

I regarded her with fond affection. "You're wonderful," I told her and started to eat.

I had almost finished the meal when someone tapped on my door. In answer to my invitation to come in, my youngest sister, Vangie, entered and surveyed me from the other side of the room.

"How come you're ready for bed at this hour and what in hell have you been doing to yourself?" She asked. "You look like the wrath of God."

"Never mind what I look like," I snapped. "I've been working since yesterday morning and I'm sick and tired of being told I look like an accident going someplace to happen."

"Poor Margaret." She sat down in the low chair by my bed and reached over to help herself to a piece of cake from my tray. "What kind of a Carnival did you have? Did anything exciting happen?"

I gazed at my beautiful, bright-haired kid sister, whose neck I often wanted to wring but whom I loved dearly. I didn't feel like retelling the story of Carnival and the rest of it, but the big blue eyes were so lively and full of interest, I soon found myself telling her all about the night before at Gaston's and the aftermath of the scene in the café.

"What did you say their names were?" She asked when I had ended the story about the suicide and the missing wife.

"I didn't say. But it is Barnett, Don and Nita Barnett. Her stage name is Annette Jeans."

The astonishment that spread over Vangie's face jolted me out of my weariness.

"What are you so pop-eyed about? Surely *you* don't know them?"

"But I do! Is she a tall, snooty, brunette with queer green eyes?"

"That's her! But where in the world did you meet them?"

"At a Mardi Gras party Julie Dupuy gave last Sunday."

"Where did Julie ever meet them? They hardly fit in that crowd?"

"Don't be a snob," Vangie advised, blandly. "She met them through her papa. You know he owns horses and Don had been a jockey and a trainer."

"I know, but, even so, few owners hobnob with their jockeys and trainers."

"Why Margaret, where have you been all these years? It's getting to be quite the thing for the jockeys to marry the owners' daughters."

"Maybe some owners find themselves in that spot. I can't see Jacques Dupuy doing it though."

"Well, he introduced the man to Julie at the track last week. Julie took a liking to him, he *was* handsome, and invited him to the party she was giving Sunday. He said he'd like to come, but he was expecting his wife to arrive any day. There wasn't anything Julie could do but include her in the invitation."

"Did Nita behave herself or did she act all over the place?"

"Oh, she behaved well enough but she looked as if she was bored to tears. Funny thing was that Mike O'Leary turned up with some girl he's been crazy about for years, Bette something—"

"You know them too? F'Pete's sake, they were along with Nita and Don on Carnival night."

"I know Mike. He went to school with Theo Dupuy. I'd seen him lots of times with the same girl but I'd never met her before. Anyhow, it turns out that Don and Nita also knew Mike and the girl. And, if you ask me, Nita was anything but happy to see either of them. She sulked all over the place."

"She did more than sulk at Gaston's and the whole scene was brought on because of her jealousy of Bette. There's a tie-in there that doesn't meet the eye. Bette was in love with Don, that was as plain as the nose on your face."

"Oh, indubitably!" Vangie exclaimed. "I felt right sorry for poor Mike. From the time Don showed up she had eyes for no one else. I wonder where that green-eyed hussy has herself holed up?"

"The cops were wondering about that too, the last I heard," I said. "As for me, I'm not capable of wondering about anything right now except how soon you're going to get out of here and let me sleep."

She giggled, picked up my tray and chanted in a low voice, "Maggie's got a hangover, Maggie's got a—"

I hurled a pillow at her, snuggled down under the covers and the next sound I heard was the alarm going off in my ear. It was six a.m. I had slept the clock around. All rested and with my eyes and temper restored to their natural colors, I dressed and trotted down to the kitchen, poked my head in the door and sang out a cheerful good morning to Bertha.

She grunted and asked, "Whut you gwine eat dis mawnin? A lil ole cup o' cawfee an' a piece o' toast?"

"Not on your life. I'm hungry. I want orange juice, bacon and eggs, toast, and coffee. The works."

She gaped at me. "You feels good, doesn't you?"

I nodded. "Fine—and hungry too."

She gave me a look. "Ah is gittin' yo brekfuss fas' as Ah kin. Hit's too bad you wuzn't feelin' lak dis yestiddy. Mebbe you wouldn't jump po ole Scotty lak you did."

"Never mind that." I beat a hasty retreat to the dining room, got the morning paper and looked for the suicide story. It was tucked away on an inside page and there was nothing new in it. The woman had not been found but police, as usual, expected to locate her any moment. I went out to the hall, found the Home edition of the paper with my story in it and saw Dennis had given it front page. He'd used both pix and the caption under her's read:

"If you know this woman's identity or whereabouts, please notify the police. She is wanted for questioning in the death of her husband, Donald E. Barnett, 1010 Baronne Street. Barnett was a former jockey and race horse trainer."

Bertha brought in my breakfast and while I ate I checked the story. It read okay and I'd just laid the paper aside when Mother and Marian, my older sister, came in. Both gave me a cool good morning which I returned in kind. Marian always irritated me by reflecting Mother's moods and actions. I gulped the rest of my coffee and got out before Mother could get settled to start on the Scotty subject again. The object of that subject, however, was waiting for me in the garage. I rummaged hurriedly through my purse, grabbed a bill and before he could open his mouth I shoved it at him and said.

"Here, Scotty, buy yourself a drink and forget what I said yesterday. I didn't mean a word of it. You know that."

He grinned delightedly. "Sho, Ah knows hit. See how Ah done polish yo cah ontil hit shines lak a mirror?"

I admired the wax job extravagantly, got in the shining convertible coupé and drove to the office, where I picked up some stuff Dennis had got from Morgan the day before, and then went on over to police headquarters.

Thursday passed without incident. The missing woman didn't turn up and no one called in to say they knew her. I managed to practice sleight of foot well enough to avoid running into the new police boss and when the nightside reporters came trundling in, I checked out and went to the office. It had been a dull day and, Morrow being off, there hadn't been anyone who was fun to jaw with. Back at my city room desk, I finished up what few things I had to get out for the last edition and left the office at a few minutes before five.

Dennis wasn't around but I knew where he might be, so

instead of heading for home I ankled over to Sammy's bar, a place which has a duplicate within easy walking distance of every newspaper office. I found Dennis and plopped into a seat across from him.

He greeted me pleasantly. In Sammy's I am Dennis' pal.

"Well, I got through the day without Elison carving me from ear to ear." I grinned at him.

"That's good. He'll soon get over being sore at you, but it was a dumb thing to do."

"I suppose it was," I assented. "But that's just how I felt and still feel."

"Me too, but I got better sense than to tell it to the guy's wife."

I giggled. "Don't you know how that happened?"

He shook his head and ordered us another round of drinks.

"Well, Elison is married to a twin sister of Tommy's. The unmarried twin hates Ted's guts. I'd had a few drinks and even when I'm cold sober those two look alike to me. I thought I was talking to Edna when, worse luck, I was griping to Edith."

Dennis roared with laughter. "That's rich!" he howled. "That's the most beautiful boner you've ever pulled."

"Okay, so it is," I agreed. "But don't you ride me about it. I haven't told this to anyone but you."

He wiped tears of glee from his eyes, told me that was worth another drink, bought it and then asked if anything new had come up on the disappearing wife.

"Nope. Oh, hell, that dame is well on her way to New York by now," I said.

"I suppose so. But it's a hell of a way for a wife to treat a poor bastard who loved her that much."

I shrugged. "Chances are she doesn't know he took the gas pipe. But I doubt very much that she gives a damn. Well, I better go. I'm in my family's doghouse—again."

"F'crissakes, Maggie, what did you do now?"

I drew back coldly. "Nothing. And don't call me Maggie!"

"Sorry, kid. Well, what's your family mad at you about?"

"Only Mother and Marian are angry—and Marian does as Mama does. My dear mother does not like the people I work with or the work I do. She is a very sweet person but much as I love her she is a headache to me at times. This is one of the times. I often wish I had a place of my own, maybe I'd be better off away from my family."

"No, you wouldn't." Dennis shook his head sagely. "Much as you love that brother and kid sister of your's, you'd be miserable. So go on home and make up with the others. You got the same beat to cover tomorrow."

"I know. Well, if I managed today I guess I can get through tomorrow without becoming a casualty. If I do get shot my family can sue the city. So long now—"

I waved him good-bye and went to get my car and go home. While I was digging in my bag for my car keys I pulled out a crumpled bit of paper. It was the piece I'd picked up on the table in the Baronne street apartment. I'd forgot all about it and wondered why I'd lifted it in the first place. I smoothed it out and saw it had some figures on it. Four figures: 1210. I wondered what they meant and decided they could mean anything from a sum of money to an hotel room. The latter thought brought me up abruptly. Hotel room! That could be just what they did mean. It could be the number of the room where she had gone when she left the apartment. Then I saw that was foolish. If she had engaged a room the police would have found her. They'd checked all the hotels and she wasn't in any of them. I chucked the whole idea, got in my car and drove on home.

The gates were open and I drove on in and put the car away. The family was sitting down to dinner and I arrived with the entrée, a large baked ham. It looked good and I said so, sailing my hat and purse into a corner and taking my seat at the table.

Mother frowned at me, then at the chair my things had landed on when I tossed them.

"I do wish you would stop throwing things around helter-skelter," she complained. "It's not ladylike."

"Nothing I do lately is ladylike," I retorted, acidly. "I'm getting sick of it."

"Her aim is always pretty good," my brother, Brett, said mildly. "The things landed smack on the chair and nothing got broken."

I grinned at him. "Thanks, darling. Where have you been besides Hammond?"

"Flying."

"Oh, fiddle! I know that. But flying where? I haven't seen you for over a week."

"I was floating around Texas and Oklahoma with a crowd of oil men and self-satisfied politicians. Both groups had pot bellies and inflated egos."

"Sounds deadly." I dug into my dinner, surprised at how hungry I was. I'd had a big lunch.

"It was deadly. Guys like that give me a pain. One knew a little about flying and he kept trying to tell me how to fly my own ship. I finally told him to take the controls or get off the pot—oops! Sorry, Mother!

Mother frowned at him and Marian followed suit. I sighed and wished they had a little more *common* sense of humor. Much as I hated to admit it, they were inclined to be a little priggish.

Brett saw the frown and hurriedly turned back to me.

"What you been up to?" He asked me.

"Dennis put me back on police after he sent Morgan to Hammond on that killing. I drew a suicide and a missing wife—"

"Oh, sure. Vangie was telling me. Don Barnett, the poor sunnavabitch."

"Now don't tell me you knew him too?" My surprised query halted the reprimand he was about to get.

"Slightly. I flew him from Chicago here."

"You *flew* him?" I was incredulous. "When?"

"About a month ago. We got pretty chummy on the trip and he said he would like to learn to fly. I told him I had an instructor's license and he said he'd get in touch with me. That was the last I heard of him until I saw the story in the paper and Vangie filled in the details about the show his wife put on in the café."

"Did he talk about his wife on the trip?"

"Nope. We talked about flying and some race track chatter. The fellow sure knew his horses. He said he was a trainer and I remembered him when he was a jockey."

"She hasn't been found yet, has she?" Vangie asked.

"I shook my head. "No, and she won't be found, if you ask me. She'd made herself scarce and she'll stay that way."

Brett turned his twinkling dark eyes on me.

"I don't suppose there's any doubt of it being suicide?"

"Technically, none." I smiled back at him.

"What do you mean, technically?"

"Well, there seems little doubt he propped the chair against the door, wrote the notes and turned on the gas. So, technically, she isn't a suspect of murder but morally she's guilty as hell, the rotten bitch."

Mother's look acted like a lever to raise me from the table. I didn't wait for dessert, but marched out of the dining room in a silence as thick as tapioca. Going up to my room I thought: I'm damned if I don't get me an apartment. This constant disapproval of my every word is getting a bit thick to take.

I stalked into my room, undressed without calling Ida, read for awhile and fell asleep with the book in my hand and the bed light on. When I woke to the sound of the alarm, the light had been turned off and the book was on the table. I got up, put on a beige wool dress and went downstairs. I stopped at the kitchen door and called out cheerily.

"Good morning, Bertha, darling. How are you this lovely spring morning?"

She eyed me suspiciously.

"They ain't nuttin lovely bout dis hyar mawnin. Hit's reenin lak de furies."

"Is it now? I hadn't noticed. My shades were down."

"Yo eahs wuzn't close, wuz dey? Anyone ain't deef kin heah dat ole reen."

My morning cheer began to evaporate. "I hear it now. You might know I'd draw a day like this just when I have to be around Ted Elison."

"Who Ted Elison? De pleeceman? Whut he got to do wif you?"

"Nothing—I hope." I grabbed the glass of orange juice she'd just finished squeezing and drank it. "Now give me a couple of fried eggs, some toast, and coffee. And hurry. I want to get out of here before Mother and Marian come down."

She gave me a searching look out of bright, beady eyes.

"Miss Marget, you hadn't oughta werry yo maw de way you does. You fixin to brek huh haht an' ruin yo own helt."

"Mind your business," I snapped.

"Hit is ma bizness. Ah bcez hyar when you wuz bohn an when you is ackin lak you is ackin hit's ma bizness."

I knew this could go on indefinitely and I knew Mother would be down any minute. I turned on my heel without a word and headed out of the house into the rain.

Driving down St. Charles Avenue, the rain almost blinded me. It was coming down in swirling, windswept gusts that made driving a chore. But it wasn't until I had almost reached Lee Circle that the real deluge let go. My wipers quit and the visibility was zero. I pulled to the side of the street to wait for it to slack. I had loads of time, even if the rain kept up for thirty minutes I wouldn't be late. For twenty-five minutes by my dash board clock, I sat and watched as solid sheets of rain cascaded out of the invisible heavens. My top began to leak and I slid over to the other side of the seat and huddled there while another fifteen minutes ticked inexorably past. I was twenty minutes late before the rain stopped.

I wiped the water off the seat and slid back under the wheel, stepping on the starter. Nothing happened, not even a polite rumble. The car was drowned out. I wasted more time cussing it, then yanked open the door and trudged two blocks to the nearest service station.

"My car's drowned out over near the Circle," I told an attendant. "Can you send someone with me to dry out the points?"

The man called a coverall-clad mechanic and we went back to where my balky car was parked. He dried the points with a rag soaked in kerosene and I drove him back to his station. When I finally walked into the city room I was forty-five minutes late and I'd had nothing to eat. I was in a foul mood and Dennis did nothing to sweeten it.

"Goddammit, Slone," he greeted me angrily, "where the hell have you been?"

"Have you noticed the weather?" I asked acidly.

Dennis pointed a finger at the window where bright sunlight was streaming into the room.

"Yah! What's wrong with it?"

"It wasn't like that ten minutes ago and you know it!" I snapped. "It was pouring rain when I left home. My wipers quit and I stopped the car. It drowned out and I had to go get someone to dry the points."

"It was raining when I left home too, but I didn't get stuck in it."

"Well, f'crissakes!" I exploded. "I didn't plan to get stuck in it either. I can't help it if the car drowned out."

"You oughta buy a decent car. That heap you drive is about to fall apart."

"That heap suits me. Besides, how can I buy a new car on my salary?"

"That, sister, is your problem. Right now my problem is getting police coverage. So get in that junkpile of yours and see if it will take you to headquarters without breaking down."

I marched out of the room without answering, went down and drove on over to police headquarters in the Criminal Courts building. I went to the press room, found it empty, put my stuff away and went out to check the beat. The blotter listed the usual catch of drunks and prostitutes, brawls and negro cuttings. A trolley motorman had been held up early in the morning on the cemetery run and a few minutes later a taxi driver in the same vicinity had reported being robbed of his nightly take. I made a few notes and went on back to the press room. It was still empty.

I was sitting there wondering where everyone was, when hurried footsteps sounded in the corridor and Shem barged in so excited he didn't seem to find my being there unusual.

"Hello, Margaret. Where's Johnny?"

"I was wondering about him. Why? What's up?"

He waved a piece of paper at me. "Here, take a look at this. The rest of the guys have gone over there and I gotta beat it. If you don't see Johnny before you leave, stick this in his typewriter." He handed me the slip and hastened from the room.

I read the few words. Read them again and reached for the wire to the city desk. Dennis answered.

"How would you like a nice murder before lunch?" I asked him.

10. *Cold Horror of Murder*

"WOULD you mind repeating that?" Dennis asked.

I obliged and added, "I think they've found our missing wife."

"You mean she's been murdered?"

"It looks like it. Shem just brought in a report from the Third Precinct. They've found the body of a woman in the rear of 602 Toulouse Street. They think it's the missing woman from the suicide case."

"You better get on over there and make sure."

"That's just what I'm about to do. You send me a camera. I'll meet him over there." I hung up and got my things together, typed a hasty note to Morrow, stuck it with the police slip in his machine, and beat it out to my car.

When I stopped in front of the Toulouse Street address, I found a knot of curious people crowded by the alley gate and clustered in the doorway of the combination ice cream parlor and Italian sundries shop. Ed Grady, another uniformed homicide squad cop, and Joe Shem rode herd on the excited residents of the section. Dr. Rollins was just climbing out of his car, reaching for his medical bag. I parked in back of his jalopy, got out and joined him on the sidewalk. The round cherubic face was grave and thoughtful.

"Well, Doc. I didn't expect to see you so soon after our last meeting."

"I thought you were not covering police anymore, my child?" The words were a question.

"It's just until Morgan gets back from Hammond. By the way, Doc, you had the inquest on that suicide?"

"Of course. I sent the report to the press room. Didn't you get it?"

"No." I walked alongside of him to the gate. "It wasn't on my desk. Not that it matters a lot, it was a suicide verdict and I can add it to the new story."

"Is there something new on that story?"

"Why, Doc! Didn't you know? They think the woman who has been found dead in back of here is the missing wife, the *femme fatale*."

"No, Margaret, I didn't know. Detective Gross called me. He merely stated that a woman's body had been found at this address and that she had been murdered. I came as fast as I could."

Just as we started to enter the alley, Miles Hansen drove up and parked. He got his camera and supply case out of his car and joined us by the gate.

"Who's the stiff?" he asked.

"The general opinion is that it's the body of the woman missing in the suicide case. The wife we accused of running away."

We entered the narrow alley, which stretched between the tall buildings, single file, and followed it to where it ended on a partly enclosed court. The court was paved with round cobblestones and in the center was a small fountain, the stone bowl littered with leaves and torn bits of paper; the pipes rusted and about to fall apart. The court was enclosed by a tall cypress fence with a gate set in the dead center. The gate was secured by a common type of hardware store bolt and it and the hinges had been recently painted a bright green.

Most of New Orleans' French Quarter yards are patios, enclosed on all sides by the building they enhance. This semienclosed court and building seemed odd and out of keeping with the usual. From the ground you couldn't see over the dividing fence.

Off to the corner of the rear fence was a group of people,

clustered about an object that sprawled brokenly on the cobblestones. I made a beeline for Tommy Gross, Chief of Detectives, whom I thought should be Chief of Police. He was leaning against the fence, frowning and absently pulling at his lower lip.

"Hi, Thomas," I greeted him. "What gives here?"

"Murder, Margaret. See for yourself." He waved a hand at the still, contorted figure at his feet.

"Is it the missing wife?"

"It is. Of course we have no positive identification yet, and she certainly doesn't look anything like the pictures in the papers, but we're pretty sure it's the woman in that case."

"I guess I can identify her," I said. "I saw her Mardi Gras night."

"Yeah, so I gathered. Well, she's been dead since that night. That's almost a cinch."

"Murder at the Mardi Gras!" I exclaimed. "It's almost like the old days of the vendettas."

"It is, worse luck." He sounded gloomy. "Well, take a look and see if you can give us the identification."

I looked down at the corpse. The twisted body lay on its side with the legs drawn up under it. Dr. Rollins was tugging at one limp leg. My gaze traveled on up toward the face, then my eyes stopped at the throat and I gazed in cold horror at the black silk cord which was knotted tightly under her right ear.

"Garroted, by God!" I exclaimed in a hoarse, shocked whisper. "Garroted in true Apache style!"

"Why the Apaches never done nobody like that!" An indignant voice in back of me protested. I turned to see Les Beton, Tommy's pet aide and my pet hate. Les and I never worked on a case without having words and most of the time they were unpleasant.

"Apaches scalped people," he continued. "They didn't choke 'em with cords."

I laughed derisively. "Cripes, if that isn't just what you'd be expected to say! I wasn't talking about the Apache Indians. I mean the French thugs who are also called Apaches. Didn't you ever see a dance team do the Apache? Never mind, you wouldn't know what it was if you had seen it. What's important, is that this is a French—or anyhow a Latin—method of killing. It's quick and quiet and the victim hasn't a Chinaman's chance to get loose. It's all a trick to the way the cord is twisted. Something like that."

"Is that so?" He sneered. "You know everything, don't you?"

"Not quite," I answered. "You don't have to be so snippy about it, either. I'm just trying to be helpful."

"We can do without your help. I thought we'd got rid of you. How come you covering police again? I bet Elison hasn't seen you."

I opened my mouth to snap at him, but Morrow came steaming up, breathless and perspiring. I turned my attention to him.

"Well, if it isn't the late Mr. Morrow. Where you been for the past hour?"

"Shut up—and thanks for the note. Have I missed anything?"

Before I could answer, Beton spoke.

"Naw, you haven't missed anything much. Except you did miss hearing about how this dame got strangled by an Apache. Of course we knew right along that she'd been strangled but it took Margaret to tell us an Indian done the job."

"I told you once the French Apaches aren't Indians," I said acidly. "They're gangsters. Nor did I say one killed her. I merely said the style had been used. Don't go putting words in my mouth."

"*Me* put words in your mouth! Now that is a laugh!"

I glared at him and turned back toward the corpse, just as Dr. Rollins succeeded in turning it partially on its back. I looked at the grotesque mask that had been a thing of beauty and was now a congested, purpled blotch, with a dried, blackened tongue protruding from the puffed, swollen lips. The emerald eyes were glazed green glass now and they were wide open and bulging from the effects of death by strangulation. I turned away, remembering how bright and compelling those eyes had been only three nights before. I thought: The cold hotness of beauty is frozen in the cold horror of death.

"What's the matter, Margaret?" Morrow asked.

"Nothing. I was just thinking that she's certainly not a thing of beauty any longer."

"I'll say not. She fits right into the mess of this court."

I looked around and agreed with him. There were piles of empty fruit crates and food barrels and beside the body was a large stack of big burlap bags. Oversized, unemptied garbage pails stood about and people were milling around, some drawn by morbid curiousity. Among those who had business there was a trio of husky Negroes; the garbage men who had found the body. They huddled in a crowded, scared looking tangle as far from the figure on the stones as they could get. A white man, who appeared to be in charge of them, stood talking earnestly with the three blacks. With something of a shock, I recognized the Italian couple, Mr. and Mrs. Pacelli, in whose place I had often eaten spumoni ice cream and drunk homemade red wine. I'd been so occupied with the murder I had not realized until then that the sundry shop and the building was the one operated and occupied by them. A pretty dark-haired girl of about fifteen hovered close to Mrs. Pacelli, her big brown eyes tremendous in her heart-shaped face. It was Christina, the eldest Pacelli daughter.

It seemed to me Doc was taking a long time with his primary examination and just as the thought crossed my mind, he straightened up and dropped one of the burlap sacks over the dead, distorted face.

"Finished, Doc?" Gross asked.

"All through, Tom. Fire away with your questions."

"Well, you know what the first one will be—how long has she been dead?"

"A long time. I can't say exactly how long, but it's more than forty-eight hours."

"Making it sometime early Wednesday morning."

"Exactly. If you want me to set a tentative hour, I'd say between the hours of three and six a.m. Wednesday."

Something rang a memory bell in my mind. I'd heard almost the same words spoken not too long ago. Doc had been the speaker then. He had given the exact same time for the death of the suicide.

"I'm sure the attack was unexpected," Doc went on. "It must have taken her completely by surprise, in a relaxed moment when she was unaware of danger. She was, as Margaret said, garroted in the manner employed by French thugs."

"My, my, what big ears you have, grampa," I murmured.

"It's part of my job to listen for comments, Margaret." His tone was pleasant enough but I had the feeling he was displeased and I didn't want him to be angry with me.

"I know, darling. And a good thing you do listen. I needed you to back me up on that particular score."

"You seem to do very well without my backing," he said, a bit tartly, and turned his attention back to Tommy. I shrugged and looked at Morrow.

"What are you grinning about?" I snapped.

"Nothing. Nothing at all. Maybe someday you'll learn to keep that big mouth of your's shut and not talk when you should be listening. Now, take that crack you made to Elison's—"

"Oh, go to hell!" I invited and turned my back on him.

Gross directed an annoyed look at me. "You were saying, Doc—?"

"I was about to say there is no evidence of much struggle. Her clothing is not torn, there are no bruises on her hands or arms and no shreds of skin under her nails. That is, none show under my glass. Indications are that she was attacked from behind and died within minutes of the assault. The autopsy will probably show more. But this I do know now; she died very quickly and with little pain."

"I always thought strangulation was a slow and painful death," Morrow objected.

"Not when a garrote is used. Manual throttling, when the bare hands are used, is something else again. So is the hangman's rope."

"But the rope breaks the neck."

"Not always. The modern trap gallows does, but the old style of hanging simple strangled out life and any struggle from the victim merely hastened the end. Even when the hands are employed, if the killer knows just the right artery to press, death comes quickly. Not many people know that, however—which is likely a very good thing. But, in this case, death came almost as rapidly as it would had she been hanged from a gallows."

"That sounds as though she'd been condemned and executed," I put in.

Rollins passed a hand over his face in an often used gesture. "Condemned and executed," he repeated, musingly. "That's a strange way to phrase it, Margaret, but she was certainly executed in the manner of the French underworld."

"And she was French."

Tommy wheeled to face me. "That's so, she was! I'd forgot that angle for the moment. You say you saw her Mardi Gras night. What happened?"

I told him the story of the scene in the café. He looked very serious and thoughtful, pulling at his lower lip in an habitual gesture.

"All that ties in with this murder, somehow."

"Dr. Rollins placed the death of her husband between the same hours he placed her murder," I offered.

"That's right, I did." Rollins looked at me. "Both deaths occurred at about the same time."

"There has to be some connection between the two," Tommy said decisively. "We'll find it, too."

"I'm sure you will, Tom." Doc smiled. "May I go now? Shem has sent word that my boys are here to take the body away. I'd like to do the post mortem as soon as possible. I've a busy day ahead of me."

"I'm through with it," Tommy answered. "You guys got all the pictures you want?" He included police and press photographers in the query. They replied they were all done and Tommy turned back to the coroner. "Let your boys come in, Doc. Send me a lab report if I don't get over for the p.m."

"Very well." Rollins moved away and summoned the morgue attendants. For the second time in a little less than forty-eight hours, I watched the grim wicker basket go past me. They carted it to the rear corner and dumped the womans' body in it as if it was a bundle of laundry. I felt a pang at the sight of that once lovely body, now just a loose lump of flesh, being taken away in what was very likely the same basket that a short while before had held her husband's corpse. I wondered, somewhat morbidly, if the two would lie side by side in the steel cases of the morgue, that huge filing room for the dead. A sudden, unwanted surge of pity swept over me and for a second I felt almost dizzy with the emotion it awakened. Morrow grabbed my arm as if to steady me.

"Take it easy, kid," he warned.

"I'm okay," I assured him. "It was just that this coming on top of that suicide unnerved me for a second."

That was when I got a real shock for Johnny spoke angrily from between set teeth.

"I'd like to take a poke at that goddam Mick editor of yours!" He exploded. "I don't know why he sends you on these things when he could and should send a man."

I gaped at him open-mouthed. Protection—and from such a source! Suddenly I recalled other odd times when he had seemed somewhat protective toward me. I wondered if he was getting soft about me. Then I resolutely pushed the thought away. Johnny had made the usual number of passes at me when I first went on police work, he'd been given the brushoff Dennis had advised me to give any of the guys who got bright ideas along those lines, and we had finally developed an amicable and sexless sort of friendly rivalry. Nevertheless, being human and also feminine, I looked at Johnny with a stirring of new interest. Johnny's a personable lad, taller than average, with curly brown hair worn a little too long for exact neatness, blue-gray eyes and a generally pleasing ensemble of features. His smile was attractive and he had a lot of charm. I'd seen that charm in action and if it hadn't been for the editor's warning, it might well have worked on me. Besides, this attitude was not the usual pass. It was something more subtle and therefore it meant more. At that point I pulled my thoughts back to earth, irritated with myself for entertaining silly notions, and announced tartly.

"You can just mind your own business, Johnny Morrow, and I'm no part of it. What's more, I'm as good a police reporter as you are."

He shrugged. "Okay, you needn't get on your ear. I was just expressing an opinion and I still think the police beat should be covered by men. There are times when it is too dangerous for a female."

"I never asked you for any protection against danger, did I?"

"Nope. But there were times when you should have."

"That's beside the point. I didn't and I'm still here and all in one piece."

"Yeah, but most of you is in Ted Elison's dog house."

I had no answer for that one, so I turned my back and marched over to where Tommy was talking with the garbage workers. Johnny trailed behind me and as we drew within earshot I heard the foreman bellow at Gross.

"Godammit, Captain, how much longer are you going to hold up the job of cleaning this section? The Department of Sanitation hires this crew to clean streets and collect refuse and not to hang around waiting for the high and mighty cops to ask them questions. This area has to be cleared by noon or the super will have my hide. So f'crissakes let's get going on those questions."

"I'd advise you to keep a civil tongue in your head," Tommy retorted shortly. "If you'll also keep it still for a few minutes, I'll soon be through with you and your crew."

"Okay. Okay." The man was angrily sullen. "But let's get on with it."

Tommy turned to the giant blacks and began asking questions. They had recovered from their first fright and with the body gone from the spot, they were beginning to enjoy their importance.

"Which one of you found the body?" Gross asked.

The biggest Negro answered. "Well, suh, Cap'n, we come in hyar dis mawnin foh to git de gabbidge. Hit wuz late. Fack is, we wuz runnin' late kase ob de reen. So hit wuz about seben-thutty when we gits hyar and usual we finish de block by dat time."

"Usual we is finish de block by seben-fifteen." The shortest of the trio had made the correction and the first speaker glared at him.

"*Mistuh* Eben! Is we agree Ah'm to do de talkin' to de man?"

"Yassuh, Mistuh Jackson, we is agree an' you is to talk." Eben subsided hastily, drawing off to one side of the fore-man.

"Den kinely lemme do hit. Well, suh, Cap'n, we comes in hyar an' stahts to heft de pails foh to empty 'em."

"And then you found the body?" Tommy tried to hurry the tale along.

But Jackson was not one to be rushed. "Nossuh, boss, hit wuzn't des lak dat. We neveh got to de emptyin' of dem pails atall. Eben, he wuz heftin' one, an' Ah took a look at de bags to see effen dere wuz enuff to tote away—and whut you think Ah seed?"

"A dead woman," Tommy answered promptly.

"Dat's exackly right! She wuz hid undah de bags, wif bofe she laigs pokin' out fum whar Ah had pulled off a couple sacks. Ah tuhned to mah boys, Joe, and dis sorry li'l ole Eben, whut got wish offen me las' week, an' Ah sed; 'Put down dem pails, boys. Dey beez someone daid ovah hyar.' Des whut Ah sed, suh." He paused dramatically.

"Then you investigated?"

"Did which, suh?"

Tommy concealed a grin. "You looked to see if the girl was dead or just unconscious, didn't you?"

"Ah knowed she wuz daid, but, lak you says, Ah 'vestigated. We left de bags—"

"*Ah* lefted off de bags," Eben interrupted, firmly.

Jackson favored the new helper with a glare. "Kase Ah tole you to do hit. You wuz all foh runnin' fas' as yo laigs would carry you foh a pleeceman. Ontil Ah tole you to left de bags."

"Des right—but Ah wuz de one whut lefted dem."

Tommy had a sudden coughing spell and Beton picked up the questioning.

"It makes no difference who lifted the sacks. The point is that one of you found the woman and I take it that one was you, eh Jackson?"

"Yassuh. Des de livin' trufe. Yes, Lawd, Ah foun' huh 'n she wuz daid as a mak'rel."

"Then you called the police?"

Jackson shook his head negatively.

"Well, suh, not jest den. Ah knowed about not techin' anything at a murder an' Ah figgered hit wuz dat. Ah went to git de boss man, Mistuh Miles ovah theah. Ah figgered bein' Ah wuz top crew man, hit wuz mah place foh to go git him."

"Went kase he wuz skeered ob dat daid gal," Eben muttered in his teeth.

The big black drew himself up and and flexed his powerful arms.

"You sez dat jes once moh 'n Ah gwine flatten you. Ah means hit. Ah ain't tuhned de color ob ashes lak some Ah knows."

"So you went and got Miles?" Tommy interrupted the threatened quarrel.

"Yassuh. Soon as he saw whut happened, he call de pleece. Ob co'se, long foh dey gits hyar, de place wuz full ob peeple an' bofe Mistuh 'n Miz Pacelli wuz hyar."

Tommy thanked him and began to question the foreman.

"On garbage collection days, don't you take the bags and boxes as well as the refuse?"

"Bein' a cop you oughta know we don't." The man was sarcastic. "Boxes and crates are picked up by the trash crews. The burlap bags belong to the store owners and they get rid of them in the most profitable way. These people leave them for the men as a sort of tip."

"The men sell them?"

"Sure. Some stores get cash or credit from the supply houses they deal with. Some people sell them to rag men and some, like the Pacellis, give them for tips to the garbage men. My crew collects them about every two or three weeks. They're worth ten to thirty cents a sack, depending on the size and condition." He kicked aside a large burlap sack, the one which had recently covered Nita's face. "One like that will bring a good price. It's almost new, has no markings on it and is closed with chain stitch that can be pulled out without ripping the cloth."

"Ummmm." Tommy squinted at the sack. "Then a pile of those could lie here for some days before being taken away?"

"Sure thing."

"So, if a body was hidden under them it might be a couple of weeks before it was discovered?"

"That's right."

"Which seems to indicate the killer is someone familiar with the section and the practices, Tommy," I put in excitedly.

"Not necessarily." Tommy tossed cold water on my idea. "The bags being there could have just been a stroke of luck for the killer. He'd be looking for some way to hide the body and he saw the bags in the light from the moon. There was a moon, wasn't there?"

"There was indeed. I saw it set as well as rise."

"See here, Captain, can't we go?" Miles was irritated.

Tommy looked as if he would like to tell him off, but he just nodded and, after getting the names and addresses of the four men, he let them leave. The blacks filed out of the court, gabbling excitedly. Tommy watched them go, a wide grin on his face, then directed his attention to the Pacelli couple.

"What do you know about this?"

Mrs. Pacelli answered. "*Madre Mia,* your honor! But we know nothing about it. Nothing at all!" She spread eloquent hands in a sweeping gesture. "All we do is put the bags there every day. Yesterday, even, we put more on the pile and already she lies dead!" She shuddered at the grim thought. "But we know nothing until the screams this morning."

"Screams? What screams?" I asked.

"The screams of the trash men. They holler, real loud, 'Murder!' So Papa, Tina, and I, we run out quickly and then we see what they have found. *Povre bella!*" She shook her head pityingly. "She was so young, so beautiful, to die in such an awful way."

"How do you know she was beautiful?" Beton, as usual, was directing his suspicions in the wrong channel.

"But signor, I hear you all say she is wife to the man who has kill himself. I have seen the pictures of her in the papers and I have seen she is beautiful. *Povre donna. Povre bella.*" Again she shook her head sadly.

"Beautiful she was, but she probably got just what was coming to her," I said bluntly.

"Now that's a fine thing to say!" Beton exclaimed.

"Well, it's just about what—" I stopped abruptly. I'd almost said it was about what Gaston would think. Why drag him in?

"Just about what?" Beton prodded.

"Oh—what usually happens to a woman who is too beautiful." The substitution was lame and I knew it.

"Ummm. Seems to me you have a lot of ideas about this case. First you pop up with the tale of Apaches having killed her and now you allow she got what was coming to her."

"I didn't say that! I said *probably*—and I told you once this morning to stop putting words in my mouth."

Beton turned away, scowling. Tommy began to query Mr. Pacelli, who hovered close to the ample girth of his wife as though her bulk strengthened and protected him. I grinned and waited to hear what Papa would have to say about this murder in his back yard.

11. *Verdict: Murder and Suicide*

TOMMY made his approach negative. "I don't suppose you know anything about this either?"

"Me? Not one thing, your honor. Only what Mama she tells you. That's all."

"And I take it neither of you heard anything in your yard that night or morning?"

"Nothing." They spoke in unison. Then the man added, "It was noisy, being the Carnival night. The streets, they are like the cabarets with everyone singing and making noises with horns."

"Were you both right on the place all during Mardi Gras?"

"Oh, yes, your honor. We have the busy night. Everyone, she wants to drink to the repeals. Lotsa friends come to drink the *vino* with Mama—"

Mrs. Pacelli's shrieked "Vincente!" interrupted his speech. There followed a rapid flood of Italian, liberally dotted with the words *vino* and *politica*. Papa was catching hell.

Tommy suppressed a grin. "Make your own wine?" He asked casually.

The couple turned to him, terrified. The grin broke through. "You needn't be afraid of me. I'm no revenue man and there isn't any prohibition now. But you better get a license to sell the stuff, just to be on the safe side."

"Oh, we do not *sell* the *vino*," Mrs. Pacelli asserted virtuously and untruthfully. "We make it only for to drink with our friends."

"And they have no enemies," Morrow muttered.

114

I smiled broadly. "They make good spumoni too."

She beamed at me. "Thatsa right! This lady, she is a friend who comes to eat spumoni or drink *vino* with Papa and me."

Tommy's grin widened. "Oh, so you're old friends with Miss Slone? That's fine. Was she here Mardi Gras night?"

"She wasn't," I answered for myself.

"What time did you close on Carnival?" Gross went back to the subject in hand.

"We close the *doors* at twelve-thirty, your excellence." There was a stress on the word *doors.*

Beton had a thought and brought it out. "If she was killed about then, or earlier, the shop must have been filled with people. Maybe some of them heard something?"

"She couldn't have been killed that early," I objected. "She was in the apartment building about that time, or later, arguing with her husband. She was killed *after* she left the apartment."

"Now ain't you bright?" Les sneered. "How'd you figure that out?"

I realized it had sounded stupid. Realizing it only made me angry. I wheeled on him furiously.

"See here, you big flatfoot! I'm getting sick and tired of your baiting me. One more word out of you and—"

"That's enough you two," Tommy intervened. "I'm getting sick of your bitching at each other every time you meet. Cut it out or I'll find a way to make you stop it."

I shrugged and walked away, ending up close to the gate which split the odd fence. The bright green of bolt and hinges struck me again as an incongruous note amid the general lack of paint. They intrigued me and something else I'd noticed earlier about the bolt also intrigued me. I was about to check it when I heard Tommy ask the couple what time they went to bed Carnival night. I walked back to where I could hear better.

"I am not so sure what the time was," Mrs. Pacelli replied. "We were so busy until all go home. Then we close up and go to bed. It is about three o'clock of the morning, I expect."

"You said you closed at twelve-thirty. Now it's three o'clock." Beton jumped at the discrepancy.

"Only the doors we close at twelve-thirty, so that no one else comes in. But those who are here, they stay much later. Papa, he goes to bed before me. He has worked longer."

"You mean you were still doing business when this woman was dragged in your alley, killed and thrown under those sacks, and none of you, customers or family, heard anything suspicious?" Beton sounded incredulous.

The distressed woman appealed to Tommy.

"Signor, you must believe me! There was the noises outside and Papa is snoring asleep. Tina," she indicated the girl, "is asleep long before even midnight. She hears nothing—did you Tina?"

A frightened look came into the girl's eyes, which had been wide and alert all through the morning's show. She shook her head in an emphatic negative and moved closer to her mother.

"You see? She hears nothing. I hear nothing. Vincente, he hears nothing. Nobody, he hears a thing."

Tommy patted her trembling shoulders.

"Now stop getting excited," he advised her. "I'm sure you've told us all you do know about it. Only one more question: Did this woman ever come to your shop? Have you ever seen her alive?"

Three heads shook in vigorous negation.

"She is not the one you would easily forget," Vincente submitted. "I see the pictures of her in costume. *Que bellissima!*"

Mrs. Pacelli directed a withering look toward him.

"You! Always you have an eye for the young girls, is it not? You must be thinking you are *Don Giovanni*, eh? With the gray hair and the grown sons, it is time you start to think of the Masses you have missed instead of the young girls!"

"But Rosa!" He protested. "You say yourself she is *bellissima*. I am only agreeing with what you say."

I smothered a laugh and turned around, facing the rear gate with the bright green hardware. Suddenly, something I'd wondered about just popped out in a question.

"Where does that gate lead to?"

No one answered. No one seemed to have heard the question. I started to repeat it but before I could phrase the words I caught a glance from Tina. It was a definite invitation to join her near the back door of the store. I walked over to where she stood.

"What is it?"

"Shhh!" She warned me. "I want to talk to you." Her voice was barely a whisper.

"Go ahead." I wondered what was so secret.

"I do not want them to hear." She indicated the group by a slight nod.

That made me stop and think. I'd been in trouble several times for doing what the police call tampering with evidence and with witnesses. I'd made a solemn vow not to do it again and this had the look of leading to just such meddling.

"If it's anything to do with this murder, child, you had best tell it to the police," I cautioned her, righteously.

She drew back, a look of fear in her big, dark eyes.

"Oh no! To you, I will tell it. But not to them."

I dumped my scruples. If it was important, I could tell Tommy.

"Okay, then. You tell me. What is it?"

"Promise you won't tell the police?"

I hesitated, children are very funny about broken promises.

"Why are you afraid of the police?" I hedged.

"Once they come and take away my brother, Victor. They put him in jail for a whole year for selling whisky in the hotel. And Papa, he too has been in jail for just selling wine. I do not like the police."

"But the men who arrested your brother and father were not city police, Tina. They were government men and that was their job. But this is a murder case, honey. A terrible crime has been committed and these police have the job to find who did it. If you know anything—*anything* at all— you must tell them."

Her face closed against me and she shook her head stubbornly.

"No! I will tell them nothing. I won't tell you either, now. You would just go right back and tell them and I'd get in trouble with everyone."

I'd run up against the stubborn inconsistencies of kids before. My sister, Vangie, had taught me a lot about girls this age when she was growing up. I told myself I had tried my best to make her go to the right authority with her story, then I proceeded to coax and wheedle her into telling it to me. It took plenty of coaxing and I had to go through the ritual of crossing my heart and hoping to die if I breathed a word of it to the cops. Finally she began to talk.

"I sleep right up there—" I followed her glance to the second floor balcony.

"Yes?" I prompted.

"The noises kept me awake Carnival night. Mama made me go to bed early, but I couldn't sleep. I'd—I'd been naughty—" She cast a sidelong glance at me. "I let a boy kiss me and Mama caught us and sent me up to bed. I finally got up and went out on the balcony, to sit for awhile in the moonlight. I was sitting there a long time, I'd heard Papa come up and go to bed and I squeezed in the corner so he wouldn't see me outside. After awhile, I heard him start to snore. I think, maybe, I fell asleep too. Suddenly I heard a noise and then I saw—" She stopped abruptly.

"What did you—" A warning look shut me up. The reason for her silence was standing at my elbow.

"What are you two so interested in—murder?" Beton asked, with heavy humour.

"Tina is worried about her parents losing money," I improvised. "She's afraid customers might be superstitious about going to a place where anyone was murdered."

"It is sorta tough to have your joint chosen for a murder," Beton said, saying the wrong thing—as usual.

"That's ridiculous," I snapped. "Personally, I think it will improve their business. Curious people will come, just to see the spot where a murder was committed."

"Oh, sure they will." He turned to Tina. "Don't let your imagination run away with you, girlie. Your folks will probably make a lot of dough out of this."

The word he'd used, "imagination," set me to thinking. Kids always have a large share of it and it was not at all unlikely that Tina had simply imagined she saw something. Perhaps even dreamed it; she had said she thought she fell asleep. The tall fence would cast weird shadows on a moonlit night. If she had been up, it wasn't likely she had stayed up much after one or two a.m. I was ready to discount the possible importance of what she had been about to tell me; to dismiss it as part of an imaginative child's dream. How wrong I was I couldn't know and it wasn't the only mistake I was to make in this case. But I turned to Beton and asked gibingly,

"Got any theories, Watson?"

"Yeah. You being so smart, it's a wonder you haven't got it all figured out already."

"Is that so? Well, maybe I have. You tell me what you think and maybe I'll tell you who done it."

"Okay. Her husband did it. He killed her, then went back to the apartment and turned on the gas."

I gaped at him. Obvious as the solution seemed, it hadn't occurred to me at all.

"How did you figure that one out?"

"It's simple deduction. She walked out on him. He followed and caught up with her. When they got down here, he pulled her aside, out of the crowds and through the gate. Then he tried to talk to her. She wouldn't listen, so he killed her, pulled her body into the yard, found the sacks and covered her up. Then he went on home and bumped himself off."

I tried to make the picture come clear. It didn't fall into focus at all. I grabbed at the first objection I thought about.

"You've forgot the note he left for her. He never wrote that to a woman he knew was already dead." ·

Beton frowned, then his face cleared. "Sure he did. He didn't want it known he killed her—some guy's minds work that way. But you remember what he said about eternity?"

"He didn't mean he was on his way to join her there," I said impatiently. "He was using that as just a figure of speech. Besides, Dr. Rollins said she was throttled in the manner of the French gangsters. There's a trick to that, you know. How would he, an American, learn such a trick and where would he get such a garrote cord?"

"Why, he learned it from her. She was French."

"Oh, sure! She was French, but she wasn't the type to teach a man an easy way to murder her, let alone leave the weapon lying around where he could get to it. And Doc said she was attacked from behind, taken by surprise. After the fight they had on Baronne Street, she'd certainly have been on her guard against him. You're stupid. The poor guy was dying on Baronne Street while you have him killing a woman on Toulouse!"

"Stop riding Les," Tommy commanded. "It could have happened just as he described. I can tell you how it could have been done."

I wheeled on him. "Oh, can you now? Well, go ahead. I'm open to conviction. Try to convince me."

"I will—if you'll keep an open mind and not give me any

argument. As Les said, he could have followed her when she left the apartment and caught up with her. He walked along, talking and trying to persuade her to come on back home with him."

"In heaven's name, Tommy, why would she walk clear down here?"

"Listen, have you ever started walking when you were good and mad and walked for blocks without noticing where you were going or how far you had gone?"

I had. I nodded.

"Well, then, that's what she was doing and he trailed along. When they reached here, he noticed the gate and drew her inside of it to get her away from the street—" He stopped and turned to the Pacellis. "The gate was open, wasn't it?"

"Oh, sure, your honor. It was open."

I looked at her narrowly and knew at once that she had no idea if the gate was ajar or tight shut.

"He saw the open gate and drew her aside—no one would pay any attention to that on Carnival night. It would just look like a petting party."

"Don't you mean *necking* party?" I muttered.

He gave me an impatient look and continued.

"Call it what you like. She probably started to walk away from him—"

"Where? On the street or inside the alley?"

"Inside, of course. She turned her back and started to leave him and that was when he used the rope."

"Cord," I corrected. "That's very neat, Captain Gross, but I think you're as nearly nuts as Beton. How come he had the cord with him? If he only followed her to talk her into coming home with him, why would he carry the garrote?"

"He probably meant to kill her if she refused to go back with him. He meant to kill himself, he intended to take her along with him. After he had killed her, he dragged the body back by the fence, found the bags and hid her under them. Then he left and went to finish himself off with gas."

"Rollins said she was relaxed and unaware of danger when she was attacked," I insisted stubbornly. "Now, please tell me, what woman would be relaxed if she was being yanked around through gates by an angry husband?"

"Why not? She wasn't afraid of him? She was angry too. She could have been as tense as a tight wire and still not afraid of his doing her any harm."

"If she'd have been as tense as a tight wire, she wouldn't have died so quickly and easily," I said, caustically. "The minute he touched her she'd have started to fight back."

"She didn't have a chance to fight back. As soon as that cord went around her throat she was as good as done."

"I don't believe it," I said flatly. "No one can convince me that boy ever killed her."

"Slone liked his looks," Morrow said teasingly.

"You keep out of this," I snapped and turned back to Tommy. "All right. Admitting it could have happened the way you and Beton said, you can't expect me to believe he went home and wrote her that pitiful note."

"I don't expect you to believe anything logical," Tommy said tartly. "You never have before. But that's exactly what we think happened."

I saw the police had made up their minds. I knew there was no use arguing about it any longer, so I just shrugged and repeated my belief that Don Barnett had killed no one but himself.

"Each man kills the thing he loves—" Morrow quoted.

"Oh shut up!" I said, irritably. "You're as bad as the rest. You can't see the forest for the trees."

Beton was jubilant. "Yeah, Chief, we got it tagged right. I guess we can get along and file our reports, huh?"

"I guess so." Tommy sounded relieved over the easy solution to what had looked like a tough case. "Good-bye, Margaret. You ought to be glad this was so quickly cleared up."

I grunted ungraciously and dropped back beside Morrow, muttering,

"Verdict for the coroner—all nicely wrapped up and delivered with the compliments of the Homicide Squad—suicide and murder while temporarily insane. I don't see it that way and I'm beginning to doubt if Tommy Gross is as smart as I thought he was."

"You wanted some excitement," Morrow teased. "You're just sore because all you got is a routine murder and suicide story. Seriously, Margaret, the time element for everything fits okay. All events have been placed between one and six Wednesday morning. I guess the boys are right. After all, this is their business."

"I know that, but I still don't see how he could have killed her, then got back and killed himself."

Morrow looked at me in surprise. "Why, Slone. That's the simplest part of the whole thing. He could have had plenty of time to kill her between, well, say two and three. Then he could have gone back to turn on the gas and easily be dead by six. Even if he was walking slowly, even with the crowds he had to get through, he could have made it. It's the logical solution."

"Oh, logical! I never trust the logical in murder." I was stubbornly unwilling to admit to myself that a man could write such a note as he had written to a woman he knew he had killed. Also, there was something tugging at my memory. I couldn't quite pin it down but I knew that when I did it would kick their fine solution high and merry.

"That garrote business sticks in my craw," I mused. "Both Beton and Gross—and you too—are nuts to think she taught him how to use it. Where did he get it and who taught him the stunt?"

"I don't know who taught him to use it. I'm inclined to agree with you that it was hardly likely she would be such a sap. But the cord could have been hers. A stage prop. She was a dancer."

"Was she? Who told you that?"

"Why those pictures I took! They were made in a dancer's costume."

"Show girls—who can't dance a step—wear such costumes. And, if the garrote was hers, it would have been locked up in her bag."

"Yeah—and the bag was so securely locked you opened it with a tin hairpin. But you can't understand how a race track guy, who is used to using all the angles of the chisel for a living, would be able to get it open. F'crissakes, honey, make some sense!"

"I'm trying to—and don't honey me. They—oh, hell! Why should I give a damn whether he killed her or not? If the cops are satisfied, why should I worry? Let's go. I'll drive you to headquarters."

We filed out of the place together and I turned to close the gate behind us. Tina was standing there. She crooked a finger at me, her eyes pleading mutely for a chance to talk. I stepped back with a muttered excuse.

"Well, what is it?" I was a little impatient.

"Close the gate," she whispered.

"Look, honey, I've got to get to work. I'll come back and talk to you later. Right now I'm in a hurry."

"How much later will you be back?"

"Oh, I don't know. Don't you have to go to school?"

She nodded. "I get out at three o'clock."

"Well, I'll come back after school."

"You promise? And you won't tell the police?"

I nodded and she steppd back, eyes lit up with the glow of a fellow-conspirator.

"Don't forget!" She ran back toward the rear, curls flying.

I shook my head, smiling and convinced she knew nothing of real importance and was just having a lot of fun imagining things. I climbed in my heap, shoving Morrow's long legs aside and out of the way of the gear shift, and drove off toward headquarters. We rode several blocks in silence, then Johnny spoke.

"Margaret, you've done some pretty keen work in murder cases you covered—like the time Dr. McGowan was killed." *

"Thanks." I thought back to the time Ned McGowan was murdered—with a toothbrush as the fantastic weapon. I recalled the cops had been ready to call that one suicide too. They'd had it all nicely solved.

"You needn't be sarcastic," Johnny remonstrated mildly. "I mean it. What I mean is that when you get a hunch that something smells wrong it usually does. You've got such a hunch now, haven't you?"

"I don't know that it's much of a hunch. I just can't seem to accept the verdict that will be dished out. But I'm not sticking my neck out. If that's the way the cops figure it— that's the way I'll write it."

"Yeah?" He lit a cigarette, handed it to me and lit another for himself. "Yeah? Well, you may be right about his not doing it, but I'll bet you nothing ever turns up to prove it. Want to bet?"

* *Poison, Poker and Pistols*, Sheridan House, 1946.

12. *Bait for Trouble*

I HAD slowed for a traffic light. I looked at him sharply.

"What are you trying to do? Bait me for trouble? Well, I'm not having any, thank you."

"That's fine. Then you must have decided he did kill her. If you hadn't, you'd be planning your crusade to clear his memory of the stigma of murder."

"Why should I crusade for a guy I never even knew?"

"Because you're the type of idealist who goes in for that sort of thing."

I said nothing to that crack.

"You know," he went on half musingly, "it's almost a sure shot he did kill her—but, if he didn't and some one could prove it—say you—wouldn't Beton catch hell from Elison and the D.A. for grabbing the easy solution? It's his idea. He suggested it to Tommy before he mentioned it to anyone else. Tommy went along with him. Boy! What a riding they'd both get!"

"I'm not looking to get Tommy a riding," I said shortly.

"Oh, I know that and, of course, Beton will get the credit for solving the case. Tommy's fair as hell about things like that. It would be a shame if the guy hadn't killed her and then had to get the blame while Les got the glory for being smart enough to figure it out the wrong way."

That did it. "How much will you bet and what odds will you give me? Mind you, I'm not betting I can find the murderer. I'm only putting up dough that I can prove the husband didn't do it."

He grinned all over his face. "I'll give you two to one. Ten bucks to your five."

"Taken. Who'll hold the stakes?"

"How about Nick?"

"He's okay by me."

"Good. We'll stop in there now and get a beer at the same time. I'll buy and charge it to the cab I didn't take."

"You can buy me a coke. It's too early for beer. How much time do I get before I forfeit my fine?"

"Well, today's Friday—how about four weeks from now? That should give you enough time."

"Cripes, you're generous!"

"All right—make it six weeks."

"That's better. And if I lose this five, I'll promise you one thing: I'll never play detective again. It's too damn expensive and I have a strong hunch this is not going to make me popular with the police."

He laughed and I joined him, a bit ruefully. It had been a neat job of baiting me and I had a neat job cut out for me to win that bet. I pulled the car to a stop in front of Nick's, a little joint just like thousands of other little joints that are always to be found near buildings such as police headquarters and newspaper offices. We went in, ordered and headed for the phone booths in the rear. I was still talking to Dennis when I saw Morrow leave his booth and go sit down at one of the tables. I sighed and wished I worked for an editor who didn't insist on hearing all the long, dreary details of a story.

At the end of the tale, Dennis said he didn't think it was much of a murder yarn and if he had anything better he wouldn't even give it front page.

That stung me to retort. "You may think it isn't much of a murder, just because Les Beton, the dumb head, has decided it's the old suicide-murder business. But, if you ask me, he's wrong and there's more to this than meets the eye—his eye, at least."

"What do you mean by that? What have you got up your sleeve?"

"No aces—yet. But there are some strange angles the cops have overlooked and I want to follow them up. In fact, I'm going to do just that."

"You'll do nothing of the kind," he commanded. "You keep out of trouble and that means you keep your nose out of police business. You hear me? That's an order."

"You sound like a general, instead of a city editor," I said blandly. "Here I have some good leads and instead of figuring on us getting a story—a real story—you tell me to lay off. Okay, you're the boss."

That had the expected reaction.

"We-ell, if you really have something to go on, go ahead. But don't pull anything out of a hat just to pad the story."

"What do you think I am—a magician? First you want to know what I have up my sleeve, then you tell me not to pull anything out of a hat."

"You know what I mean. I don't want you to bring me in a hand-embroidered yarn that you have to rip apart to find the facts."

"I have never done anything like that," I said, with great dignity, and hung up.

When I joined Morrow at the table, he was on his second beer. I sat down and picked up my coke, which he regarded with distaste.

"How can you drink that stuff this early?"

"I learned it in Georgia. A coke and an aspirin is a Georgia breakfast. Didn't you know?"

"No. What did Dennis want that took you so long?"

"All the minute details."

"Did you tell him you meant to prove the guy innocent?"

"Not exactly. I just said I had some ideas I wanted to work out."

"What did he say?"

"Guess?"

"To stay out of trouble and let the police run their show?"

I grinned. "Just about, but he came around finally. Dennis usually gives me plenty of rope. He's always hoping I'll hang myself and then he could park me in society for punishment."

"Seriously, Margaret, he should keep you off this stuff. And I think maybe we better call off that bet. You may get into some real trouble. Why not skip it? If you got hurt it would be my fault and I'd feel like a heel."

It was the second time that morning he'd pulled the protective act on me. I couldn't quite figure it out, but I meant to call a halt to it and fast.

"The bet was your idea," I said, coldly. "If you want to welch on it, okay. With me, it stands."

He reddened angrily and called to Nick to come over. When he got there, Johnny pulled out his wallet and extracted two five dollar bills. I got out my five and laid it beside his elbow.

"We've made a bet, Nick, and we want you to hold the stakes. Okay?"

The big man smiled. "Sure. I hold them. How much?"

"Fifteen bucks. I'm laying her odds she can't do something. She says she can and will. She's got four weeks—"

"Six weeks," I corrected.

"I mean six weeks. So six weeks from today, I'll come in and collect the dough."

"That's what you think," I jeered. "Nick, I'll be the one to collect that dough."

Nick laughed and went to the cash drawer to get one of his brown bank envolopes. He came back to the table, picked up the money and placed it in the envelope. Then he made us sign our names and the amount enclosed and seal the flap.

"Now I put this in the safe and when you win the bet, you both come in and I'll buy the loser a drink."

"Johnny, remember that. Nick is going to buy you a

drink." I got up, smoothed down my skirt and picked up my purse. "I'm going. You coming with me?"

"With an unfinished bottle of beer sitting in front of me? Don't be silly. Run along, girl detective, I'll see you later."

I shrugged and walked on out, crossed the street and entered the courts building. I headed for the other end of the hall and went down one flight of steps, then along another hall until I came to a heavy green door marked, "City Morgue." I turned the knob, pushed hard and walked into a small office, with one desk enclosed by an oak railing. Ricky Edwards was sitting at the desk reading a Western magazine. He didn't look up, just went on reading.

"Hi, Rick," I greeted him. "How come you're not reading a detective tale?"

He hastily swung his big feet off the desk, then, seeing who it was, replaced them and grinned at me. "These stories are better. They got more action in 'em."

I smiled, then sniffed and turned up my nose. Even out there, with another heavy door between the room and the morgue, you could smell the odor of death and decay and formaldehyde.

"Hey, lookit! You needn't turn up your nose!" He sounded aggrieved. "My feet are flat but they don't smell."

I laughed aloud. "You fool! I wasn't turning up my nose at your clodhoppers. I just got a whiff of the morgue smell. What are you doing on cold storage duty? I thought you were out on the Ridge."

"I was, until my feet started bothering me. They put me on here so I could rest 'em for a spell."

"Oh? Well, you've got the same kind of company here as you had on the cemetery beat."

"Not quite. Out there they were already planted. In here, they're just filed for a few days. What you want?"

"I want to see that murder that came in this morning. The strangling case."

He consulted a big black ledger—the register for the dead.

"That'll be number twenty-seven. She may still be out for posting. If she's back you can see her. I'll have a look."

"I'll go along with you."

He led the way through the heavy iron door and down a flight of twisting iron stairs which ended in the file room for the public dead. The odor of formaldehyde and death grew stronger with each step and the air grew colder. I shivered, not only from the drop of temperature. The room, lined with large steel cases, always gave me a creeping sensation.

Rick halted in front of a case on the left side of the room.

"Twenty-seven—here it is." He pulled on a handle and the slab slid out with a protesting creak. It was empty.

"She's not in from posting yet." He pushed the bare slab back into place. It creaked again.

"Why the hell don't they oil those runners?" I asked, somewhat irritably. "This place is bad enough without noises like that."

He chuckled. "The maintenance crew doesn't like to work in this part of the building. I haven't seen any of 'em since I came on this duty. Well, your gal isn't receiving yet. Maybe she's still in the receiving room, though."

"Oh, hell. That means I have to go clear around the building."

"Uh uh. You can get into it through that door over there." He indicated another heavy iron door on the far right side of the room. "Want to take a look? I can get you in this way."

I nodded and we went up a short flight of stairs and through the door into a long, narrow, hall-like room. Here, the bodies were checked in and tagged. There were five stretcher tables standing alongside of the wall. One was occupied by a sheeted figure.

"There she is." I pointed at the stretcher table.

Rick walked over and lifted the sheet at the foot of the rolling slab. A delicately arched foot, with a tag tied to the big toe, came into view. Delicate as it was, it was not a woman's foot.

"Nope. This is the guy that bumped himself off. He was her husband, wasn't he?"

"Yes." I stepped to the head of the stretcher and pulled back the, sheet. For several minutes my eyes lingered on the still, placid face. In those few minutes—or maybe it was only seconds—I knew, by some strange, occult means that he had never killed Nita. I had the uncanny sensation of holding converse with the dead man and that he told me he had harmed no one but himself. The feeling was so powerful I answered him.

"But the police think you killed her," I murmured.

"Huh? What did you say?"

Rick's startled question snapped me back to reality.

"Oh! I just remarked that the police think he killed her and then committed suicide. That is, Beton and Gross think so. I don't believe it." I took another last look, then gently dropped the cover back over the quiet face.

"Why not?"

"Well—I don't know, exactly. I just have a feeling. Call it woman's intuition, if you like, or maybe it's a reporter's instinct."

He snorted. "You reporters! You're all alike, Always trying to make a mystery out of something."

"What about you cops? You're all alike too. You dress alike, think alike, and have flat feet. But you rarely have an original idea. You make me sick!"

Rick stepped back a pace, startled by my tirade.

"Well, f'cripes sakes, don't get sore at me! I didn't know the guy was a pal of yours."

"He wasn't. I didn't know him from Adam. What's he doing out here?"

"He's been claimed," Rick consulted the tag again. "Mr.

James A. Dunn." He read off the name. "He's going to the Brent Funeral Home. Their wagon must be on the way to pick him up."

"So Dunn claimed him? Apparently he's fulfilling the request Barnett made in his note. Where does that guy live, by the way?"

"Who? Mr. Dunn?"

"Obviously I cannot mean Barnett," I said drily.

"What's the matter with you, Margaret? I didn't do anything to make you get nasty with me."

"I'm sorry," I apologized. "I've had an irritating morning. Can you get Dunn's address for me?"

"I guess so." He walked down to the far end of the room and I tagged behind him. A small alcove held a large desk and in front of it·sat a white-coated morgue attendant.

"Charlie, there's a reporter here who's working this suicide-murder case. She wants to know the address of the guy who claimed the man's body."

The attendant gave me an incurious glance and pulled out a file box. He handed the whole box to Ricky. The cop leafed through the cards, took one out and handed it to me.

I read the typed words: "Barnett, Donald E. Resided at 1010 Baronne Street. Permanent address unknown. Cause of death, monoxide poisoning. Coroner's verdict, suicide. Body claimed by James A. Dunn, 611 Baronne Street. Apt. 4F. Deliver to Brent Funeral Home."

I scribbled Dunn's address on a piece of copy paper and gave the card back to Ricky. He replaced it in its space in the metal box and returned the file to the attendant.

I thanked them both, a little ashamed over the way I'd snapped at Ricky. "I'll just go out through the driveway." I motioned to the double doors at the end of the room. "I'll see the other body later, no sense waiting until she gets back from posting. Right now, I have some work to do."

Rick grinned at me, his peeve forgotten. "Bee buzzing in your bonnet?"

"Loudly. How'd you guess?"

"Oh, I'm smart about things like that." He hesitated. "Well, good luck to you—and stay out of trouble."

"Thanks. I'll try to." I went on out and down the drive to the street. Before getting in my car, I glanced in Nick's to see if Morrow was still there. He was—but Beton was sitting with him and they were both laughing about something—probably me. I wasn't having any more of Beton that morning, so I jumped in the car and drove off. The dashboard clock said eleven-ten. That meant I had almost two hours to follow my leads and get a story in for the one-thirty edition. I pulled to a stop in front of 611 Baronne Street.

The building was a small and quite modern hotel-apartment setup and the section was a lot nicer than the address four blocks further up the street. Like many neighborhoods, Baronne Street changes its personality in the space of a few blocks. Around this end were apartment hotels and small hotels of fair quality. I got out and went into the miniature lobby. A desk clerk presided at the switchboard.

I stepped up to the counter, picked up the handset and asked for Dunn's apartment.

The clerk made no move to connect me. "I'll have to announce you first. Mr. Dunn left an order to put through no calls without the party was announced."

I had been afraid of that. Still, there was no reason why he should refuse to see me. I gave the man my name and added that he was to tell Mr. Dunn I had some important news for him.

He inserted a plug into the board and a moment later I heard him repeat my message. In another moment, he turned back to me.

"Mr. Dunn wants to know what your news is about?"

"It's about Mr. Barnett's wife."

He repeated that, listened again and then said, "No sir. She's in the lobby. Shall I send her up?"

Apparently Dunn vetoed that, for he told me to pick up the phone on the counter, that Mr. Dunn would speak to me over the phone.

As soon as I heard Dunn's voice, I spoke rapidly.

"Mr. Dunn, something has come up that I think you should know. I don't care to discuss it over this phone, however. May I come up for a moment?"

There was a short hesitation, then he spoke, not too graciously.

"Very well. Come up—if you feel you must."

I smothered the temptation to tell him to go to hell and thanked him nicely instead. Then I headed for the elevator.

"It's automatic," the clerk told me.

"So I see," I answered and got in the small cage. It labored painfully up to the fourth floor and I got off and found the apartment I wanted. A voice bade me enter and I went into a neatly furnished living room. In a quick glance, I saw that several tasteful personal touches took the furnished apartment curse off the appearance of the room. As the touches included a fair-sized bookcase, a sandalwood chest, and a teakwood coffee table, I concluded the tenant spent a good part of the year in the city.

Another attractive touch was the red-haired girl, Bette. She would have been more attractive if she hadn't been huddled in a large chair weeping into a soggy handkerchief. Next to her, sitting bolt upright in a straight-backed chair, was Mike O'Leary. At the moment he looked pretty grim and it was evident he had no desire to see me. Dunn stood to the left of Bette's chair, his hand on her shoulder in a rather protective manner.

I studied the glum tableau for a moment then said, stiltedly,

"I'm sorry to intrude on your grief, but I really think you should know what has happened and what the police think about it."

"We know all about what has happened." Dunn's tone was not at all encouraging. However, the words surprised me. The City edition, in which was printed the story of Nita's murder, would not be on the street for another ten or fifteen minutes. How then, could they know all about what had happened? I watched them narrowly.

"You know that Nita Barnett has been found?"

"Nita found? Good God, no! When?" Dunn's surprise was genuine.

"This morning. Didn't you expect them to find her?"

He gave me a searching look. "Not particularly. Why should I?"

"Why shouldn't you?" I countered.

"No reason, except that knowing Nita I didn't think she would stick around for the police and the newspapers to get hold of her. She wouldn't care for that sort of publicity."

"She would have loved any kind of publicity!" Bette said viciously.

I whipped around to face her squarely.

"Why did you use the past tense?" I asked sharply.

She cringed back in her chair, eyes bewildered. Dunn spoke for her and, I gathered, for all three of them.

"See here, Miss Slone. You said you had something important to tell us. Well nothing Nita does is important to any of us any longer. She has done her worst and with Don gone, she is out of our lives completely."

"She's out of everybody's lives. She's been murdered."

13. *A Bit of Unmasking*

~~~~~~

THERE was a moment of dead silence while I tried to watch three faces at once. Bette was the first to speak.

"Murdered? Nita?" Her voice came out a hoarse whisper.

I nodded, looking squarely into the pansy-colored eyes.

"But that's incredible!" Dunn exclaimed in shocked disbelief. "Who but—" He bit the rest of the sentence off.

"Who but Don would have killed her?" I finished the query.

"That's not what I meant." His protest was weak.

"Well, she sure needed killing," O'Leary spoke up. "I hope whoever did it made a good job of it."

"He did. A quite professional job," I said, drily.

"When—when did it—it happen?" Bette asked, hesitantly.

"Early Wednesday morning and about the same time Barnett died. Some time between the same hours, that is between three and six."

"Where?" Dunn's voice was strained and unnatural.

"In a yard in the French Quarter."

"How?" O'Leary completed the cycle of questions.

I didn't answer that last right away. I'd been looking around and had taken note of several interesting things. I spoke to Dunn.

"I see you've traveled in France?"

He followed the direction of my eyes and saw I was looking at some French stickers on a large chest.

"Why, yes, I have. What has that to do with Nita's death?"

"Ever hear of a garrote?"

137

"Certainly. Why? Oh my God! Was that how—?"

"It was."

"What is a garrote?" Mike asked the question.

Dunn answered, explaining the manner the strangling cord was used and adding that death at the hands of someone who knew his business was generally quick and painless for the victim.

"Damn sight more than she deserved," O'Leary asserted.

"You liked her, didn't you?"

"Yeah!" He sneered at me. "I *loved* her. Many is the time I'd have relished killing that bitch myself."

"But you didn't, of course. You didn't even know what a garrote was until it was described to you."

He gave me a dirty look, started to speak but apparently thought better of it and turned away.

"Who—who do they think did it?" Bette asked, half-fearfully.

"Do any of you have any ideas on that?" I stalled.

Three heads shook in negation.

"I didn't expect you would have. No one ever seems to have ideas in murder cases except the police and the reporters. And the cops seldom have any original ones. They follow strict logic which, in this case, is that Barnett killed his wife then went home and turned on the gas. That's what they've—" I broke off as Bette rose to her feet and threw out a hand in a gesture of appeal.

"Please! I can't bear it! I won't have it!" Her voice rose to high C and I stepped back wondering what the hell gave now.

Her next words spilled out like a torrent released after a long period of being damned up behind a barricade.

"Wife?" She faced me, shaking like a nervous breakdown. "Wife! *She* wasn't his wife. But *I* was and, oh God, what a fool I've been! I loved him. She didn't. She took everything from him, even honor. Now they try to say he killed her. He didn't! Do you understand? He didn't do it!"

She was shaking me by the shoulders, screaming the words in my face. I pulled away, staggering back as her hold on my padded shoulders came loose. I began to edge toward the door but my exit was blocked by a grim-faced O'Leary.

"Not so fast, my girl. Where do you think you're going?"

"Back to work. Where the hell do you think I'm going?" I tried to match his belligerency. "Move out of my way."

He stood there, as solid as a concrete block.

"If you think you're going to spread Miss Marshall all over your dirty paper, you're crazy."

I made a mental note of the name Marshall and then tried to reason with the furious Irishman.

"See here, bub, I'm a reporter. I came up here to give Mr. Dunn some information I thought he'd be interested in knowing. I got some news I know my paper will be interested in printing. Now be sensible and let me out of here."

"Not on your life. You stay right here until you make up your mind this is one story you won't write."

He was being foolish but I had no time to argue with him and he looked mad enough to take a wallop at me any minute. I decided my best chance lay with the newly unmasked Mrs. Barnett.

"Look, Mrs. Barnett or Miss Marshall—whatever you call yourself—your boy friend is giving me trouble."

She stopped wetting down Dunn's shoulder and faced me, lips quivering.

"I'm sorry I broke down."

"That's okay with me. I guess you had plenty of cause to break down. But the kind of stuff this guy over here is pulling is not going to help you one bit. Sooner or later this story will have to break. I've tried to be nice to you people. You'll be much better off if you don't try to hold me here. You can't keep me very long. My editor expects to hear from me very shortly and if he doesn't he is sure to start checking. The guard at the morgue knew I was coming here. He gave me the address just after I took a last look at Barnett's body—"

Bette screamed and fainted. Both men jumped to her side and I leaped for the door, wrenching it open and hightailing out of there. I took the stairs in high, skidded into the lobby, scattered out of it and flung myself in my car. I headed for the office. Dennis greeted me with a blast.

"I've been trying to get you for an hour! Why the hell don't you leave word where you're going?"

"I'm sorry," I said mildly. "I've been chasing down those leads I told you about and I think I have something pretty good."

"Okay. Write it and get back to the beat." He turned his back and I went to work.

I did about three hundred words on the story of the unmasked wife and took it over to him. He read the first few lines and his face lit up.

"How'd you get this? Who else has it?"

"No one else has it but us. I got it by following those leads I told you about earlier. Morrow could have had it but he—"

A ringing phone interrupted me. Dennis reached for it, then handed it to me with a laconic, "I think this guy wants you."

It was Dunn. He wanted to know if I would please come back to the apartment. He said he felt that if the story had to come out it was best that I should have all of my facts straight. I agreed with the latter but suggested he come over to me, bringing the real wife with him.

He demurred. "Miss Marshall is not in a condition to go to a newspaper office."

I replied·to that by saying that Mr. O'Leary was not anyone I cared to encounter twice in one day.

"Mike won't be here," he assured me.

I debated a second. I did want fuller information than I had and Dunn and the girl were the ones who could best supply it. On the other hand, any one of the three could be the killer and I might well be walking into a trap. But the urge to get the full story was strong.

"All right, I'll come over. But if you think you can pull any funny stuff and get away with it, you're nuts. If I'm not back in my office in one hour from the time I leave, the cops will be looking for me."

"We have no intention of pulling any funny stuff," he said stiffly. "But you can do as you like about insuring your safety."

"I intend to and I'll be there in ten minutes." I hung up and faced an impatient Dennis.

"What the hell was that all about?"

"That call was from James Dunn, the man who claimed Barnett's body and the guy who received one of the suicide's notes. I just left his place, after a scramble with a pal of his. He wants me to come back and get the facts in correct order. But there are certain things about going over there that I don't like. That O'Leary looked like he'd enjoy throttling me. Do you think I should go back? He, Dunn, said O'Leary was gone."

"Well, if he's gone he can't hurt you," Dennis said, with good logic.

"How can I be sure he has gone? After all, this is a murder case and those three are suspects as far as I'm concerned. This may be a gag to get me in where they can go to work on me."

"I'll send Hansen with you."

"No. A photographer would queer the deal, if it is a straight one. That girl has been bawling for hours and looks like hell. I'll go alone and if I'm not back by one-thirty, call out the police. No, wait, I'll call you if everything is okay and I'll say—just so you'll know I'm not calling under pressure—'Hold this for page one.' If I don't call or get back, send for the riot squad. Dunn's address is there in that story."

Dennis looked dubious. "You better take Hansen."

"I don't want Hansen," I said impatiently. "It would take too long to wait for him to get ready, anyhow."

"Okay, then, but be careful. The last time you got nosy you wound up with a lump on your noggin. Anyhow, the cops say this is murder and suicide. Why can't you just settle for that and keep away from this joint? You got a good enough story."

I shook my head. "No, I haven't. And it isn't murder and suicide. There are too many angles for the verdict to be that simple."

"What angles, for instance?"

"Well, the note he left her. Oh, I know it could have been meant to mislead the police but I don't believe it. The woman in the next apartment told the police she heard Nita leave—alone—then come back and demand her bag and he wouldn't give it to her. And the record he was playing on the phonograph when he died—oh say! That does it!"

"Does what?"

"Don't you *see?* If that neighbor heard the vic playing from the time Nita left the building until it ran down then he had to be right there to wind it up. That being the case, he couldn't have been on Toulouse to kill her!"

"Maybe the machine was electric and the connection blew out?"

"But it wasn't!" I was remembering it all now. What I was recalling gave me the answer to the nagging suspicion I'd had all along that somewhere I'd seen something that made it impossible for him to have done the murder. If that woman had heard the vic and if it had played the same record for several hours, she would surely remember that. Even if it had been playing other records for a long period of time, she'd have been annoyed as hell.

"How do you know the machine was run down? Maybe he just stopped it and then went out."

"I tried the handle. The vic was completely run down. It started to play after I had wound it for a little while."

Dennis grinned at me. "Christ, Maggie, you're a fool for luck. Why don't you go see this other woman and skip the extra wife?"

"No, I want to see that one too. I'll go back to the other building as soon as I leave Dunn's apartment."

"Suit yourself, you're on a hunch bet now. But don't forget to call me by one-thirty."

"Make it one-forty-five." I looked at the clock "That gives me an hour and five minutes."

He made a note of that and I collected my things and took off. I planned to get the story from Bette, call Dennis, go on over to the other apartment and check on the vic and scoot back to the office. Then I'd go down and see Christina Pacelli. It had begun to seem possible that she could have seen something.

When I entered the small lobby for the second time that day, the clerk told me to go right up. I got off the elevator at the third floor, climbed the stairs to the fourth and tiptoed down the hall. I listened for a couple of minutes, meaning to trot right out of there if I heard O'Leary's voice. I didn't, so knocked and was bidden to enter. O'Leary was not in sight but the bedroom door, which had been standing open when I left there, was now closed. I eyed it warily and took a seat where I could watch it.

Bette was back in the easy chair but she had stopped bawling and was sipping a tall drink. It looked like a highball. Dunn read my mind and asked if I would have one. I would—and thanks.

While he fixed the drink, I studied the red-haired girl and waited for her to begin talking. I'd heard of situations such as must have existed in her life, but it was the first time I'd actually met one in the flesh. It was a brand new angle on the wronged wife story.

She said nothing until after Dunn had handed me my

drink, then she merely remarked that she hardly knew where to begin.

"At the beginning," I advised.

"It's a long story and a sad one," she warned me.

"I'm used to both. Go ahead."

14. *A Pretty Sorry Story*

"IT began eight years ago, when I was sixteen and met Donny at a dance on the steamer *Capitol*." She started her story. "I'd gone with Mike. I—I was Mike's girl, sort of— just kid stuff, of course.

"I was standing by the orchestra when Don came up and asked me for that dance. I'd never seen him before but on the boat no one bothered with introductions. I'd often danced with strange boys as long as they looked like nice kids. Don looked nice.

"From the first step we moved in perfect harmony. I'd never known dancing could be like that. I don't know if he had dated any other dances, but I do know if he had he didn't keep them. Neither did I, except the two I had with Mike. The rest of the evening I danced only with Don."

"What did Mike have to say to that?"

"Oh, he just sat and sulked." She shrugged her shoulders. "It wouldn't have made any difference anyhow. You see, I fell in love that night. It does happen that way. It did to me."

I settled back in my chair. I could see she had meant it when she said it was going to be a long story. If she was going to cover eight full years of her life, it was going to be a longer story than I wanted to hear.

"Don took me home that night. It was a dirty trick to play on Mike, but I couldn't help it. It was a lovely night, full moon and early spring with the jasmine in bloom. We stood in front of my house for several minutes, just talking of one thing and another and finally he did what I had hoped he would—"

"Kissed you, of course?"

She nodded, her eyes wide and starry with remembering that moment. "Yes, he kissed me and then told me he was leaving for Maryland the next day. He said he was a jockey and would be back the next year. Then he laughed and told me that by then I should be grown up enough to go places with him, wrote down my name and address and said he would write from Maryland.

"He never wrote at all. Not even a card."

I smothered a yawn and began to think that after all it was a highly unoriginal version of boy meets girl, so far. I was only interested in the part that started when Nita entered the picture.

"In late November, right after the races began, I saw him standing on the corner of Canal and St. Charles. He was in riding clothes and I walked over to speak to him. I told him I was all grown up now and he seemed glad to see me. He asked me to have dinner with him. We went to his hotel so he could change clothes—

"Next morning we took a ferry to Gretna and were married."

She paused and looked at me, half-defensively. I said nothing and she continued.

"I knew my parents would never consent to my marrying a race track man, so we didn't even call my family for a week after we were married. It was too late then for an annulment."

I thought: It was too late before you went to Gretna.

"I learned a lot of unpleasant things in the next few weeks. I found he was not a jockey—he—he was—"

"A tout." I supplied the word she stuck on saying.

"That's right." Dunn spoke for the first time since she had begun the tale. "Don rode for me until he got too heavy, then I began to break him in as a trainer. He had a way with horses but he got in with some gamblers and they paid him to hop one of my horses. I fired him that summer in Saratoga and he went on the tout. But I couldn't help liking the kid and when he called me and said he was married and also broke, I let him have a couple of hundred—"

"We won a thousand dollars with that money." Bette took up the story, sadly. "That spring we went to Louisville, then to Chicago, and on to other tracks all over. It was a strange and exciting life. One week we stayed in the best hotels, the next in dumps. One week we ate in expensive cafés, the next in hash houses. One week I wore diamonds, the next they were in pawn. But it was exciting and I had Don."

"I'll stick to reporting," I muttered.

"I was in love," she said, simply.

"Love or no, it sounds like the hell of a way to live."

"You don't understand. Until you have loved someone so much that just seeing them across the room from you makes you thrill all over, you can't know what being in love that way means."

"I'll take vanilla. Oh, I'm sorry, really. Go ahead."

For a second I thought she was going to freeze up on me and I'd never find out where Nita came from, but she picked up the story again, saying that they had traveled that way for several years, five to be exact, and that she and Dunn had become close friends.

"Jim and I knew Donny was weak and we formed a sort of team to take care of him. Jim even put him to work again and things went fine until summer three years ago. Don wanted to go to Chicago and we left Jim in Saratoga and traveled to Chi. Don went broke there and couldn't seem to get a break. He pawned my jewelry one day and just disappeared."

"You mean he just left you flat, with no dough at all? Just left you to shift, starve, or lie in the gutter?"

She smiled bleakly. "Just about. I got a job and worked

until I had enough money to get to New York. I meant to look for him in any city where they had racing. I knew sooner or later I'd find him."

"And you found him with Nita?" It was hardly a guess.

She showed no surprise at the question. "I located him through another former jockey, Lionel Garson, who had been a good friend. He brought him to my hotel and Don treated me as if I was an unwelcome stranger. He wanted to know why I had followed him and said he had written and told me to go home and get a divorce."

"Kee-rist!" I was incredulous. "And you let him get away with that?"

"Not exactly. I told him I'd had no letter and asked what he meant. He said he had written me that for the first time in his life he was really in love and wanted his freedom. I demanded to know who the woman was and where he had met her."

I began to grow really interested. At last we were getting to the information I wanted.

"And he told you?"

"Yes. She was a French-Canadian actress named Annette Jeans. She claimed to have been born in Paris. He was living with her in New York as man and wife."

"Fine thing."

"I demanded a chance to meet and talk with her. I had a crazy idea that if he saw us together he would realize he didn't love her and come back to me."

"And you'd have taken him?" I gazed unbelievingly at her.

"Of course! He was my husband. I loved him."

"I'm sorry. I just can't understand that kind of love."

"You're fortunate, I suppose." Her voice was bleak.

"And when did you meet her?"

"He wouldn't take me until I agreed to go to the apartment as a friend of Lionel's and not tell her who I really was."

"And you agreed to that too?" I was fast losing sympathy for the woman.

She nodded. "When I saw her, I began to understand things. She was beautiful—like an animal is beautiful. I felt a sense of defeat, a feeling that I could not compete with her kind of beauty. But by then I didn't care. I would have done anything just so I could be near Donny. I even cultivated her friendship so I could be with him."

"How long did that little play last?"

"Until we ran into Jim one evening on the street. He didn't know anything about what was going on and, naturally, he gave the show away. Nita was wild with rage and Jim and Don almost came to blows on the street.

"The next day I packed up and came back home. I didn't see him again until this winter. But I didn't divorce him, although Mike kept trying to get me to file suit. I just couldn't bring myself to do it."

"What can you tell me about Nita? Other than her name and nationality?"

"Nothing much. She was in a musical comedy when I met her. It was called *Let's Carry On*. And then she was in *The Rounders*. She had just left that show when she got down here. She claimed she came from French royalty and had been brought to Canada by a nun when she was a child. To Quebec, she said. She used to hint at some sort of mystery in her life and she'd get quite excited about a vow she had sworn to avenge someone's death. She was always acting, so I paid no attention most of the time. She *was* French—"

"Oh, indubitably."

"How do you know?" She gave me a keen look.

"I sat next to you in Gaston's Carnival night."

"Of course! That's why you seemed familiar. She asked about you. The waiter told her you were a reporter. She was angry because you kept looking at her."

"I wasn't the only one she got angry with," I said blandly.

"I know. If that hadn't happened—"

I broke in hastily, that line of thought would lead to more tears.

"How come you were dining with her if she knew who you were?"

"The same reason as always. I was content to be near Don. But it had not been since that winter in New York that I saw him until he showed up down here a couple of weeks ago. He called me and said he and Nita were through and that he had been ill but was well now. I didn't know then that his illness had been caused by his taking poison."

"So he had tried it before?"

"Yes. Jim told me about it. However, we began going around together and had begun to talk about trying marriage again when one day he called and said Nita was with him. The rest you know."

I did, but I was still curious about a couple of things.

"Do you really suppose you two could have made a go of it after everything that had happened?"

"I don't know. I was willing to try, though."

"And you humbled yourself to the extent of going out with them, after all he had done to you?"

She drew herself up a fraction. "I didn't exactly humble myself. It was Nita who called me. Said she knew no one in the city and would like to be friends with me if I would let her."

"And you fell for that line?"

"It didn't matter whether or not it was a line. I could see Don and that was all I cared about. I knew they had broken up once, I thought it could happen again. I hoped it would, but Carnival night I knew once and for all that I'd been hoping for the impossible."

"Well, that was quite an amazing story." I smiled at her. "Don't worry about publicity. The story will soon die down as far as your part is concerned." I hoped with all my heart I was right about that but suspected I wasn't. If anyone in the world was suspect to this murder, it was the red-haired girl sitting across from me.

"You've given me some pretty good leads to work on to find out just who Nita was and that's a big help. So now I'll get—"

I stopped abruptly and with a sinking feeling looked at my watch. The hands pointed inexorably to two-twenty. I jumped for the phone just as it began to ring. Simultaneously there was the sound of a heavy fist pounding on the door and a baritone voice shouting,

"Open up! This is the police!"

15. *Alibis and Excuses*

I GROANED. This was not going to endear me to either the cops or Dennis. Dunn picked up the phone. All he said was, "They're here."

"They're looking for me," I said forlornly. "They—well, never mind. I'll straighten it all out."

Before I got to the door, I'd decided how to play it the best way for myself. I flung the door wide open and two uniformed officers almost fell on their faces.

"What the hell is the idea of trying to break the door down?" I asked irritably. "All you had to do was knock and be admitted."

Tim Vestor of the riot squad stared at me, jaws slackly open.

"Well, come on in. Don't just stand there with a mouth full of teeth."

Vestor scratched his head in a bewildered gesture. The two men moved aside far enough to let me get the door shut and then Vestor spoke.

"Something's screwy here. Your boss called us and said you was in danger of getting your head blown off. He gave us this address and told us to get right on over. Now *you* ask *me* what the hell is the idea. Well, just what *is* the idea?"

"I'm sure I don't know." I made sweeping denial. "But since you are here, how about a drink?"

Vestor and his partner, Emmett Blanding, clouded up like a thunder storm.

"Never mind the drink." Tim was furious. "If this is one

of Dennis McCarthy's lousy gags, I will personally throw that Mick in the can. Gimme that phone."

"Oh, don't do that!" I blocked his way. "I do know what it's all about but there's no sense getting mad about it."

Tim eyed me suspiciously. "I thought as much. Okay, let's hear it—and it better be good."

"Well, Dennis probably meant this call in perfectly good faith. I'm covering a murder story and these people knew the party who was killed. You guys both know I have had my head busted while working a murder case and Dennis didn't want me to come over here alone. I didn't want to wait for Hansen and I told Dennis I'd either call him or be back by one-forty-five. But I forgot to watch the time and I guess Dennis got worried and called out the rescue detail."

I watched the two faces, hoping the story had gone down without too much effort. Neither looked too convinced, so I started to talk again.

"Honestly, fellows, that's how it was. Come on now, have a drink." I threw a glance of appeal to Dunn, who started for the pantry.

"We-ll, okay—" Vestor grumbled, beginning to grin at the end of the grumble. "Seems funny Dennis would worry about you, though. The way I hear the story, he'd enjoy seeing you get your throat slit."

"That's not so!" I denied, indignantly.

"Aw, hell, Margaret. Everyone knows you two have had battles that set a record—even for a reporter and the editor."

"I *beg* your pardon. Dennis and I—" I stopped abruptly. "Record! Oh good glory! What time is it? Never mind, I have a watch. Oh, Lord—two-thirty! I gotta beat it—" I started for the door just as Dunn came in with a tray of drinks. I came to a halt and accepted a glass.

Blanding whooped. "What happened to your hurry?"

"Quiet please. One drink won't make me much later."

"My name is James Dunn." The belated introduction brought me to a realization of my lack of manners. I repaired them hurriedly by completing the introduction for Dunn and then turned to Bette.

"And this is—"

"Miss Marshall." She supplied the last name hastily, then slumped back in her chair. I walked over to her and lifted the pretty chin.

"Keep that up," I advised her. "At least you know where he is now and that he isn't sleeping with other women."

She pulled away angrily.

"Don wasn't like that. It was just that he couldn't help himself where Nita was concerned."

Vestor's look was bright and questioning.

"Don? Nita? Oh say—are you covering the case of the guy who bumped himself off after killing his wife?"

Bette leaped from the chair, jostling Vestor and spilling most of his drink.

"That tore it," I muttered.

She advanced on him furiously, hands clenched into fists. Tim backed off, a funny look of surprise on his face.

"He never killed her!" She screamed at him. "Don't you dare say Don killed her! One of her other men did it—not Don!" She collapsed back into her chair, sobbing wildly.

"What's eating her?" Vestor gave her a bewildered look, then gazed sadly at the almost empty glass in his hand. "Lookit, she spilled my drink. What's she to that guy?"

"It's a long story." I turned to Bette. "What do you know of her having other men?"

"Oh go away and leave me alone," she wailed.

"But you must—" Fists pounding on the closed bedroom door interrupted what I was going to say. Mike O'Leary's furious voice demanded to be let out or he'd break the door down.

"That's Mike," Dunn said, unnecessarily. "I locked him in there. He wouldn't go home but he promised to behave if I let him stay. I slipped the lock on to insure his behaving."

"Well, let him out—f'evvins sakes. What are you waiting for? I'm not afraid of him." I sidled close to the stalwart arms of the law.

"*Now* what the hell goes on?" Vestor wanted to know.

"The guy who is in there threatened me when I was up here once before. That's part of why Dennis got worried about me when I didn't call."

"Oh? Is he mixed up in the murder?"

"Maybe." I shrugged. "He's got a foul enough temper to be a killer—and he did hate the woman. You might check his alibi."

O'Leary charged out of the bedroom just as I finished the sentence. Then Blanding provided a surprise.

"F'crissakes, Mike! What the hell are you kicking up a fuss about?"

O'Leary grabbed him and started pounding on his back.

"Emmett! Damn, but I'm glad to see you. I was going to call you and see if you could help us."

"Nice you two know each other," I said drily. "Now, I'll be on my way and you can get together."

"Just a minute, Margaret." Vestor restrained me. "You said this guy threatened you? Why?"

"We-ll, he didn't *exactly* threaten me, but he did try to keep me from leaving here to go write my story and he *looked* as if he'd like to wring my neck."

Vestor gave me a disgusted look. "Dames on newspapers," he snorted. "Cripes, if the guy only looked mad you can't call that threatening you."

"He tried to keep me from leaving," I retorted.

"I was only trying to protect Bette from the po—I mean the newspapers and things. That's all."

"You mean the police and the newspapers," I said, tartly.

He gave me a dirty look. "All right, maybe I do. I was afraid it would be a messy scandal so I tried to persuade you not to write it."

"*Persuade* me, he calls it! He blocked that door like a granite slab."

"Look, Emmett." He appealed to his friend. "I want to marry that girl someday and scandal won't help either of us. She's had her share of heartache. Why can't they let her alone?"

"What in hell is he talking about?" Vestor demanded.

"Let him tell you. Ask him where he was between two and six Wednesday morning."

The big Irishman had moved his hulking frame over beside Bette. He sat on the arm of her chair and cuddled her hand in his big fist. He favored me with a glare.

"I was home in bed—and I can prove it. You needn't try to pin any murder on me."

"I'm not trying to pin it on you. I'm only trying to eliminate you as a suspect."

Vestor assumed his official dignity like a hastily donned cloak.

"I think that is a job for the police, Margaret."

"Well, you're the police. Why don't you get on the job?"

Vestor cleared his throat but O'Leary began to tell his friend Blanding the story.

"I got home about two-thirty and went to bed, Emmett. I talked to both Mom and Dad, before I went upstairs. You know where I live. I couldn't have gone from Shrewsbury to the French Quarter and got there by three or four —which was when the coroner said she was killed."

"Coroner? How do you know the coroner said that?" I was pretty sure I had not mentioned the coroner.

He scowled at me. "Well, you said it and you must have got it from the coroner."

"I said she was killed between three and *six*, which is what the coroner gave as the time. Where did you get the figure four from?"

"Look, Emmett, this dame is getting in my hair. Make her lay off of me and Bette. I mean it. Mom and Dad know

I was home. I took Bette from Gaston's to the Blue Room, where we had a few dances. We stopped at the Sazerac and then dropped into the Ritz bar for a last drink. About midnight or a little later, it may have been twelve-thirty, we got a cab and I took her home. I'd parked my car by her house and we sat in it for awhile just talking. Then I went on home myself."

"Okay, Mike." Blanding directed an unfriendly look at me. "I don't believe you killed anyone. Women, particularly newspaper janes, are always going off half-cocked."

Vestor had been listening, growing more puzzled all the time.

"If I knew just what this was all about I'd feel better," he said. "Where does this guy fit into the picture and who is she?" He pointed to Bette.

"They can tell you." I started for the door. "Me, I'm going."

They didn't try to stop me that time and I marched out into the hall, caught the elevator and left the building. I had driven two blocks before it dawned on me that I had not called Dennis and I also wondered why he had not tried to call the apartment after having sent out the police. I looked at my watch. It was almost three and the next edition would carry the story of the unmasked wife. I figured Dennis would keep until I got back from this checking of the record. He no doubt knew, or figured, by now that I must be okay or the cops would have called him. I drove on over to the other apartment and was mildly surprised to see Morrow turning in the doorway.

"Hey, wait up for baby," I called from the curb. He looked a bit annoyed but halted. I joined him. "What you doing here?"

"Just checking an angle to this thing. Why?"

I grinned at him. "Could it have anything to do with a victrola?"

"It could—and does." He shook his head, sadly. "Someday I'll have a hunch that you missed. How'd you get on to it?"

"Same way you did, by using my head. I do have one, you know. I figured if the woman next door heard the vic going until he passed out, then he couldn't have killed his wife— oh, say—that reminds me. She—" I stopped. Why not just let him read the story in my paper?

"She what?"

"She won't have her body claimed by Dunn," I substituted a little lamely. "He claimed the man's body, though. Did you know that?"

"Yeah, I knew it. Well, someone claimed her too."

I stopped on a stair and looked at him. He was smiling smugly.

"Who? A relative?"

"Nope. At least I don't think he's related to her. He's French, though. Gave the name of Maurice De André. He came in to claim her while I was checking her body after the posting."

"De André? Sounds like a hair dresser."

"Doesn't look it. Looks theatrical, but prosperously so. He must have dough, he sent her to Livaudais. He's sure cut up plenty. Acted like she was *his* wife. Or something."

"Did he now?"

"Uh huh."

We had reached the top of the long climb and turned down the hall to the apartment next to the one which had recently been the setting for tragedy.

I rapped and a blowzy blonde opened the door. I saw what Joe had meant when he had called her a floozy.

"Whatcha want?" She asked sullenly, shoving back tousled bleached locks with one hand and holding her soiled robe together with the other.

"We'd like to speak to you for a minute," Morrow said.

She didn't look anxious to speak to anyone.

"What about? Jeezus, I wisht I could get some sleep. For

three days cops and other people have been running all over the joint. I told 'em all I know and it ain't much. If my rent wasn't paid to the first, I'd get to hell outa here."

"I know it must be awful to try and sleep in such confusion." I took over the conversation. "But we won't keep you long. We're from the newspapers and we believe you can help us out on something very important. In fact, you are about the only one who can give us the help we need."

She thawed perceptibly. "Is that so? Well, I dunno, but come on in." We entered a messy duplicate of the next room. "Don't mind the looks of this dump." She waved a hand vaguely around. "I work nights. I'm a singer. I don't have much time to do housework. Here, sit down." She tossed a pile of soiled clothing off of the two chairs and settled herself on the unmade bed.

16. *The Music Went Round and Round*

"NOW Miss—?" I gave her a questioning look.

"Desire. Elise Desire."

"Is that your stage name?" Morrow asked, with a perfectly straight face.

"Oh sure. Do you have to know my real name?"

"Not at all," I put in hurriedly. "We just want to know what you heard Carnival night. From next door, I mean."

"What didn't I hear! Them two, between 'em, kept me awake all night pretty near. First they were battling and she was yelling and calling him all kind of names in French and English. Then she left. But about half an hour or so later, she come back and began to pound on the door. My boy friend was here. Pete and I had both worked right through Monday night until Tuesday night. Pete had brought a bottle and we were having a few.

"She, the second time she come back, banged on the door with her shoe heel. That was when I went out and told her to shut up and let decent people get some rest. She didn't answer me, didn't even turn her head. She just yelled at him that he could keep her bag, that she'd get plenty of new clothes where she was going."

"That's highly unlikely," Morrow muttered.

The blonde looked at him curiously, but he said no more and she went on. "That was about one-thirty, I guess. They'd been at it ever since Pete and I got in about eleven. Well, she finally went tearing down the hall and he started to walk up and down. These walls are made of paper and I could hear him walking and sort of making noises like he was crying. Anyhow, kinda talking to himself."

"Did you hear the victrola? You must have, if you could hear everything else so plainly."

"I hope to spit in your eye I heard it! He began to play that thing about an hour after she left—"

"Wait a minute. He didn't go out after her at all, did he?"

She shook her head emphatically. "Oh, no. He went no place. First he walked up and down, up and down. Then I heard him dragging stuff around and in a few minutes he started the phonograph going."

I gave Morrow a triumphant look.

"What did he play?"

"Well, he started off by playing some classical numbers but he only played about three or four and then he put on 'Among My Souvenirs.' Jee-sus, I sing that number myself and I like it, but I got good and sick of it that night. I was going to bang on the wall but Pete said to let tho poor bastard alone, he was probably having himself a crying jag."

"And he kept on playing that one piece?"

"Over and over and over until finally I got to where I was nearly used to it. When it finally stopped I missed it."

"What time was that?"

"It was exactly four-ten. I happen to know because Pete said he had to get dre—had to go home. Just as I looked at my watch the vic ran down. We figured the guy had fallen asleep and it had run on out."

"Looks like you can kiss that dough good-bye," I told Morrow.

"What dough?" The blonde asked.

"We had a bet that he didn't kill that woman, that is I bet I could prove he didn't."

"You mean that dame got killed?"

I nodded.

"Well, whadda ya know!" She sounded awed.

"I know you've been a big help. The cops thought the man had killed her and then came back and turned on the gas. Your story busts that little theory into a million pieces. If the vic was going all that time, it was impossible for him not to have been here to wind it up. He was here dying while she was out getting killed."

"Gee. The poor bastard. And me griping about the noise."

"Well, you can't be blamed for that. It's too bad you didn't get a smell of the gas, though."

"My windows and doors were closed and the walls ain't *that* thin."

Johnny and I got up to go.

"You'll have to tell that story to the police," I said.

"Oh, sure. I don't know how come I didn't think to tell them about that music going round and round anyhow. How about a drink before you leave?" She motioned toward a bottle of gin on the dresser.

"Thanks, no. I never drink when I'm working."

Morrow gave her the same excuse and we left. Going down the hall, Johnny opined that we were a pair of lying hypocrites.

"Since when has work ever interfered with our taking a couple of quick drinks?" He asked.

"I spoil easily. That cheap gin reminded me too much of the bathroom junk I've ruined my stomach with by drinking just to be drinking. From now on, I mean to be choosy about my liquor."

"Me too. Well, you called the turn again."

"I know—and I'm ten bucks richer than I was this morning."

"Yeah. Well, it's lost in a good cause. If that floozy heard the vic going until her piccolo-Pete got up out of a warm bed and went home, then the poor bastard, Barnett, I mean, had to be there. Even though he's where he can't get hurt, it would be kind of nasty for him to take the blame for a killing he didn't commit."

"That's exactly the way I feel about it." I smiled at him. We had reached the street and I got in my car. Johnny climbed in after me.

"Just where are you going?" I asked. "Have you changed papers?"

"Huh? Who? Oh, me? Hell, no. I thought you were going to the station to gloat over Beton and Gross. I figured I'd ride with you."

"I have to go to the office first. I have to explain something to Dennis." I didn't say what I had to explain.

"Okay, then, I'll grab a cab. When you going to collect that bet? Nick has to buy me a drink for losing my ten."

I laughed. "I'll meet you in Nick's right after working hours."

As he stepped out of the car, a newsboy came by calling the latest edition. The imp that dwells within me came alive at once.

"Why don't you buy a good paper and read all about it?"

"I'll do that—I mean I'll waste a nickel on this sheet just to see what you dreamed up." He gave the boy a coin and unfolded the paper. He hadn't read much farther than the headlines when he howled,

"You louse! Where did you get this beat?"

"I got it while you sat and drank beer with Beton," I said, blandly. "I found out Dunn had claimed the body and decided to go see if he could tell me anything. I looked in Nick's, meaning to ask you to go along, but you were busy with your pal. I went on to Dunn's apartment and when I got there the real Mrs. Barnett spilled the beans. She, by the way, is the Bette that note he wrote was meant for. They had been married eight years. But read the story—all the details will be in the next edition."

He was still glowering at the paper as I put the car in gear and slid off down the street. I was still chuckling when I walked into the city room, but the chuckle died in a hurry.

My entrance was the signal for Dennis to blow skyhigh. I knew I was all wrong, so I stood silently while he called me every kind of a jackass he could think up; while he told me, vividly and profanely, that I could bloody well get killed before he would ever do anything about it again and finally wound up by howling he ought to fire me on the spot and have done with it.

When the bellow died down to a bluster I said meekly that I was awful sorry to have caused so much trouble but that I'd figured he'd call Dunn's apartment before he actually sent for police.

That brought on another outraged sermon, in which he swore I had flatly told him not to call that apartment under any circumstances but just send out the cops. I knew he was wrong about that, but I had better judgement than to argue with him, furious as he was. I waited again until he had stopped sputtering, then I repeated my apology and added that the story I'd heard had been longer than I expected and I'd failed to watch the time. I promised never to do it again. It was hardly likely such an occasion would arise again so I felt safe in making the promise.

"Anyhow, O'Leary was still there and he roared like a lion. If Vestor and Blanding hadn't shown up, Lord knows what he *might* have done to me. However, I'm truly sorry I worried you."

"Worried me!" He spluttered. "Dammit, you didn't worry me any. But I'm shorthanded now and I didn't want you laid up. But the next time—"

"Shhhh." I held up an admonitory finger. "There won't be any next time. And I have a story, a good one. I have the proof that Barnett didn't kill that woman."

"Huh? No kidding? The phonograph?"

"The phonograph. The music went round and round until after four a.m. It kept the blonde and her boy friend awake. She's a singer and he's a musician. They both heard Barnett walking around his apartment for some time after Nita left and before he began to play the victrola. She's ready to swear he never left the building."

"Good stuff, kid."

"You're darn right it's good stuff. So's that ten bucks I won from Morrow."

"What ten?"

I told him about the bet and he grinned at me. Then his face fell. "Morrow onto this story?"

I nodded. "He had the same hunch as I had," I admitted. "I met him in front of the building and we went in together."

"Too bad. But we got the beat on the real wife."

"*We?* You mean, *I* got that beat. Please don't forget it."

"I'm not forgetting it, Maggie," he said, a little wearily. "It's things like this that keep you on the payroll. You do have the damnedest luck."

"Luck my eye!" I protested angrily. "I worked hard for that beat. Luck, he calls it."

He leaned back in his swivel chair and regarded me with a jaundiced eye.

"I suppose you knew when you went to that guy's apartment the real wife would be there and lay the story in your lap."

"I didn't say that," I retorted heatedly. "But, by God, if I hadn't brains and ambition enough to go there—to follow up the story when I found Dunn had claimed the body— we wouldn't have had the beat, would we? Morrow didn't get the story and he had the same chances at it that I had. He's just before a fit because I beat him on it. You didn't *send* me to Dunn's. I went on my own hook and hunch and I think I deserve some credit for having the initiative to go dig up a beat. It's just such initiative that makes the difference between a *real* reporter and a hack writer."

"You can get off the soap box now," Dennis said, after I had run out of breath. "You'll get credit—in a by-line. Now go write the follow up and the new story. Beat it." He waved toward my desk. The discussion, as far as he was concerned, was ended.

I walked away muttering under my breath, sat down and put copy paper in the machine. I wrote the two stories and took them over to Dennis.

"We'll use that pix of Nita again," he said. "I'll check the files for anything on the Marshall girl. Maybe her folks had her reported to the Missing Person's Bureau when she ran away to marry Barnett. Did you get a picture of the blonde —this Elise Desire?"

I shook my head.

"Well, we can do without it. You better get back to the press room. And you better tell your pals, Gross and Beton, about this. I don't want those guys jumping me. They'd be sure to say they knew all about it but kept it quiet hoping to lull the suspicions of the real killer. I'm in bad enough with the cops—thanks to you."

"Johnny will tell them," I said hurriedly.

"You tell them too," he ordered. "Or maybe you got another hunch about something?"

"I thought I'd check that kid's story. I promised her I'd see her right after school and I'm way late now."

"What kid? What story?"

"The Pacelli's daughter, Christina. She's about fifteen and this morning she said she had something important to tell me. She wouldn't tell the cops and made me promise not to either. I thought at first she was just imagining things, but, in view of what's happened since, it's possible she does know something."

"The trouble with most grownups is that they don't give kids credit for having any sense," Dennis said pompously. "You better go down there right away."

"All right." I started to walk out, then turned back to his desk. "I almost forgot something else. I did forget to put it in the story, but you can add it. Nita's body has been claimed by a rich Frenchman. At least, Morrow said he looked like the money and he sent the body to Livaudais Parlors. His name is Maurice De André. He—"

"*Who?*" Dennis was positively livid.

"De André. Maurice De André," I repeated, slightly taken aback. "Why? Do you know him?"

"Do I know him!" It was the first time I'd ever heard Dennis actually screech. "Do you mean to say you don't?"

"Why no. Should I? Is he somebody important?"

For a full moment Dennis looked at me fixedly, then he leaned his arms on his desk and addressed the room in general.

"Is he somebody important, she wants to know. Oh, Christ, what's the use? De André is one of the world's most famous dancer-actors and one of the wealthiest. Do you guys, any of you, know about him?" He looked at the solemn faces around the copy desk and in the slot. They all nodded their heads.

"Sure, you know him, but *she* knows nothing about him. He's here in the city, he claims a murdered woman's body, she knows all about it, but does she tell me? *Only* as an afterthought. Does she put it in her story? No, she tells me it can be added on. I've spent ten years trying to make a reporter out of her and—oh, well, skip it. Only tell me just one thing, Maggie. How come you never heard of Maurice De André?"

I blew up.

"Why the hell should I have heard of him? I don't write the amusement page and I'll bet no one but you and the amusement editor knows about him!" I glared at the suddenly busy copy desk men. "I don't give a farthing for men dancers, anyhow. Most of 'em are pansies. And don't call me Maggie!"

"This one is no pansy. How come he claimed her body? Is he related to her?"

"I don't know any more than I've already told you. Morrow saw him in the morgue when he went to claim her."

"Does Morrow know who he is?"

"I don't think so. If he does, he didn't tell me."

"So I notice. Where's De André staying?"

"I don't know that either."

Dennis looked like he was going to explode again, but he only reached for the phone on his desk and made a couple of calls. Then he spoke to me again.

"He's at the Monterey Hotel on Royal Street. In room 1210. Skip the kid for now and beat it over to see De André. Find out why he claimed that body. There ought to be a story in it somewhere. And don't bother to announce yourself at the desk—he's not receiving but make sure he receives you."

"What am I supposed to do, climb in the window?"

"I don't care if you climb through the transom. You might put on an act of being the maid and then duck in under his arm. But don't come back without seeing him."

"I'm off at five-fifteen," I reminded him. "It's quarter of now."

He said nothing. He didn't have to. His look was enough. I took the blue assignment slip with the room number written on it and marched out of the room. When I got in my car I looked at the slip. Then I looked again. The numbers, 1210, and the color, blue, looked very familiar. I was sure I'd seen just that combination before. I sat there for a second, puzzling over it and suddenly it hit me. I rummaged in my bag and found the slip of paper I'd picked up in the Baronne Street apartment. It was blue and it had the same number written on it, but the handwriting was feminine. I got going in a hurry.

I had a lucky break and found a parking place just around the corner from the hotel. I walked in and went right to the elevator, gave the operator the floor number and rode on upstairs. I knew the floor plan, so I turned in the opposite direction and away from De André's room. When I heard the elevator descend, I turned about and trotted down the

hall to the door of 1210. I had been trying to figure a stunt
to get in and the only thing that came to my mind was
what Dennis had suggested about the maid. I knew they
employed Negro help and I'd always been pretty good at
mimicry. I leaned on the door and knocked. When he
opened the door the position I was in would just naturally
carry me into the room. I knocked again and an impatient
voice called out,

"Yes? What ees eet?"

"Hit's de maid, suh," I drawled. "Ise got towels foh you."

"But I 'ave towels," he answered.

"These hyar is fresh towels, suh. De housekeepah ohded
dem."

"Oh, ver' well. Come in."

I turned the knob. The door had been open all along and
I could have walked right in. I stopped near the door, expecting any kind of reception but the one I got—which was
none at all. The man was seated with his back to me, talking on the phone. The room I'd entered was the parlor of a
suite and he was parked in an easy chair. The bedroom
opened off of my right, which was away from his sight. I
went toward it and shot a quick glance around. A heavy,
light tan leather suit case was on the luggage stand, a dark-
blue brocaded silk robe hung from a hook on the open
closet door and a pearl gray felt hat, snap brim, sat on the
top of the dresser. Outside of those things, and a pair of
lounging slippers, the room was neat. I stepped back out
into the living room. Without turning his head, the man
spoke to me.

"Maid, be so·kind as to close the door when you leave,"
he asked, then to the phone—"I was speak with the maid,
not you. To you, I say make her ver' beautiful. She was mos'
beautiful in life and she mus' be so in death."

He listened awhile, then spoke again. "Yes, I know the
garrote makes great damage but you mus' do all you can to
restore her beauty."

I listened with interest. The man was speaking with someone from the funeral parlors. I heard him instruct them to
buy the most beautiful white gown in the city, "like a
wedding robe," he said. Then he replaced the receiver,
sighed deeply and sat for a moment with his head sunk on
his chest. In a moment he rose, turned about and saw me.
His eyes popped and he gaped at me.

"Who are you? How deed you get in?"

"You told me to come in." My voice was calmer than my
heart.

"I? I told no one but the maid, the black woman, to
enter."

"That was me. I changed my voice. M'sieu De André, I
must talk to you. It's very important. That's why I pulled
that trick to get in. I knew you had given orders no one was
to come up."

"Ah, so you play on me the trick, eh? So, I shall call at
once the *gendarmes* from the 'otel and 'ave you put out. He
reached for the phone again.

"If you're smart you'll put that thing down," I said
quickly. "You're mixed up in a murder and I've been sent
to find out why you claimed the body of a woman who was
living as the wife of a man she was not married to at all. I
wouldn't call for the house dick if I were you."

His hand continued to rest on the phone, but he didn't
pick it up. I went on rapidly, hanging on to the small advantage I had gained.

"Nita Jeans was a French dancer. So are you. She was
killed a short distance from here. She was hardly up from
the posting in the morgue when you claimed her body. Yet
you aren't a relative." I took a stab at that last and he didn't
deny it or explain what his interest was. I went on, in a surer
tone than ever.

"The man with whom she was living killed himself, as
you must know by now. In the apartment where they were
living there was a piece of paper found with your room

number on it. That means she or he knew you were in this hotel. Don't you realize you are a suspect of her murder?"

His eyes flashed and he clenched his hands into fists and came toward me. I shrank back against a table on which sat a portable victrola. I leaned on it at an angle where I couldn't help seeing the record on the turntable. I read the title and went cold all over. It was a French recording of the *Danse Macabre!*

17. *Dancer on a Spot*

MAURICE DE ANDRÉ was a lithe slim man of about thirty-five. He had the build of an athlete and the liquid movements of the trained dancer. Right now he looked mad enough to perform the *Danse Macabre* with me as his unwilling partner.

"Now wait a minute," I warned him. "Getting angry with me won't help you any. I haven't accused you of murder, I only said you were a suspect." And I thought: And so you are, my fine Frenchman.

He regarded me for a moment, then recovered control.

"I ask your pardon. You make me mos' angry for a moment. Sit down please and tell me what it is you mean by saying all these things to me."

"I was just stating facts. It's your turn to talk now."

He moved the big chair around from the phone and offered it to me. I refused and perched gingerly on the edge of the divan. He took a seat in the chair.

"What do you wish me to say?"

"I want to know what Nita was to you and why you claimed her body and behaved as if she was your wife—or something."

"She was my love," he said, simply.

"What about Don Barnett?"

"She cared nothing for him. That is why he killed her, not me. I had not the cause. It was I she loved. The papers say he killed her and himself."

"The papers were wrong, thanks to the police going off
172

half-cocked. He didn't kill her. He couldn't have done it."

"No?"

"No." I told him the story of the victrola and the music which had been heard all through the important hours. He listened, gravely attentive, until I had finished talking. Then he rose and began pacing the floor, moving with an easy rhythm that reminded me weirdly of a panther. When he finally spoke, it was in a low, musing tone and almost as if he was talking to himself.

"She was my love. I adored her. I would 'ave made her great. For over the year now, I 'ave plead with her to leave this gambler and go away with me. I would take her to London, Vienna, Berlin, and to the Paris we both loved so well. I would train her and make of her the greatest dancer the world has known since Duncan. All that I 'ave and know would 'ave been hers. All of it. She loved me, she told me this long ago, but she is feeling sorry for that man. When he sent for her in Chicago a short while ago, she say she mus' come to New Orleans for a little while. She mus' see him and, she said, there was someone else she mus' see also and he, too, was here. She made the promise to arrange everything to leave Don, but she does nothing."

"What do you mean, nothing?"

"She has promise to return to Chicago to me over and over. But she calls and says she cannot come right away. I became impatient and came here my own self. I arrive on Monday and soon I see her—"

I interrupted. "You saw her on Monday? Where?"

"Right here, M'selle. We met and talk and this time she is promised to leave Don at once. I warn her that I am tired of this fooling. Before I weel let her to stay with another man, I weel keel her!" His accent became pronounced and his eyes flashed again.

"And did you? Kill her, I mean?"

He sat down quickly, as though the question had knocked his legs out from under him.

"*Mon Dieu, non!*"

"M'sieu De André, do you do an Apache routine?" The question was seemingly irrelevant.

"The greatest in the world," he admitted.

"Modest, aren't you?" I couldn't repress the grin.

"I 'ave no need for false modesty." His eyes were wide and serious. "I am the greatest of the Apache dancers."

"I wouldn't know," I said drily. "Do you use a knife or a garrote in your dance?"

"Always the garrote. It is of a great dramatic effect and the death looks more real than the fake knife stab with the rubber knife." His eyes widened suddenly. "Ah, I see! Nita was killed with the garrote and you ask that question trying to—how you say it—? Trap me, is it?"

"Not at all," I denied. "But the garrote used on her was a silk cord such as dancers use. Or do they?"

"To be sure, the cord is always silk. Nita had a garrote which I gave to her. It was one like I use in a routine in which things are reverse and the woman kills the man."

"Was it black silk?"

He stook his head. "No, the woman uses white."

"Not very sensible. I thought the cord was black so it would not be seen in the dark of a night."

"It is, but in the dance one may take liberties with reality. I 'ave a black silk cord. Several of them, in fact."

"She was strangled with a black silk garrote."

I watched him narrowly, half-wishing I'd stopped off and told Tommy Gross where I was going. But the dancer showed no fresh anger at what was a pretty obvious insinuation. He regarded me with sad eyes.

"It is plain to see you do suspect me, M'selle. Better we call the *gendarmes* and let them question me."

I felt better. If he was prepared to be questioned, he couldn't be too worried. If I got a really good story from him, Dennis might forgive my ignorance of the stage.

"Wait a bit. You can call them anytime. But I think you

can tell me a few things about Nita. Do you know who she
was, where she came from and if she had any family?"

"She had no one, poor little one." His face was moody.
"She told me a few things of herself. That she was born in
Paris and her mother was an actress. The mother died when
Annette was quite small and someone placed her in a convent in Normandy. She could not remember the man's
name, but knew he was not her father and, also, she knew
he was the lover of her mother. This man paid her bills for
many years."

"And she didn't know who he was, not ever?" I asked
somewhat bewilderedly.

"No. Although she told me she tried to find out and she
had some suspicions."

"Perhaps she was seeking him in New Orleans? A lot of
expatriate French live here."

He shrugged. "Perhaps. I had a feeling this may be so.
Nita told me she remained in the convent in France until
one of the Sisters was sent to an academy of the same
order in Quebec. She arranged with Nita's unknown protector to take the child with her. She remained in Canada
until she was of age."

"Odd, that the man kept his identity such a dark secret."

"Not too odd. Many Frenchmen bury natural children
in convents where they will not embarrass them."

"But you said he was not the father?"

"Nita thought not. I do not know that for a fact. He may
have been, you know."

"I suppose so. It's strange for anyone to do so much for a
child unless they are related someway."

"Not if he was the lover, as Nita said he was."

"I guess not. Well, what happened when she became
of age?"

"On her eighteenth birthday, the good Sisters turned over
to her quite a large sum of money. She wished for a career
in the theater, so she traveled to New York to study drama

and dancing. Also, she believed her unknown patron was in this country."

"What gave her that idea?"

"One time, when she was in the Superior's office, she happened to see a bank draft with her name on it. It was drawn on a bank in the United States. She made out only the first signature and part of the second when the Sister caught her. She was reprimanded for picking up the paper and sent to her room."

"What was the name?" I was growing excited. This began to lead someplace.

"That I do not know. She would not tell me, always insisting she was making this search alone."

"Oh nuts," I said inelegantly. "Where did you meet her?"

"In New York, when she is in *The Rounders*. I fall in love with her at once. I make it my business to meet her. This is easy for one as great in the theater as I am. I know she feels the same appeal for me as I do for her. For both of us it was destiny we should meet and love."

"But she wouldn't leave Don for you?" I asked, with some irony.

"Oh, yes. She was leaving him. But she was very sensitive and wished to do this in a way to hurt least. I followed the show to Chicago and, while there, she and Don had the falling out and he came to New Orleans. She was finished with him then, but he calls and threatens to kill himself. So she said she must make the trip here and talk to him."

"So she moved right in with him and began to talk. Sure must have been a long conversation. Now I'm going to tell *you* something, M'sieu De André, much as I hate to spoil your illusions about the sensitive Nita. She came here mainly because she knew that Don was considering going back to his wife and she couldn't stand the idea of anyone else having him, even though she didn't want him herself. I'd be willing to wager that if it was possible to check on that telephone call, you'd find it was she who called Don.

It happens I saw a scene she put on Carnival night and it was a fine display of green-eyed rage, the root of which was jealousy. And when she did leave him that night, she knew, in her heart, he would kill himself. That was what she wanted, she couldn't have borne it for another woman to re-build him into a man."

I paused and thought of what Dennis had said about the soap box. "I'm sorry," I muttered. "I guess I had no business to talk like that about her."

"It is all right. One understands your sympathies are with the wife. I knew she lived here and Nita told me of the quarrel on the night of Mardi Gras."

"You saw her *Mardi Gras* night?"

"*Oui.* She came to me about two of the morning. She is without baggage and said Don would not let her take her things. I procure for her a room, saying she is my sister—"

"You got a room in this hotel on Carnival night?" I asked skeptically.

"With enough money one can do even that."

I thought: He knows all the answers. He knows them too well.

"She went to her room, saying she would be back in only a few minutes. I wait for an hour and she does not come. I call the room and she does not answer. I grow frantic and all night I pace the floor, wondering, wondering—"

"You didn't leave the hotel that night, or morning?"

"No. I call her room every few moments until finally, about daylight, I fall asleep with exhaustion and worry."

"Can you prove that you didn't leave the hotel?"

"Perhaps the operator would remember I make all those calls."

"No good. She was killed only a few blocks from here. A person could have made the round trip and done the killing in a short time. Between phone calls, for instance. The elevator boys wouldn't be much help. What with the Carnival crowds, it isn't likely they would recall whether they saw you or not. Looks like you are without an alibi."

"At about five I have coffee in the room."

"That won't help. She was killed between three and six."

"Right after I have coffee, I send for the morning paper."

"She was killed between three and six," I repeated flatly.

"*Mon Dieu,* M'selle! It would seem I am in a bad position."

"You are clunk on a spot," I said, bluntly. "However, it may not be too bad. You have absolutely no alibi, so don't try to make one up out of whole cloth. Often no alibi is better than one you could shoot holes through."

"Pardon?"

"I mean you're better off with no alibi than a too pat one."

"Pat?"

I gave up. "Look, M'sieu De André, we don't speak the same language, so—"

"I speak almost perfect English," he protested, haughtily.

"That's just it. I speak American English. What I was trying to say is, don't attempt to manufacture an alibi with the hotel employees by using the same stuff you used to get these rooms. The cops would soon break that down and then you would be in trouble. American cops are pretty smart people. Just tell them the same thing you told me."

"*Oui,* M'selle. You are very kind to—to, how you say? Tip me off?"

"That's okay. Well, how long did you sleep Wednesday morning?"

"Only about two hours. My worry will not let me rest, so I arose and shaved and go to that apartment where she was living with Don. I knock many times, but no one comes and finally I go away."

"You were at the door of Barnett's apartment Wednesday morning? What time was that?"

"It is about nine."

"My God! Didn't you smell the gas?"

"No, Mamselle. I am thinking only of Annette and that she is in there lying with him. I am wild with jealousy and I notice nothing of smells."

"I wonder what she had that I haven't," I muttered.

"Everything, M'selle," he said, brutally honest. Then he realized how it sounded and tried to cover up. "Of course you are a mos' attractive—"

"Skip it." I cut him off, shortly. "What happened after you left that Baronne Street building?"

"I return here to wait some more and, once more, I fall into troubled sleep. When I awaken again, I send for more coffee and for the papers. Her picture is on the front page."

"And my story about the suicide and her disappearance."

"Oh, it is your story?"

"Mine or Morrow's. It doesn't matter. Go on."

"I read of the suicide and realized that even as I knocked the man was dead in that apartment."

"He died between the same hours as she did. There must be some sort of ironic justice in that."

"Justice? There is none in this world, M'selle."

"Perhaps not, but you better hope there is. Innocent men have been executed for murder, you know."

For the first time since I had pointed out he was suspect, he looked a little worried. I proceeded to add to his worry.

"First thing the police are going to want to know is why you didn't come to them at once with your story. You read the paper, you knew her and you knew the cops were looking for her and you knew she was registered in this hotel— oh, say! If she was registered here, I wonder how come the clerks didn't spot her name or recognize her from that picture."

"She was registered here as my sister, under my name. The clerk did not see her. When I procured the room, I took the key. Annette came directly to this suite and no one saw her."

"What about the elevator boy?"

"You, yourself, said they would not notice one person in the Carnival rush."

"Yeah, but she was different and elevator boys are men."

He shrugged that off. "I did not go to the *gendarmes* because I felt Annette had her reason for disappearing and I would not interfere. So I remain here, feeling she would call when she was ready to tell me of her actions. Today, I find that she is dead."

It all fitted very neatly. Almost too neatly. I recalled my earlier thought that M'sieu De André seemed to know all the answers.

"She was dead when you read that story."

"I know that—now."

"But you didn't know it then?"

He threw out his hands in a helpless gesture.

"*Voilà*, M'selle! You do think I am the strangler."

"I don't know just what I think about you. But that woman was never destined to die quietly in bed. Gaston was right about her, more than right."

He jumped from his chair as though someone had exploded a bomb under it.

"Gaston? Gaston who? What has he said of Nita? Who is he?"

"Who is Gaston? Why, he's a café owner in the city."

"What did he say of Nita?"

"A number of things, among them that she was a vampire and a destroyer of men who would one day be destroyed herself. He just happened not to like her looks, that's all."

"All! *Mon Dieu!* He wishes her destroyed and you say that is all—as if it means nothing! And she *has* been destroyed."

I realized then it must have sounded pretty bad and tried to amend things.

"I didn't say he wished her dead. He simply didn't like her because she reminded him of someone who had done him dirt when he was young."

"What is this café he runs?"

I knew there was no sense lying. He could find out which café Gaston owned. I told him the name of the place.

"Le Coq d'Or—" He repeated the name. "But, that is the place where Nita and I lunched on Monday."

I looked at him sharply. Gaston had not said anything about the woman ever being in there with anyone but Don. It seemed to me he would have mentioned it as an example of what a double crosser she was. Then I recalled that Gaston seldom appeared during the luncheon hour, leaving it to his maître d'hôtel, Martin.

"I don't see any reason to get excited about that," I said. "Gaston's is the finest café downtown, except for Antoine's. She probably ate there often."

"Why should a café owner say such things of a good client?"

"I told you why. Her type of woman was a sort of fixation with him."

"Fixation? Ah! *L' ideé fixe,* eh? This has often led to murder, M'selle."

"Not this time. Besides, he was annoyed because she created that scene in his place."

"That took place in Le Coq d'Or? She did not tell me that."

"It was nothing to be proud of, M'sieu. She left—at his request."

"This thing I mus' look into." He leaned back in his chair, a speculative look in his eyes. "Yes, it will have to be explained better than you have done it."

"Nonsense," I said bruskly and rose from the couch. "I suggest it would be best for you to go see the police and let them handle their business. My car is downstairs. Come on, I'll drive you to headquarters." I looked at my watch, five-thirty, and Morrow was waiting for me to collect that bet and, naturally, to set up some drinks.

"*C'est bien.*" He rose from his chair and went into the bedroom. As soon as he got out of sight I began to worry.

He *could* be the killer and he *could* figure maybe I knew, or suspected, too much. In that case, where would I be? Dead, too, maybe. As that unhappy idea crossed my mind the door resounded to loud knocking. The wave of relief washed me right up to the door and I opened up to Gross and Beton. I was right glad to see them.

"What you doing here?" Beton asked.

"Earning my salary, what do you think?"

Before he could crack wise, De André came up, hat in hand and a topcoat over his arm. He looked questioningly at the two men.

"We don't have to go to the cops," I told him. "They've beat us to the call."

I introduced the dancer to the policemen and Gross began to question De André about his connection with Annette Jeans. The story was virtually the same as the one he had told me. When he finished, Tommy looked dissatisfied.

"You don't mind coming over to headquarters, do you? The District Attorney wants to see you."

The Frenchman smiled a bit grimly. "Would it make a difference if I did mind? I think not. So let us go and have this done with."

Beton opened the door and De André followed him out and down the hall. I started after them, but Tommy held me back. His eyes were unfriendly and I wondered what he was mad about. I found out right away.

"Now, Miss Smarty-pants, having disproved the murder-suicide theory with your phonograph hunch—which you never let me in on—and having spent some time alone with this man, perhaps you learned a few things that might help the police. If so, will you share them with me?"

"I don't like your tone of voice, Mr. Gross. Morrow had the same hunch on the phonograph business as I had and he was already going in the building when I caught up with him. When he left me he went back to headquarters. I didn't. Why didn't he let you in on the thing?"

"I wouldn't know. I'm always doing favors for you fellows."

"Well, you needn't gripe at me. If I'd gone back to the press room, I'd have told you."

"Okay, skip it. You could have called me. What do you know about this man?"

"Nothing more than you know. I heard the same story."

"How come you to be here?"

I smiled sweetly. "*Morrow* told me De André had claimed the body of the woman. I'd just come from Dunn's apartment where—hey! How did you like my story about finding the real wife?"

"Very much." His tone was dry. "Christ Almighty! You would dig up a triangle just to make things more difficult."

"De André makes it a quadrangle. Honestly, Tommy, I should think you cops would show a little appreciation to reporters who uncover such details for you. You make me sick. You're as bad as Les Beton. Both of you would have been perfectly content to close this case the easy way and let the real killer get away scot free."

"That's what you think. You reporters never seem to give the police credit for having enough intelligence to do the work they are trained for. You always have to go sticking your nose into things. The phonograph hunch was good, I'll admit—"

"Nice of you."

"You're welcome. But you ought to know we'd have uncovered the wife before long."

"Oh, sure. But it happens I beat you to it."

"Yeah—and almost got your ears pinned back too. Dennis had to call out the riot squad."

I couldn't help grinning.

"It's not funny. You were just wasting taxpayer's money and meddling in things that didn't concern you."

"I'm a taxpayer," I retorted. "And I wasn't meddling. I was covering a murder story and Dunn was part of my job."

"You carry your job too far sometimes. Well, if you have no ideas about this Frenchman, have you any on O'Leary or Dunn? Or the wife?"

"None. That comes under the heading of police business —for which the taxpayers pay good money. You handle it."

"Thanks. I will, if you'll let me."

Without another word he turned away and joined the other two men. I went downstairs with them and went to the phone booth to call Dennis and tell him what I had and that I was going home. When I got him, I gave him all I had on De André and told him the police had taken him for questioning.

"Gross is peeved with me because I didn't let him in on the phonograph business."

"Got the big boy's goat, huh?" I could almost feel the grin over the phone. "Good. It's time those guys gave reporters some credit."

"There are others who could learn about that." I hung up and left the hotel.

18. *Broken Date*

I WAS in my car and headed uptown when I remembered the date I'd broken with Christina Pacelli. The dash clock said five-forty-five and I thought: It's almost too late to bother. But, even as the thought crossed my mind, I turned the wheel of the car and swung into a downtown bound street. When I entered the spumoni parlor, it was filled to overflowing. Rosa was bustling happily about filling orders. She saw me and came forward, smiling widely.

"Well, Rosa, it's an ill wind that doesn't blow some good." I smiled at her.

"Ah, Signorina Slone! It is good of you to come back with Tina to have some spumoni. Or maybe you would rather drink some *vino?*"

"Come back with Tina?" I repeated, blankly, then turned and looked behind me, expecting to see the child standing there.

"But, I came here to see Tina," I said.

Rosa looked puzzled, then a worried expression came into her eyes.

"She is not with you?"

"Why no. I was supposed to meet her here after school but I got tied up and just now managed to get free."

"But Maria Braggiotti, she told me Tina was going to meet you."

"She was. But right here."

"Maybe, the Sisters have kept her in school for punishment for her lateness this morning?" The question was pitifully hopeful.

I looked at my watch. It said six on the dot. I opened my mouth to say that the Sisters wouldn't keep her this late but Rosa was swooping down on a bunch of teen-agers who had just come into the store. She singled out a little brunette beauty, with long shining curls and dark brown eyes.

"You, Maria! You are the one who told me Tina is meeting this lady from the newspaper. Why you do not tell me the truth, that Tina is being kept in school for penance?"

The child ducked back a step.

"But Mrs. Pacelli, Tina left school with us. Really she did. And she did tell us she was going to meet the newspaper lady, didn't she?" The child appealed to her followers who all nodded silent heads.

My throat went suddenly and terribly dry.

"Look, Maria, what time did Tina leave you and did she tell you where she was supposed to meet me?"

"She left us right after school was out but she didn't say where she was going to see you. She acted sort of mysterious but she promised to tell us all about it later. We thought sure she would be here by now."

"But you came earlier, Maria," Rosa accused. "You came to tell me Tina had gone to meet this lady."

Maria turned wide eyes on the upset mother.

"No, Mrs. Pacelli. We came to see if Tina was back. You asked us where she was and I told you what she had said. She told us she would be home by four or four-thirty."

I began to shake inwardly.

"Where was she when you left her?"

"Standing on the school steps."

"But she crossed the street after we left." One of the other girls made the statement. "I looked back when I got to the corner and I saw her crossing the street."

"Which way was she walking?" I couldn't keep the tremble out of my voice.

"Toward the river front."

I began to shake in earnest. The conviction that Tina had

seen something which put the murderer in danger took hold of me and didn't let go. With it came the dread thought that he knew what she had seen and meant to silence her forever. I thrust aside the fear that he had already done so. Rosa's eyes looked in mine, begging for an assurance I couldn't give her.

"Where is your school?" My voice was a croak.

She told me and my heart slid further toward my shoes. The river front in that section was flanked with large, barren warehouses, most of them deserted and tenantless for the years of the depression. Rosa was showing signs of approaching panic and I knew I'd have to try and stop that while I figured what to do next.

I tried to smile brightly and failed miserably.

"Now, Rosa, don't start worrying. Tina probably went to a show."

"Tina went to no show! She is a good *bambino* and always comes home unless she has permission to go someplace."

I saw it was no use to try that tack. Perhaps the best thing to do was let her realize the child was in danger, but not explain just how serious the danger was.

"Well, that's bad. That section she was going toward is not a good neighborhood for a girl that age. Toughs hang out all around it and they might get fresh with a girl alone. I think we had better call the police and report that she is missing. Maybe she was playing around one of those old warehouses and hurt herself. No one would ever hear her calling if she was in an empty one of those devilish places."

Too frightened to speak, Rosa bobbed her head up and down. I went to the phone behind the counter and called the Third Precinct. I told the desk sergeant the story, evading any mention of the possible connection with the strangling case, described Tina and suggested he had better send someone to search the area she had last been seen in.

He wasn't a bit enthusiastic about sending a man out. I

began to insist and finally he agreed to look for her. If he had kept on arguing, I was going to tell him the whole thing, even though Rosa was hanging over my shoulder and listening to every word.

"Okay, we'll send a man out," he said ungraciously. "But these kids who play hookey make me sick."

"She didn't play hookey," I said tartly. "She strayed off after school was out."

"Probably went off with a boy friend. Kids who pull this stuff ought to be sent to the juvenile court for making a lot of trouble for everyone."

"Look, if you don't want to do this I'll call headquarters and tell Tommy Gross. We'll get some action from him." My voice had turned from tart to acid.

"I said I'd send a man, didn't I? Well, he's practically on his way."

I hung up the phone and turned to face an almost distracted Rosa.

"Stop worrying," I told her, almost beside myself with fear. "The cops will find her."

But Rosa was too far gone in worry and a torrent of tears was the answer to my weak comfort. I decided I needed the moral support of someone and picked up the phone to call Dennis, hoping he was still in the office. He wasn't, but I called Sammy's bar and got him on the wire.

"Denny, that Italian kid I told you about is missing from home."

"You mean the girl you were supposed to see this afternoon?"

"Yes. I had to go to see De André instead and I came here as soon as I left the hotel, even though it was past office hours."

"Maybe she went to a show, or to a friend's house."

"I was hoping that was the answer, but her mother said Tina has never stayed out without permission. That kid must have seen something the night of the murder and I'm worried to death about her." I kept my voice at almost a whisper.

"Take it easy, hon." Dennis' voice was gentle. "There's no sense getting all upset until you know she's been hurt. How old is she and how long is she overdue from home?"

I told him.

"Well, stop worrying. Only a sadist or a sex maniac would kill a kid that age."

"I can't stop worrying. Besides, how do we know the killer isn't a sadist or a sex maniac? If I'd only had sense enough to realize she really knew something and let her tell me about it this morning, this wouldn't have happened. A child that age talks too much anyhow. God alone knows what she might have said or hinted at around the neighborhood. If the killer got wind that she knew something, it would be simple for him to trick her into meeting him someplace. All these little friends of her's knew she was to meet me. If anything has happened to that kid, it's all my fault."

"Stop talking like that," Dennis said sharply. "It was natural that you should have thought she was imagining things and you've nothing to blame yourself about. Go on home and get some rest. She'll turn up all right."

"I'm not going anywhere until I know she's all right. If the killer lives in this section, and he most likely does, then he has heard something that made him dangerous to Tina. I'm staying right here until I hear something from the Third Precinct."

"I can tell your mind is made up, so there's no need of me wasting my breath on advice you won't take. It's after hours and you're on your own, so I can't order you off the job. I'll be home if you need me, I was just leaving when you called."

"I'll let you know if anything happens," I promised and hung the receiver back in its hook. Then I squared my shoulders and prepared for an hysterical session with Rosa.

Rosa was weeping noisily and praying in Italian between sobs. I walked over to the table where she was sitting and sat down in a chair beside her.

"Where's Mr. Pacelli?" I asked.

"Papa is working at unloading bananas way uptown. I have sent the friend from next door to get him."

We settled down to a vigil which grew more nerve wracking with every moment that crept by on rusty, laboring wheels. When it seemed to me that hours must have passed since I had talked to Dennis, it was actually only ten minutes. I sat as long as I could, then got up and prowled restlessly around the shop, wandering out into the back room where the supplies were stocked and finally on out into the cobbled yard. Dusk had settled over the city and was creating strange shadows in the enclosed space where I stood. They brought to mind the morning mistake, when I had thought shadows in the moonlight had made Tina imagine things. Sequent to that, I recalled I had meant to look at the bolt of that queer gate. I went over and studied it by the light of a match. Excitement surged through me and I knew, almost certainly, what Tina had seen in the early hours of that grim Ash Wednesday morning. I ran back into the shop and grabbed Rosa by the arm.

"Rosa, where does that back gate lead?"

"The back gate? Oh, it goes into the next—"

The phone shrilled loudly, interrupting her words. I jumped past her and grabbed the receiver off the hook. It was just six-forty-five.

"This is Sergeant McEvilley, over at the Third," a gruff voice announced.

"Yes?" I began to tremble and felt myself grow clammy with the sweat of uncontrollable fear and I prayed, silently and fervently: "Please God, don't let Tina be dead. Don't let her even be hurt bad, God. Please, let her be all right."

There was a second of silence, then the sound of a throat being cleared. Finally, "We—er—we—we found the girl."

Hope drained out of my heart, suctioned out by the tone of his voice. My voice was shaking so I could hardly get out understandable words, but I managed to ask if she was all right.

"Well, she ain't dead." The relief that surged through me was cut off by his next words. "But she's in bad shape and she's been taken to the hospital."

"What happened to her?"

"We don't know all of that yet, she was unconscious when we found her, but she hadn't been hit or mauled and she has no bruises on her."

Rosa was hanging on my arm, begging incoherently to be told what had happened to her *bambino*.

"Wait a minute, Sergeant." I turned to Rosa. "They found her, she was unconscious but she hadn't been hit or anything. They took her to the hospital. Now let me find out all about it and then I'll tell you and take you to the hospital."

She nodded dumbly and I went back to my conversation with McEvilley.

"Where did you find her?"

"In an old warehouse down by Pier Twelve. It's been empty for years. Our man just looked in there on a hunch, the door was partly off the hinges and the opening was big enough for anyone to get through. She was trussed up with rope, gagged and lying in a far corner. It was just luck that he caught her in the beam of his flash. She's been covered with some tarpaulin but had managed to wiggle partly out from under it before she passed out. The doc on the ambulance said she hadn't been criminally attacked."

"Gagged and tied up and thrown in a corner under tarpaulin! My God! What do you call criminally attacked."

"Now you know what I mean, Miss Slone."

"Oh. Oh, of course."

"Her attacker must have been in a hurry and he probably meant to come back after dark and finish her off. Fortunately, we found her first and when we find him, he's going to be sorry he was ever born. I can promise you that." His voice held a grim note that was assurance of his keeping that threat.

"Have you any idea who he is?"

"Not now, although we found tire marks on the dock. Fresh ones. And we found footprints of a man's feet in the dust on the warehouse floor. Men from the laboratory are over three now, taking casts of the prints. But, even if they lead nowhere, we'll know as soon as she comes to what he looks like and, most probably, who he is. I have a feeling it is someone known to the kid. As soon as she regains consciousness, she'll tell what happened."

"Yes, of course." I agreed with him, and neither of us had any idea of how wrong we were.

"Well, I'll take her mother to the hospital right away. She's at State?"

"Yes ma'am. And, look, Miss Slone—I'm sorry about what I said when you called here. It's just that we get so many calls about kids that never mean a thing except work for nothing for us, we just darn near go nuts some days."

"It's all right," I assured him. "You went out and found her and got her out of danger before it was too late. That's all that matters."

"Thanks. Will you bring her parents over here so they can make a formal complaint?"

"I'll be glad to bring them. But first we're going to the hospital." I said good-bye and replaced the receiver just as a wild eyed Vincente burst into the shop.

"Whatsa matta? Whatsa happen?"

I told him. "We're going right to the hospital now," I added.

He stood there, his big hands clenching and unclenching and his face a study in bewilderment.

"But who would hurta my *bambino*? Tina is a gooda child, never she gives anyone trouble. Why should anyone hurta her? Who did this thing to my girl?" His voice rose as anger overcame puzzlement and he shook me by the shoulders.

"I wish I knew." I didn't even protest about the grip he had on my shoulders, although he was pinching me.

He relaxed his hold and turned to his sobbing wife.

"Estop crying, Mama. I finda out who did this and I maka him pay."

"We'll all know soon enough," I said. "Tina will be able to either tell us who he is or give a good enough description for the cops to trace him in a hurry. She may already have talked to the doctors."

I spoke too confidently—for little Tina was not going to tell anyone anything. We found that out shortly after we got to the hospital.

19. *Scared Speechless*

WHEN we got to the hospital door, Morrow was standing in front of it.

"What are you doing here?" I demanded. "You're off hours ago."

"So were you," he said, blandly. "I sat in Nick's and waited for you until after six, then I went to the press room to see if you had called. I couldn't understand what could be important enough to keep you from collecting that bet. While I was there a flash came in from the Third about the Pacelli girl. I saw her talking to you this morning and I figured it connected up with the murder. I also figured you would come here and need my help. So I rushed right over. Johnny on the spot, that's me."

"Well, I don't need your help. I do all right without you." I brushed past him and guided Rosa and Vincente into the hospital. Johnny followed right behind us.

"Your friend, he likes you very much." Rosa smiled for the first time in hours, distracted for a moment by the inborn Latin interest in anything resembling romance.

"Don't be silly," I said shortly, then grinned. "That guy isn't my friend. He'd cut my throat in a minute if he thought it would help him beat me to a story."

"Oh, no, Signorina! You are wrong, and if you do not see how his eyes are when he looks at you, then you are also blind."

"Nonsense." I retorted, but a pleasant glow crept around my heart.

The desk attendant sent for the doctor as soon as she

194

learned the Pacelli's identity. When he appeared, the upset parents rushed to meet him, bombarding him with questions. Morrow and I crowded close behind them.

"She's had a very bad shock," the medic explained. "She's conscious but I'm afraid you can't see her just yet."

Rosa and Vincente protested excitedly, then appealed to me to make him let them see their girl. I didn't think I could do much about that, but I did explain about my broken date with Tina and said that we were anxious to know the full details of what had happened before we went to the police for the parents to file a formal complaint.

"Sergeant McEvilley told me very little beyond the bare facts of where and how she had been found," I said. "You say she is now conscious. If so, has she told you who did this to her?"

"She hasn't told us anything." His voice was tight and grim. "She can't tell us anything. The child has been shocked speechless."

"What?" I gaped at him, thinking this was a poor time for wise cracks.

"I mean it. Literally and medically. Shock will sometime do that, you know. She hasn't been able to utter a word since she came out of the semi-coma she was in when we we brought her here."

"Maybe seeing her parents might help, then," I suggested.

He was about to say no, then appeared to debate the question.

"Perhaps it would, at that," he said finally. "But they had better go in one at a time and they can only stay a minute or two. Unless, of course, she does regain her speech when she sees them."

Rosa went into the ward he led us to. In a couple of minutes a nurse led her out. She was sobbing bitterly.

"Papa! She looks at me like she doesn't know who I am! She just lies there like one dead with the eyes still open."

Vincente patted her shoulder with his big, dirty paw.

"Maybe she will talk to her papa. I go now and see what I can do." But when he came out of the ward, the confused, angry look in his eyes said plainly he had not succeeded in rousing the child either.

"I tell her to tell me who has hurt her and I fix him good. But she says nothing, just looks like she is not seeing me. Whatsa matta with her, Doc?"

"I told you that her voice is gone, lost from shock," the medic said, wearily. "The child has had a terrific fright and has gone into a state of shock. We're doing all we can, but often it is days before a case like this will recover the power of speech. Mainly, she must have rest and quiet. She's young, perhaps she will be all right in a day or two."

I looked at him sharply, then drew him aside.

"You can tell me the truth," I said in a low voice. "How long is it likely to be before she comes out of this shock?"

"I wish to God I knew." His voice was fervent. "She may never speak again. She may talk tomorrow. Often, loss of voice from shock is a subconscious means of escape from having to talk about what has happened. You see, the experience is so terrible the patient does not want to remember it and the brain sends that message to the vocal chords which react by closing off speech. I could give you a long palaver in medical terms but I think you'd rather have it in words you can understand. The surest cure, as a rule, is to remove the cause of the fear that controls the patient after shock has set in and make sure the patient understands there is no longer anything or anyone to fear."

"In short, if they can find the man who did this to her and get it through to her that she is safe and he can't harm her again, then she'd get her voice back?"

"That's about the size of it. As it is—" He spread his hands out in a gesture of helplessness.

"Could I see her for just a second?"

He looked doubtful. "You're not a relative and—"

"I won't upset her, Doctor. I promise. I just have a feeling that if she sees me she may remember she had wanted to tell me something this morning. Something important."

He agreed, somewhat reluctantly and I went into the ward.

It was a twelve-bed room and Tina was in the bed fourth from the right end of the ward. As I entered they were putting up a screen around her bed and a nurse was directing the orderly who was handling the curtained frame. The other patients were buzzing like a hive of bees and none of them looked very sick to me.

"It's a bit noisy in here for a shock patient, isn't it?" I asked the nurse and I didn't try to keep the critical note out of the question.

"This is really a convalescent ward," she explained. "We had to put her in here temporarily. The flu epidemic filled us up and this was the only immediately available bed."

"Put her in a private room," I instructed, promptly. "I'll guarantee the charges. My paper will pay them."

Those instructions won the nurse to my side at once. She beamed on me.

"That's splendid. In cases like this, one never knows what sort of reaction may set in and she should have complete quiet."

I nodded and slipped behind the curtained screen. The slim, pitifully inert figure hardly made a bump in the bed covers. I looked at the wan, little face and anger rose in me and made a hard knot in the pit of my stomach. McEvilley had said she wasn't bruised, but he was wrong. Her jaws and mouth had ugly purple marks where a cruelly tight gag had been tied. I gritted my teeth and forced a smile.

"Hi, Tina, remember me?" I asked softly.

She looked at me out of blank, unwavering brown eyes. I thought of how bright and lively those eyes had been in the morning and the knot in my stomach got still harder.

I took the small hand that lay limply on the bedspread

and patted it. "Look, Tina honey, remember you were going to tell me something this morning? You had a date with me this afternoon and you broke it. You were supposed to tell me what you saw in your yard on Carnival night. How about telling me now?"

She made a slight, almost imperceptible cringing motion. Not a sound came from her throat but she began to cry, the tears flowing swiftly down over her cheeks onto the pillow. The nurse motioned me to leave. I patted the now twitching fingers and left the ward, filled with cold rage and self-condemnation. If I had only listened to the child—

In the hall I found the emotional Italian parents beleaguering the weary resident. They saw me and three pairs of eyes asked the same question. I answered it with a defeated shake of my head. Then I remembered the tears.

"She did cry," I said. "And although her eyes were pretty blank, I have a feeling she knew me."

"Well, at least that was some reaction," the doctor said. Then he took me aside and in a tired voice he told me the time he had been having with the Pacellis.

"You'll have to help me out with them. They ask questions and before I can answer them they call on the Virgin and all the Saints to punish the man who hurt their child. Then they ask more questions and the mother weeps while the father swears vendettas in Italian and English." He smiled ruefully. "I wish I could speak Italian, maybe I could make some sense with them. I tried to explain why she can't talk but I made no headway and they've nearly set me nuts. They know you and they seem to trust you completely. You tell them what I told you about the case and try to get them to go home. They can't do her any good hanging around here."

I agreed to try and told him about ordering a private room. He said that was fine but in that case she really should have special nurses. It might be bad if she woke up at night and found herself alone.

"Get nurses then." I spent some more of the publisher's money. "Get her anything and anyone she needs—including specialists. My paper will pay all expenses." Old Man Phipps' money just ran through my fingers. I hoped he didn't run me off the paper for it.

"I'll have her moved at once," he said and started to carry out the words.

I went over to the couple and after several mintues of talk I managed to convince them they could do Tina no good by staying in the hospital. I said nothing about the private room, afraid it would give Rosa the idea that in such a room she should be able to stay with her child. I finally got them out of the hospital by adding the convincing argument that they had to go file the charges against Tina's assailant.

Morrow had disappeared while I was talking with the doctor, but he turned up leaning against my car.

"I'll ride with you," he said, as we stopped by the coupé.

"I don't know where you'll sit," I snapped. "The rumble of this cabriolet coupé hasn't been opened in years—there's no seat in it."

"I'll sit on the floor of it. I'm not leaving you alone until you get home. You're all upset and you need someone along with you to help keep your courage from dying out entirely."

I gave him a sharp look, but I couldn't drown a feeling of warmth over his odd solicitude even while I wondered what it was all about. He'd been acting strangely all day.

"Suit yourself." I climbed behind the wheel and Rosa and Vincente wedged their oversize frames in beside me. We drove straight to the Third Precinct station and went in to file charges and see if the police had found anything worth following.

McEvilley helped the parents make out the complaint and told us they had nothing definite yet but the big-

gest part of the police force was working on the case. I
told him about the connection with the strangling case
while Rosa and Vincente were over talking in voluble
Italian with a cop whose parents came from the same part
of Sicily as did the Pacellis. I wasn't telling him anything he
didn't already know and he soon apprised me of that.

"I figured that out as soon as I found out who the kid
was," he said. "You had oughta told me that side of it when
you first called and I wouldn't have given you an argument
about looking for her. The fellows from Homicide have
been here for an hour, they just left."

"Who was it?"

"The captain himself and his lieutenant."

"Gross and Beton, eh? What did they say?"

He grinned. "Les Beton was cussing about you having
been in a deep conversation with that kid this morning and
how you both shut up as soon as he walked over to you. He
told Captain Gross that he was going to wring your neck
some day if you didn't stop shoving your snoot in the cop's
business."

"Oh, did he now? Well, that's just too damn bad about
that big lug. I wish he'd try something with me."

"Les seemed to think the kid had told you something and
you should have gone to him with the information. Did
she?"

"No, unfortunately. She refused to say anything to the
police. She has an active dislike for the law because her
brother and papa have both been in jail for selling booze.
I tried to explain that these police were a different breed
of cop, but she wouldn't listen. Finally, I made a date to
meet her after school but I got tied up and didn't get down
there until late. When I did, she hadn't turned up. You
know the rest of the story."

He nodded. "It makes my blood run cold when I think
how easy we could have missed finding her and left her in
that place for that bastard to come back and finish the job.

He's a killer and he'll kill again and again if he has to do it to save his own hide."

I nodded and he asked how the girl was. I told him and his face fell into lines of disappointment.

"Captain Gross told me the doctor had said she couldn't talk. I just thought she was still passed out."

"Mac, could I see the gag and the ropes she was tied with?"

"You could—if I had them. The captain took them off with him to the laboratory."

Rosa and Vincente, accompanied by Morrow and the officer they had been talking with, came up to us.

"This policeman is the one who found Tina," Vincente said. "He told us he thinks she is hurt by the same man who killed the lady in our yard."

"That's right, Vincente. But the police will catch him."

"Better they do it before I find him. I will tear him apart with my hands—so!" He made a twisting, rending gesture with his brawny hands and I shuddered. Not that I blamed him, I'd have been right there helping him if he found the guy when I was around.

"Come on, let's get out of here." Morrow sounded impatient. "I don't know if you realize it, but it's eight-thirty and I'm starved."

"What? Oh, Lord! I forgot to call home and tell them I'd not be there for dinner." I hustled the couple out of the station and piled into my car again. The ice cream shop was crowded and the people came rushing out as soon as we drew to a stop at the curb. I said I'd better get right on home, but Rosa insisted I come in for a minute. When I refused, she said something to Vincente in Italian and then asked me to wait for a moment.

"I'll come down in the morning and take you to the hospital," I promised her. "Now try not to worry too much. Tina will be all right." I said a silent prayer that I was right.

"You're so kind, Signorina." Her eyes filled again. "Never will I forget your kindness and the good God, I will pray to him to reward you with a fine husband and a lot of *bambinis*." She looked directly at Johnny, who had climbed out of the seatless rumble and was standing by the car door.

"Why—why, er, that's very kind of you, Rosa," I stammered, angry with myself for stammering and for the flush I could feel creeping up to my hairline. "But you had better pray he rewards me with a raise in salary. I could use it."

"But if you have the husband, you no need the job," she said, naïvely.

Johnny grinned from ear to ear and I glared at him. Vincente came up just then and saved me further embarrassment. He had a bag in his hand and the shape of it told me just what was in it.

"Here is something for to cheer you with the spaghetti," he said, smiling. "Spaghetti without this is without cheer and is only dough and tomato sauce." He patted my hand, which was resting on the door of the car. "I am not mucha good with the words, *cara Signorina*, but my heart is full with thanks for your goodness. If my little Tina, she is going to be all right, it is because you have made the police go find her before it was too late."

I gulped but the lump in my throat didn't go down. I motioned to Morrow to get in the car and drove off without speaking. I couldn't have spoken and I knew the Pacellis understood why. As it was I only managed to get around the corner before tears blinded me and I had to pull to the curb and stop.

"What's wrong? Why did you stop?" Johnny asked.

I tried to smother a sob but it wouldn't smother. Another followed it and Johnny put his arms around me, drawing me against his shoulder. That was all I needed to release the deluge. I sat there and bawled like a calf while he patted my shoulder and said all the inane things a man says when a woman weeps all over his shirt.

I blubbered and cussed myself and blubbered some more. Finally, I pulled away, accepted his handkerchief and used it to fullest advantage.

"I'm all right, now. It was just that having seen Tina like she is, when I know so well I could have prevented it, got me down."

"I understand, baby. Here, let me drive. You look beat."

"How will you get home if you drive me? You live way back of town and I'm uptown."

"Taxis are still running." He got out of the car and went around to the other side. I moved over and we headed uptown. We were about midway to my house before he spoke again and by then I'd fully recovered my composure.

"How about a drink and some food?" he asked. "You need both and so do I. We can go to Eddie Teller's joint. He has good steaks and he's right close by."

"It sounds good to me."

He turned at the next corner and drove to Teller's. We went in and took a booth and ordered drinks. Then I remembered, again, that I had not called home.

"I better get to the phone, Johnny. My mother is going to be angrier than ever with me for this. Order me another drink and a steak, rare."

I located the phone booth and called home. Bertha answered.

"Bertha, tell Mother I was delayed on an important development in that murder case—she'll know which one—and I've had no chance to call her until now."

"You tell huh foh yo'se'f. Ah don't know nuttin bout any 'velopments."

Mother's "Hello?" had a resigned quality which I knew only too well. I told her what had happened.

"It's quite all right, Margaret. We are so accustomed to your not coming home and not calling, we just go right ahead and eat."

I knew there was no use saying anymore except that I'd

be home as soon as I had some food. When I returned to the booth, Johnny cocked an eyebrow at me.

"What's the matter? You look like Mama was scolding you."

"She was and I'm in the usual doghouse. I've been in it ever since I went to work in the city room, so I'm pretty used to it now."

"Well, the city room is no place for a girl. I wish you were out of it and I wish Dennis would stop putting you on murder stories."

20. *Romance and Restored Peace*

I LOOKED at him in open-mouthed amazement.

"Are you nuts, Johnny Morrow? I'm as good a reporter as you are."

"I'm not denying that. You're one of the best reporters I've ever known. But police coverage is tough on anyone. On you it's even more so, if you know what I mean."

"I most certainly don't know—and I wish you'd explain."

"Well, trouble with you is you've got better than the average sized bump of curiosity and a damn sight more nerve and courage than any female has a right to have. The minute I know you're on a murder detail, I start worrying."

"Just when did this over-active concern of yours begin to develop, may I ask?"

"The first time you ever covered a murder and managed to get into a pot of danger. I've tried, in my dumb way, to sort of stick around you ever since that time and when you give me the slip, as you usually manage to do, it nearly drives me nuts."

I didn't answer. I couldn't. This, coming on top of what he had said earlier in the day, was too much for me to cope with. I hardly noticed the waiter when he put the steaks in front of us. Then Johnny grinned.

"Put some of that steak in your mouth and stop gaping at me. I know you must be hungry but you don't have to sit there open-mouthed like a young bird waiting to be fed. You can use a knife and fork."

The casual tone and joking words restored in some measure my calm, but didn't abate my surprise over the way things were developing. I popped some of the steak in my mouth and began to try and figure things out. I wasn't sure I liked this new setup but I wasn't sure I disliked it either. It produced a warm and unfamiliar glow to have someone talk like that to me and the memory of various times when Johnny had tried to protect me when I was on murder coverage came to my mind. I'd had the idea he was just trying to keep me from getting a beat on him. Now I began to wonder. While I ate, I stole covert glances at him. He looked just the same as ever—or did he? He *was* good looking, almost handsome in fact. He was good company too, I'd had loads of fun with him. I studied his well-shaped sensitive mouth and wondered what it would be like to kiss Johnny—? Then I pulled my thoughts back with a snap. The situation was getting out of hand. I needed time to think this over and I'd not do that with him along. I decided to go home—alone.

"Look, Johnny, there's no sense in your going the rest of the way home with me. Why don't you call your cab from here?"

He lit two cigarettes, handed me one, and surveyed me lazily through half-closed eyelids.

"What's the matter? Are you afraid I might try to kiss you?"

Because it was right in the channel I had been letting my thoughts ride, I blushed to the root of my hair.

"Don't be silly. Besides, as you have said so many times, what's a kiss between friends? I just think it's foolish for you to drive me home when I can go alone."

"I'll ride along anyhow." There was a note of finality in his voice.

I stopped arguing and we began to talk about the strangling and the attack on Tina. We began working on the theory that someone who lived in the Quarter was our killer and that brought us to De André. Johnny had been at headquarters when Gross and Beton brought the French dancer in for questioning. He had gone over after waiting for me at Nick's and had seen the man come in with the two detectives. He didn't know what had happened at the questioning, because the flash on Tina had come in and he had figured I'd be at the hospital.

"He could have done it," I said. "He lived close enough to the spot and he admitted to owning garrotes. She may have decided to go back to Don and he followed her from the hotel."

"But she was headed the wrong way to go back to the Baronne Street house. Toulouse is downtown from the Monterey."

"That's right it is. Well, maybe he followed her out and asked her to go for coffee or something and talk it over. They walked down that way, just looking around, and suddenly he decided to kill her."

"Possible, but he had decided on killing her before he left the hotel or he wouldn't have had a garrote with him."

"That's true. Well, I'm not worrying my head with it anymore tonight. Gross and Beton will round him up again— wait! He couldn't have attacked Tina! I was with him when —no, I wasn't either. I got to his room about ten of five. But how would he know so much about the Quarter? And about Tina and that warehouse?"

"He read the paper. He knew where the Pacelli place was. He knew for *sure* if he is the killer. Maybe he went back to listen and see if anyone had seen anything. He may have heard something that put him on Tina's trail."

We were fitting the noose nicely around De André's neck when I happened to notice the time. It was almost eleven.

"Holy cow, Johnny! Let's get out of here." I rose to my feet and gathered up my things. Johnny paid the bill and we went out and got in my car. Johnny took over the wheel again and drove to my house, stopping in front of the driveway.

"End of the line," I said, sleepily. "I'll go inside and call a cab to pick you up in front of the house."

"Just a minute." He pulled me over to him and his mouth came down on mine.

My heart did a crazy dance to the tune of silver bells and I stopped wondering what it would be like to kiss Johnny. I knew—and it was pretty wonderful. I was drowning in a sea of thrills and I had no wish to be rescued. The self-sufficient Margaret Slone wrapped her arms around a rival reporter and clung like mad. I wondered what had been wrong with me all these years that I had never discovered the thrill of Johnny's lips on mine.

"I've wanted to do that for a long time," he said at last. "I've always had a suspicion you were my girl and now I know it."

"Ummmm," I said, and went back for more of the music of the bells.

After a long moment we drew apart and sat admiring each other in the light from the waning moon.

"You're wonderful," I told him boldly. "I heard bells ringing and they all sang your name."

"Darling!" He pulled me close to him again. "Margaret, love, I want you to get Dennis to take you off of this case. I don't want you running into—"

I sat up and pulled myself out of his arms. The silver chimes had become fire alarms.

"Oh, no you don't! I'm seeing this case through."

"I told you I don't want you working murder details anymore. I can't work with a clear head and be worried about you all the time."

"Then you can just stop worrying about me. I'm staying on this story."

"Not if you're going to be my girl, you're not."

"And who said I was going to be your girl?"

"Why you did—you wouldn't have let me kiss you like that and you wouldn't have kissed me unless—"

"I had a weak moment," I said, flippantly. "Now I've got my strength back. It won't happen again."

"Oh, yes it will!" He grabbed for me, but I'd anticipated that move and was out of the car before he got a good hold on me.

"You go on home, Johnny Morrow," I called, making tracks for the back door. "I'll call a cab for you." I beat it into the house, figuring I'd put my car away after Johnny had left.

Although it was late, the family was still up. I went to the alcove in the hall where the downstairs phone was kept and called a Yellow to come get Morrow. Then I joined the group in the living room.

"I didn't hear you drive in tonight, Margaret," Mother said.

"I didn't drive in. Johnny Morrow came home with me and he is sitting in my car waiting for the cab I called to come pick him up. I'll put the car away after he has gone."

Mother gave me a shrewd look. "Why didn't you ask him in?"

"It's too late for company. I'm going to bed right away."

"Another hard day, Maggie?" Vangie sounded sympathetic.

"Sort of—and don't call me Maggie."

"You call her Vangie, don't you?" Mother asked.

"Vangie's a right pretty nickname. Maggie isn't. Sounds like a washwoman."

"It does not," Mother said, somewhat indignantly. "I don't care too much for nicknames, but my mother was called Maggie and she never minded it."

"Oh, well. It's a good old Irish nickname," I grinned at her.

"You were named for your grandmother. You're a lot like her, too."

"Thank you, darling. She was a great old lady."

Mother nodded and Vangie broke in to ask what I'd done

during the day. I told them the story of the attack on Tina and filled in on details of the day's work.

"I blame myself for that child's horrible experience," I said. "If I'd only listened to her when she wanted to talk this morning I'm sure we'd have had the murderer safely in jail by now."

My family entered a concerted protest over my self-blame and Brett topped it off by offering high praise over the way I'd found the real wife and tracked down the phonograph clue.

"Not every detective would have been smart enough to figure that one out," he said. "You did a damn fine piece of work there, didn't she, Mother?"

"Why, yes. I think it was very smart of her. I'm sure I would never have noticed that the phonograph had run down and then followed the clue to prove that poor young man was innocent."

I sat back and glowed. It was a rare treat for Mother to do anything but scold about my job. I'd had two novel experiences that night. Resolutely, I thrust the thought of the first one out of my mind. That had to stop. No man was going to tell me what to do and what sort of stories I should cover. Next thing I knew he would be suggesting the safest place for me was on the society desk—God forbid!

I heard a car door slam, then the sound of another doing the same thing.

"I guess Johnny's gone," I said. "I'll go get my car and put it away now."

"I'll go do it," Brett offered and suited action to the offer. I heard him drive in and run the car in the garage. In a few minutes he came back into the room, a wide grin on his face.

"What are you grinning about?" I asked, suspiciously.

"This note was propped up on the wheel." His smile widened. "I couldn't help reading it. Besides, I didn't realize it was so personal until I'd about finished it."

I snatched the piece of copy paper out of his hand and read the printed words.

"I shall kiss you at exactly noon tomorrow in the back booth at Nick's. I shall keep on kissing you until you admit you're my girl and stop this damned police coverage. I don't want my children to all grow up to be police reporters. Johnny."

I looked around at the circle of questioning eyes.

"Johnny Morrow is nuts," I said slowly and distinctly. "And I shall make it my business to be anywhere but at Nick's at noon tomorrow."

Brett whooped. "I wouldn't want to bet on that!"

"You shut up," I said tartly. "And just forget what you read on this paper." I started to tear the sheet, then thought better of it and folded it carefully, putting it in my pocket.

Brett roared loudly.

"Now just what are you two carrying on about?" Mother asked.

I gave him a warning look but he answered.

"You and Johnny Morrow should get together, Mother. He wants her to quit covering police stories too."

Mother sighed. "Ah, well. I've learned you can't run your children's lives after they are old enough to run them for themselves. You enjoy the hazards of flying and Margaret life in the city room. Of course, if she gets married—?" She smiled a question.

"Don't worry about that, darling. I'll probably be an old maid chasing city desk assignments when all your children but me are married and grown stodgy."

She laughed. "I find that hard to believe, Margaret. When you find the right man, you'll marry and your reporting experiences will become stories to tell your children."

"Well, they won't be named Morrow whether they grow up to be police reporters or not." I got up and picked up my purse and gloves. "I'm for bed." I yawned widely. "I'll see you all in the morning."

I kissed Mother and waved good-night to the others. Peace was restored in my homelife again and I knew I'd sleep better for that fact. I started for bed, Vangie trailing behind me.

While I got ready for bed, my youngest sister sat on the foot of my mattress and talked to me. Suddenly she asked, "Sis, do you like Johnny?"

"*Like* him! I'm nuts about him, but he isn't going to run my life."

She grinned at me. "You've been in love with him for a long time, haven't you?"

I gaped at her. "No indeed! I never even thought of Johnny that way until tonight when—" My voice trailed off and I was remembering the sound of the silver chimes ringing their tune in my heart.

"Oh, get out of here and let me get to sleep," I commanded. "You're too full of romantic nonsense and I have to get to work early tomorrow."

She rose and stretched lazily. "Just the same, whether you realize it or not, you and Johnny have been crazy about each other for years."

"Scat!" I lunged at her and she darted out of the room. I climbed in bed and reached for the light switch on the bed lamp. The sight of the extension phone, which I'd had installed in my room, reminded me that I had not called Dennis and told him about Tina's being found. It was too late to bother now, he'd be asleep most likely and the story couldn't come out until morning anyhow. I'd get in early and have the story ready for him in a jiffy. On that pleasant thought came the one about the care I'd ordered for Tina. I called the hospital and checked to see if she had been put in a private room with constant nursing attendance. I was assured that everything had been done as ordered and that Tina was "resting quietly."

"That's what you always say," I told the hospital nurse and hung up. Five seconds later I was sound asleep.

21. *Look for a Frenchman*

I WAS in the middle of a fantastic dream of Morrow kneeling before me in a crowded press room pleading for just one kiss, when the shrill sound of the phone shattered my dream. I fumbled with one hand for the receiver and with the other for the light switch. I found both at the same time and saw my clock said four-forty-five. My dream of Johnny was still so vivid in my mind I just naturally assumed it was he calling.

"What's the idea of waking me up?" I demanded crossly. "And just get it out of your head that you'll kiss me at noon——"

"What the hell are you talking about?" A bewildered voice asked. "Who said anything about kissing you at noon? Hey, is this Margaret——?"

"It is." I recognized Tommy Gross' voice and was wide awake on the instant. "Never mind what I said. I thought you were someone else. What's up?"

"Your friend De André's body just came ashore near the Napoleon avenue ferry docks," he stated calmly.

"WHAT?"

"That's right. He had been killed and dropped in the river."

"My God! When?"

"Tonight sometime. I mean last night. About eight or nine. The body hadn't been in the water very long. When it went into the river, it fell afoul of an old fruit crate and the crate kept it afloat. It was a funny piece of luck for that crate to be so handy."

213

"Very funny," I said, caustically.

Gross ignored the sarcasm. "We don't know just where he was pitched in the water, but we have river experts working on it. They'll figure the tides, current, drift and so on. I thought you'd want to know. It ties up with the other murder and that attack."

"It certainly does. When did they find the body?"

"About an hour ago. Some night crew workers from the docks were taking a sneak fishing trip. They saw an object in the water and dragged it to the side of the boat. When they saw it was a body, those blacks yelled blue murder." He chuckled and I smothered a giggle.

"I can imagine they did. How was he killed?"

"Knifed—in the back."

"Find the weapon?"

"Yeah. It was just an ordinary knife, but plenty edged. A steel bladed thing that was as sharp as a razor."

"Any fingerprints?"

"Nope. The killer must have worn gloves."

"Or else the river washed the prints away. Where are you now?"

"At the morgue. We just got him here a few minutes ago. As soon as I get the full report I'm going to work with the river men."

"Wait for me. I'll be down as soon as I can get dressed. Have you seen Morrow?"

"Why no. Should I? Isn't he home in bed?"

"I wouldn't know," I said drily.

"Do you want me to call him?"

"Hell, no. I'll see you in a few minutes."

"All right. If I'm not in the cold room, I'll be in my office."

He hung up and I immediately dialed Dennis. He came on the wire sleepy and grumpy but as soon as I told him what had happened he snapped awake.

"Murdered, huh? Who killed him?"

"That's what the cops would like to know. He floated

ashore riding on an old fruit crate. Some Negroes were fishing and they saw the body coming in close to the Napoleon Avenue ferry slip."

"How'd you find out?"

"Tommy Gross called me. He ties it in with that strangling and the attack on that Italian child."

"What attack?"

"Oh, good gravy! I forgot you didn't know about that." I gave him a quick resumé of the crime on Tina, glossed rapidly over my having ordered the private room and nurses, and ended by saying I hadn't wanted to wake him up when I got home and figured the morning would be time enough to tell him about Tina.

"You could have called me when you got to the hospital," he groused. "I told you to let me know if anything happened."

"You told me to go home and get some rest," I snapped. "When I refused, you told me I was on my own."

"Okay, skip it. I only hope the main office doesn't howl when the bill comes in from the hospital. You just said you were doing things on your own."

"You wouldn't be that mean. I know you well enough to know you'll okay that bill."

"Ummm. How was De André killed? With a garrote?"

"No. He was stabbed in the back."

"Stabbed, huh? Another Latin method of killing."

"Dennis! I think you've hit it. First a garrote, now a knife. The tieup here is definitely Latin. The cops had better start looking for a Frenchman—"

I stopped suddenly and knew I had the answer. I needed to find out just one thing, one I had tried to find out about a couple of times before. If the answer was what I figured it had to be, then I was sure I knew the killer.

"Well, let 'em look. It's too early for us to worry about it. We'll get the dope later. I'm going to get some more sleep. You do the same. I'll see you in the morning."

"It is morning." I hung up and added to the silent phone.

"Sleep hell. That's what you think, Denny McCarthy. I've got a murder to help solve."

In half-an-hour I was on my way to headquarters. I drove down a silent avenue, still sleeping as dawn began to touch up the puffy clouds with fingers dipped in the rouge pot of the sun. Only a few cars were on the street and only a few were parked in the lot by the courts' building when I pulled to a stop behind Gross' car.

I went straight to the morgue where the night officer on duty told me Gross had gone to his office.

"Don't you want to see the stiff they brought in?" He asked.

"Not before breakfast, thank you." I left and made my way to Tommy's office in the other part of the building.

The room was crowded with cops and men whom I judged to be the river experts. They were charting the course the body must have taken after it was dumped in the water. Minutes slipped by and Tommy showed no signs of getting free. He'd given me a brief nod when I walked in but indicated he was too busy to talk to me then. I grew restless. After a few more minutes, I decided I'd go do some phoning, then come back. Maybe I'd have something more than just suspicions to go on by then. I left the room and went down the hall to the press room. I wasn't at all surprised to find Morrow asleep on the couch.

As quietly as possible, I tiptoed past his recumbent form and called the Pacellis on my outside line. Rosa answered. I told her who I was and then spoke rapidly and as softly as I could.

"Rosa, I have a very important question to ask you but you must promise me not to say a word about this to anyone, not even Vincente."

"I promise, Signorina. For you I would promise anything. You are so full of the goodness for us."

"That's okay. Now, where does that gate in that dividing

fence of your yard lead? Whose yard is on the other side?"

"You ask me that before." Her voice went tense. "Is this the man who hurt my *bambino?*"

"Now take it easy, Rosa. I'm not saying that at all. I don't know yet what man you mean."

She told me. It was the answer I'd expected and I couldn't help being sorry I was right. I'd been hoping I had just had a wrong hunch.

"Okay, Rosa. That's all I wanted to know," I said, dully. "The cops can have it from here. I don't want any part of it."

"Signorina!" Her voice rose to high C. "You do think he is the one! Wait, I go to get Vincente."

"Rosa!" I shouted her name, forgetting the sleeper. "Don't do it! You promised me you wouldn't. You let the police handle this, do you hear? If you tell Vincente, he may get killed himself. This man is desperate."

I could sense her reluctance but finally she promised to keep quiet until the police got there. I hung up and put my head in my hands.

"What are you hollering about?"

I looked up to see a sleepy, disheveled Morrow.

"Nothing," I said, shortly.

"Oh, yes there is something. You said the man was desperate. What man?"

"If you'd stay awake you might learn things as soon as they happen." I got up and flounced out of the room.

I went back to Tommy's office on the double. He was still busy but this time I didn't pay any attention to his warning nod. I barged right up to him.

"I have to see you for a minute. It's damned important."

"I can't leave now. Tell it to Les." He bent back over the map of the river one of the experts was working with.

"I don't want to tell it to Les." I protested. "I think I know who the killer is and I want to tell you."

"Look, Margaret, stop playing detective. If you have

something you think is important, tell Les. He's my lieutenant."

I went out of the room but Beton followed me. In the outer office he laid a hand on my arm.

"You better tell me, Margaret. You know how the captain is when he gets busy like this. I'll give him the message."

Against my better judgement, I told him what I'd learned and what I thought about the killings and who had committed them. His reaction was all that could be expected.

"You're nuts!" he exploded.

I glared. "You're the one who's nuts. I might have known you wouldn't have sense enough to see how it all ties in together."

"I got sense enough to see you are on the wrong track."

I set my jaw stubbornly and answered angrily.

"I am not. For God's sake, can't you understand how perfectly logical it is? It has to be that way."

"Boloney. Trouble with you is you had a couple of lucky breaks in covering murders and it's gone to your head. Like the chief said, you better stop playing detective. This idea you got now is just plain screwy. Go on home."

"Don't you give me orders!" I snapped. "You march right in and tell your boss what I said. If I'm wrong, no one is any worse off than before. If I'm right—and I'm pretty sure I am—it may give that kid back her voice and her future sanity. Now go tell Tommy. I'll be in the press room. He can call me there."

Beton gave me a look that wasn't pleasant and went back into Tommy's office. I raced back to the press room, sure that Tommy would see the logic in my solution. The phone was ringing on my inside line when I hit the door. I grabbed it just as Morrow reached for it. It was Tommy.

"Go home, Margaret," I heard him say, to my utter amazement. "I've told you to stop playing detective on this case. I've enough trouble without having to worry about you. Now beat it."

I began to wonder if I was losing my sanity or whether I had suddenly developed an unsuspected sex appeal. First Morrow, now Gross, had suddenly grown worried about my working on murder stories.

"You don't have to worry about me. I can take care of myself. But, Tommy, for God's sake, you must listen to me. As long as that man is free Tina may still be in danger of her life. He can't know she has lost her voice. What's to prevent him from going to the hospital, posing as a friend of the family, and finishing off that kid?"

"I'll put a guard on her, but I'm not barging down to arrest a man just because you have had a brainstorm. I need more evidence than your suspicions to arrest a man for murder. Now go home and mind your own damned business."

The phone clicked decisively in my ear and I sat there, a study in defeat.

"Who poured vinegar in your milk?" Morrow asked.

"Tommy Gross," I said, bitterly. "Damn dumb coppers, they can't see what's right in front of their noses."

He whistled. "You *must* be riled to talk about your pal Gross like that. I thought he was a little tin god to—"

"Oh, shut up." I cut him off, crossly. "You make me sick too. What's the idea of getting drunk and sleeping in your clothes in the press room? You've got a home. Why not go there instead of passing out in here?"

"I wasn't drunk. I didn't have one drink after I left you. I just came down here and laid down to think about things. I fell asleep because I was tired. I was dreaming about you when you woke me up yelling at Rosa. What were you telling her?"

"Nothing." I gave him a keen look. If he knew I had been talking to Rosa, he must have heard more than just the last few words of my conversation with her.

"Oh, no? Of course you wouldn't have been talking about anything at all. Just about some man being desperate and Vincente should stay away from him or he might get killed.

Then you go kiting off and come rushing back and then Gross phones and you get mad as hell with him. But of course it's all about nothing."

"Well, it's nothing that concerns you and Tommy isn't at all interested. Maybe Rosa is right. Maybe I should get myself a good husband."

"Will I do?"

"I said a *good* husband."

He yawned and lay back down on the couch and I resumed my brooding. Tommy had said he wouldn't go on just my suspicions but maybe if I could get him some proofs he *would* act on them. I thought fast and finally decided on two moves. I began to collect my things, got up and started for the door. A suddenly alert Morrow blocked my exit.

"Where do you think you're going at this hour of the morning?"

"None of your damn business," I retorted, sharply. "Get out of my way. Just who do you think you are?"

He hesitated, then shrugged and stepped aside. I swished past him and slammed down the hall to the nearest office that looked as if it might be empty. I leafed through the telephone directory and found Sergeant McEvilley's home phone number, called it and as soon as he came on I asked him if he would tell me what had been used as a gag on Tina. His answer confirmed my suspicions. I needed only one more thing to clinch it as far as I was concerned, then I'd go back and see if I couldn't convince Tommy.

I called the morgue but the phone didn't answer. Then I tried the coroner's office. I got an answer there and found that Dr. Rollins was on his way home. I stewed impatiently for about ten minutes, then rang his home phone. He answered and told me he had just walked in the door as the phone began to ring. I asked him if De André had been stabbed with a long, thin bladed steak knife, got the right answer and hung up. Now I knew I was right and somehow I had to make Tommy see it. I beat it down the hall to Gross' office. It was open, but deserted and so were the offices adjoining it.

For a moment I stood looking in the doorway and gazing around the empty room which was just beginning to be filled with the light of the newly risen sun. I was filled with a sense of frustration and thoroughly dejected about the whole thing. I knew I was on the trail of a murderer but I couldn't go follow it alone. Or could I? I had a gun in my car and I knew I could use it. Ironically, it was a weapon Tommy had given me as a souvenir of the McGowan murder case. He'd even attended to getting me a permit to have the thing. It only took a minute for me to decide whether I was going to follow through. Two minutes later I was in my car and headed downtown. When I parked in front of my destination, my dash clock said six-thirty. I got the gun out of the glove compartment, made sure it was ready for action, put it into my bag and, heart pounding like a trip hammer, climbed out of the car.

I said a silent prayer for help and protection and rang the night bell of Le Coq d'Or. Then I waited in front of the quiet café, looking at the drawn shade of the door and the curtained windows. There was a sound of footsteps approaching the door and I fought down a rising desire to turn tail and run down the street. I told myself sternly that I was going to confront a murderer and, cops or no cops, I would stop his bloody activities.

Gaston opened the door. His eyes were red-rimmed and he looked as if he hadn't been to sleep for a week. I thought: So murder kept you awake, did it?

He looked at me in surprise. "M'selle Slone! What brings you here so early? You know we do not open for business until ten. The chefs are not here yet. But come in, I 'ave made *café* and we shall drink a cup, eh?"

"I don't want coffee, Gaston. I just want to talk with you."

His eyes were suddenly veiled, but he ushered me into the dining room. The white covered tables were ready for the late French Quarter breakfast business. Places were set and sugar bowls, salt and pepper shakers, and honey pitchers awaited the morning gourmets who would come to eat Eggs Benedict, Omelette Apricote, and thin, crisp French pancakes.

Gaston motioned me to a table near the wall. I took the chair facing the door and sat with my back to the kitchen quarters. I laid my bag on my lap and slipped my hand inside of it.

"What would you speak with me about, M'selle?" He asked quietly.

"Murder," I said bluntly.

22. *Unmasking a Murderer*

THE slightest flicker of expression crossed his face, a mere tightening of his lips, an added veiling of his eyes.

"Murder? Of whom, M'selle?"

"Of two people, Gaston. One at the Mardi Gras and one in the first week of Lent."

"I do not understand you."

"I think you do. The first one killed was Annette Jeans, she of the cold hotness of beauty."

"Ah! But of course! She was found near here."

"She was found in the yard that backs up on yours."

"To be sure. In the Pacellis' yard it was. Now, I begin to see what you drive at with me. You think, perhaps, I 'ave seen or heard something that will help you in your business? But you spoke of two who were murdered? I understand the young man has killed himself. You see, M'selle, it was as I told you after all. She destroyed him, but someone destroyed her as well."

"Oh, you were correct enough about it, but I didn't mean Barnett was murdered also. I meant Maurice De André. He was the second victim."

The expression was no mere flicker this time. Fear and shock shone plainly in his sharp black eyes.

"De André! *Mon Dieu!*" He made as if to rise, then sank back in his chair. "He dined here last night and he questioned me about the woman. Once he lunched here with her." His eyes became veiled and cautious again. "He left here about nine. And you say he was murdered?"

"He was indeed. He was knifed in the back within minutes after you say he left here. He was stabbed with a sharp steel steak knife. Just such a knife as Nita picked up from one of your tables Mardi Gras night, Gaston. The same kind exactly."

"*C'est horrible,*" he murmured. "Why 'ave you come to me? Is it because of the things I said about that woman and because a steak knife was used to kill a man? Many cafés have similar knives—"

He stopped abruptly as if struck by a new thought.

"Do you think someone in my café has done these murders? Someone who hated these people?"

"It was someone who hated Nita, all right. But the murder of De André was done because of fear of exposure. So was the attack on Tina."

"Tina? Tina who?"

"The Pacellis' daughter. Christina Pacelli."

"*La p'tite* Christine?" His hands gripped the table edge and the knuckles showed white under the strain. "What is this you say?"

"She was attacked by the killer, Gaston. She saw him that Ash Wednesday morning when he carried his victim's body into her yard. He found out Christina knew and so he attacked her. He tied and gagged her and left her covered with old tarpaulin in an empty warehouse on the river. He meant to return and finish the job but, thank God, the cops found her before he could get back—" I had been watching Gaston narrowly as I spoke words that were plainly an accusation of murder and assault. He was staring at me, pop-eyed.

"*P'tite* Christine attacked! That child attacked. No, this is too much!"

"I agree with you," I said acidly. "Why did you do it, Gaston? You seemed—"

"Eh? Me? Why did I do eet?" He half rose from his seat, his accent becoming very pronounced. "Are you mad, M'selle?"

His sincerity seemed so obvious I began to have a small doubt. Then I shoved it aside. Everything led to Gaston. Everything was tied up in a neat package addressed to him. He had to be the one.

"No, I'm not mad. But you are. Oh, come off it Gaston, every shred of evidence points right to you." I curved my finger around the trigger of the revolver in my bag. "Nita was a type of woman you had a fixation hatred for and she was killed with a garrote, used in the French method. De André was stabbed with a steak knife like you use here and Tina was gagged with a black silk tie, just like the ones you wear. You may as well tell me the story and you can start with Nita. What was she to you?"

His shoulders slumped. He looked ten years older.

"She was the daughter of Céleste," he said, dully. "The true spawn of a devil."

"Céleste?"

"Oui. The one of whom I spoke to you, that one of so many years ago."

"The woman she reminded you of and—oh say! Was she *your* daughter?"

"Mine? *Mon Dieu, non!* She was not of my seed."

"Well, then why—?"

"She was Céleste's own image. I knew it could be none other than she when she first came to my café. She was a true daughter of a mother who gloated in making men suffer, who made men mad like a drug makes them to be mad."

"So you killed her because she was like her mother. Then you tried to kill Tina and did kill De André My God! You *are* mad."

He looked at me for a full moment and he looked as if he was just beginning to understand the import of my accusations.

"*I* kill them? *I* attack that child? It is *you* who are mad! I did none of these things but I 'ave been crazy enough to

protect the one who did them all. Now, I am *fini. C'est fini.*
I can no longer protect him and he must suffer for his
crimes. The mad man you speak of is—"

"Nevaire mind, *mon ami!* I weel introduce myself!" The
voice came from behind me and it was tense with excitement. I yanked at the gun in my bag.

"Drop your weapon, M'selle," the voice commanded. "I
'ave you covered. One wrong move and I weel keel you
both."

I dropped the gun. I dropped bag and all. I couldn't have
held them anyhow. I was shaking like a leaf. All I could
think was that once again I'd been too smart for my safety.
Tommy was right. Johnny was right. Mother was right. But
why couldn't I have found that out sooner? I sat there pet-
rified and waited for whatever was coming next.

The speaker moved into my line of vision and I got the
surprise of my life. The man who stood before me, a lethal
looking automatic held in his hand, was Gaston's maître d'
hôtel.

"Martin!" I gasped. "My God—"

"*Oui,* M'selle Slone. Martin. You seem much surprised, is
it not?"

Surprised was a mild word. Frankly, I was dumbfounded.
Gaston started to rise from his chair.

"Sit where you are, *mon frère.*" The order rasped harshly
from the lips of the unmasked murderer, the man who had
been masquerading as a head waiter.

The term, "*mon frere,*" struck me like a blow in the face.

"Brother!" I said. "Brother? Well, I'll be damned."

Martin bowed mockingly. "Now you are more surprised.
Allow me to present myself. Martin Villiere, brother of Gaston, owner of Le Coq d'Or. Can you not see how we look
alike?"

Now that I knew the facts, I could indeed see it. A fleet-
ing memory skipped through my rattled brain. Damned if I
hadn't noticed it before! I clearly remembered thinking at

least once that Martin looked enough like Gaston to be his brother.

"You may look alike but you don't talk or think alike," I said, hoping my voice sounded steady and flippant.

"I 'ave more of accent, perhaps?"

"Much more. And you go around killing people. That's bad."

"Bad? Not always. It is sometimes necessary to kill in order to save yourself."

I studied the killer, seeing him as a person and not as a suave maître d'hôtel. He was younger than Gaston by about ten years. His eyes held the gleam of the homicidal maniac. I wished I was home.

"So you are *fini* wiz me, *mon frère?*" He turned to Gaston, but kept a wary eye on me.

"I am." Gaston's voice was calmly controlled.

Martin began speaking in rapid French, not one word of which I caught. He spoke for some time and when he stopped talking he ended on a ugly laugh that jarred clear through me.

Gaston's answer to the long diatribe was delivered quietly and in English.

"You 'ave killed once too often, Martin. You are insane if you think you can get away with two more murders. The police are not fools. If you kill us, you are indeed lost."

The meaning of the last sentence struck like a cold knife of fear at my heart. I began to shake again. Gaston went on speaking.

"You say that I hate you, Martin. That I 'ave hated you since you became Céleste's lover. I did not hate you for that. I did not hate you or blame you for killing her—"

"Killing her? Céleste? Christ Almighty—another one?"

"No, M'selle. The same one. Céleste, the mother of—"

"Yes, I understand. I mean he committed another murder as well as these two."

"Ah, *oui*, M'selle." There was a slight note of pride in

Martin's voice. "I was ze last man Céleste made a fool. Ze—very—last—wan. And zen came Annette, so like ze mama eet was as if Céleste had come from her grave to torture me. I knew I mus' send her back or I will nevaire know peace again. I knew, ze firs' time she comes here zat I mus' use on her ze garrote jus' as I 'ave use eet on Céleste."

"Of course." I knew we were dealing with a mad man and I'd always heard you must humor one. "Of course you had to kill Annette. But you shouldn't have hurt poor little Tina and killed De André. What did they ever do to you?"

I was talking against time, although I had no idea what time it was and I didn't dare take my eyes off Martin to look at my watch. I knew it must be getting on toward the hour when the kitchen help, at least, had to be coming in to work. If I could only keep him talking until someone came in and sounded the alarm.

"Christine did nothing to me. But she was a danger. I found out she had seen me hide Annette's body. All the neighborhood knew of her engagement with you." He was simply stating facts and as he grew calmer his French accent dropped off to where it was not much more apparent than Gaston's.

"But you didn't kill Tina," I said. "Why not?"

"I was in a hurry and knew I could not stay long enough away to be missed from here. It was near cocktail time. I had sent her a note in your name to meet you by the docks instead of at home."

"You knew that secret stuff would appeal to the child!" I shuddered at the grisly premeditation of the act.

"*Mais certainement.* I waited for her, just inside the warehouse door. When she comes, I grab her and pull her in. She screams once and I gagged her wiz my tie. I had meant to use it for other things."

I knew too well what he meant by the last two words. I shivered again.

"I heard a car come in near the warehouse and grew a

bit frightened. I knew I could not wait there until dark, when I could dispose of her body. So I tied her up and hid her under some tarpaulin. I meant to go back after dark and finish my job. I did not wish to kill her, but it was necessary."

"But you didn't go back?"

"Of course, I did! Zat is where I keel De André who is wan beeg fool!" The accent was coming back with his excitement. "I 'ave heard every word he says with Gaston and when he leaves I follow him to ze door, jus' as if I am bowing him out. But I whisper to him to meet me at ze dock and I weel tell him all he wishes to know. He is waiting—"

"For a knife thrust in the back," I interrupted. And thought: God, won't anyone ever get here?

Martin shrugged. "*Oui.* I cannot spare my tie I am wearing and ze knife was quicker. I look for Tina, but she is gone. I came back to ze café as if nossing has happen."

"Weren't you worried when you found Tina was gone?"

"Some, yes. But I soon feel zat if no one has come looking for me then no one knows who I am. I ask about her from people in the block and learn she is not able to speak. Her parents 'ave told everyone what has been done."

"But she will be able to speak again." I forgot my fright in anger. "She'll speak as soon as she finds out the police have got you in the can!"

"You are a fool, M'selle." He spat on the floor. "As beeg a fool as De André who also is playing at being a *gendarme.* Ze *gendarmes,* weel not catch me." His eyes glittered insanely and I shrank back against the wall.

"Of course not, Martin. You're too smart for them." My laugh sounded as hollow as a vacuum. I had a sudden vision of Nita's bloated features as I'd seen them that morning. I groped for words to try and give him the idea I was his friend.

"Look, Martin. You know I'm a reporter and after you get

away I can write a good story about you, so everyone will know how smart you are and how you put it over on the police. I have no use for cops and I can help you get away. I know just how—" My voice trailed off as his expression told me just how silly my words sounded to him.

"You mus' take me for a fool, M'selle, if you think I would believe that fairy tale."

"You are insane, *mon frère*." Gaston leaned toward his brother. "If you give yourself up, the doctors will know you are crazy and you will not hang."

"Give myself up? Phoo!" He spit in Gaston's face.

Gaston shrank back and wiped the spittle from his cheeks. He sighed heavily.

"Once before you spat in my face," he said, softly. "I said if you ever did it again I would kill you."

Martin laughed crazily. "But it is I who weel keel you! You and M'selle Slone. Ze *gendarmes* weel learn you are ze wan who pays Annette's bills in Canada and of De André coming here. You weel be found dead wiz a gun in your hand and M'selle beside you, shot wiz ze same gun. Christine weel believe it was you she saw in ze yard and in ze warehouse. Ze light was not good and we look alike. I weel be mos' disturb, but, after all, I am only your employee. No wan weel suspect me of such crimes, not when zey find ze carnage here. Zey weel believe you commit zem all and shoot yourself."

My nerves tore apart like raveled threads.

"You're a fool, Martin!" I screamed at him. "You'll never get away with it. You're a cold-blooded murderer and two more killings won't save your rotten carcass from the hangman. They'll get you and you'll hang. You'll hang, do you hear? Hang by the neck until dead!"

I stopped and watched in cold terror as his finger slowly tightened on the trigger. The explosion would come any moment. I wondered what it felt like to get shot. Then instinct asserted itself and I dived for the floor. A bomb went off in my ear, something hit me with a terrific force and a stab of pain went through my right shoulder. Just before I passed out, I heard the sound of several shots and in that last moment of consciousness I had a curiously unselfish thought: Poor Gaston, how awful to be killed by his own brother.

23. *Another Sorry Story*

~~~~~~

I CAME to amid a babel of voices and the sound of general confusion.

"Lift the table off of her," someone said.

"Morrow, get some water." Another voice ordered.

"Get it yourself, I'm staying with her." That voice was Johnny's.

"Is she hurt, M'sieu?" I was a little surprised to hear *that* voice. Surprised and thankful.

"I don't think so. Just scared into a faint." That had to be Beton, the lug.

"Damned little fool. I hope this teaches her a lesson." This time it was Gross.

"Darling, speak to me. Margaret, sweetheart—" Ah! *That* was Johnny again.

Someone put a glass of water to my lips and spilled most of it down my neck. I opened my eyes and looked around at the circle of faces. Johnny helped me sit up and then lifted me to a chair.

"Hello," I said, in a small voice. "I'm glad you guys got here. I was in a little trouble."

"Little!" Gross snorted. "You damn near got your head blown off. Why can't you leave the business of catching killers to the police?"

"You said I was nuts when I told you the killer was here," I retorted tartly.

"I said nothing of the kind. Besides, you thought it was Gaston. We knew better. *We* being the police. We had all the evidence we needed with the knife and that black silk tie. But you were so smart you had it pinned on Gaston."

"You mean to tell me you knew when I talked to you that Martin was the murderer?"

Tommy looked a little sheepish. "Well, not just then. But we knew it soon after. The tie was handmade and it looked like convent work. We took a chance and checked the Little Sisters of the Poor and found a nun who made ties to order for Martin. She identified it as the one of a set she had made for him. The knife was no trouble to trace. Only one supply house in town carries that make and they sold them to just three restaurants in the city. The other two were uptown and that let them out."

"That still doesn't explain how you knew, even before you traced the tie and knife, that Gaston was not guilty."

"We weren't sure about that. But after you broke the story of the phonograph we checked the area again. We had seen those scratches on the gate bolt and it didn't take us long to find out whose yard was on the other side of the gate. We put a tail on Gaston right away and we knew he hadn't left his place at any time during the hours that Tina was attacked and De André killed. De André gave us enough information to check Nita's background and we knew Gaston had paid her convent bills. Until Tina was attacked we did suspect him. But he wasn't out of sight of one of our men since we found where that gate led, so he couldn't have been Tina's attacker."

"Well! You might have let me in on it. You'd have saved me a bad scare. Gaston and I could both have been killed by that maniac."

"We have been hiding in the kitchen ever since you came here. We got in just as you sat down at the table with Gaston and we'd have taken Martin sooner but we wanted to hear his confession."

"Martin—?"

Tommy motioned to a corner of the room where a silent figure lay under white table cloths. I looked from it to

Gaston. His chin was sunk on his chest. I reached over and touched his hand. His anguish was so apparent that tears of pity stung my eyelids.

"I'm sorry, Gaston. And forgive me for suspecting you."

He looked at me out of eyes clouded with pain.

"Your suspicions were only natural, M'selle. Even the police had the suspicions of me. My grief comes from knowing that the years of protecting Martin were wasted years."

"Care to tell us something about those years?" Tommy asked.

"Why not? They go back to our boyhood in France. Martin was the younger but when I went to Paris to the Ecole de Cuisine to study to be a chef, Martin accompanied me and attended day school there. I was working as second chef in a fine café in Paris when I met Céleste in 1908. She was a young widow, with an infant girl. I was just twenty-four; Martin was eighteen.

"I had known Céleste only three months when she became my mistress. She did not wish marriage, though I begged her to be my wife. I learned her husband had committed suicide. Martin was then going to the Ecole de Cuisine and he lived with us. For three years we had many happy times, then she began to look at the boy as a man and soon she was playing us, one against the other.

"One day, early in 1912, I came in and found them in each other's arms. I cannot remember all I said but I found they had been lovers for almost a year. I threatened to kill them and myself. She laughed in my face and told me to leave the house and drown myself in the Seine as her husband and two of her lovers had already done. I struck her and Martin spat in my face.

"I rushed out of the house, intending to commit suicide but I met a friend who had known Céleste since she was a child. He told me I was fortunate she had thrown me out, that I must save myself by leaving Paris and never seeing her again. Unlike the young man who came here with

Annette, I listened to his words and that night I left Paris and went to Cherbourg. I engaged as a chef for one trip on a steamer and landed in Boston. I arrived with nothing but the money I had drawn from the bank and one extra suit and oddments of clothing.

"In 1914, I came to New Orleans and purchased Le Coq d'Or and in 1916 Martin arrived. He had traced me, he said, through friends in France with whom I had correspondence. At first, I told him to go, that I wished to have nothing to do with him, that four years had not been long enough for me to forget what he and Céleste had done to me. He plead with me to forgive and forget. He said I must give him sanctuary. I asked what he means by that word and he told me he has killed Céleste and put Annette in a convent in Normandy. He fled France on a freighter and landed at Baton Rouge.

"I could not turn him away then. He was my brother and I had to protect him. He had the fear of the hunted and wished to work as a waiter. He said no one notices the waiter and that is the job he takes first. As the years go by, he becomes filled with the feeling of security and finally he takes the duties of my maître d'hôtel. As the years went by without discovery, we both ceased to worry."

"Don't you know you broke the law by protecting him?" Tommy asked.

"He was my brother," Gaston repeated, doggedly. "I could not send him to the guillotine."

"But when the money for the girl's board was sent, didn't you ever worry for fear the police would trace him here by the drafts? Didn't the child know he had killed her mother?"

"She knew. He bought her silence with a new dress, hat, and shoes. *Mon Dieu!* It is hard to believe that even at six she was so heartless and cold."

"Six?" Tommy asked. "Wasn't she older than that?"

"*Non,* M'sieu. It was in 1914 that Martin killed Céleste

but he did not come to me until 1916. He worked as a waiter in Baton Rouge until he found courage to approach me."

"It's odd the child never said anything all through the years of her stay in the convent."

"Martin had told her he would always take care of her if she never told the police of what he had done. He hoped, in time, she would forget what he looked like and what his name was."

"Likely she did," I put in. "De André told me she did not know who was her protector. How come you sent the money instead of Martin?"

"He wished me to take care of it. I realized it gave him an additional security and I knew if anyone did come I could always prove my innocence of Céleste's murder. I had not been in France since 1912."

"When did the nun take Annette to Canada?" I asked.

"In 1921. But how do you know of this?"

"De André told me. He told me something which may explain how Nita came to ferret you out, too." I related the story of the check the sister had tried to hide. "She must have seen that it came from New Orleans and she said she saw the first name."

"Ah, that is how she came here! She knew or remembered Martin had been in the café business. She sought out the French cafés until she found this one. When she came the first time, I thought I was seeing a ghost, so like the mother she was. Martin saw the likeness, too. From that night, he was like one frantic with fear. But she gave no hint of knowing either of us until Mardi Gras night. You recall, do you not, M'selle, how she spoke to me when she was leaving?"

"Yes, indeed. I also recall how insistent you were about not knowing her."

"I knew then for certain who she was and that she must have some knowledge or suspicion of me. Until then, I had hoped it was a chance likeness. I meant to make Martin leave the city, but she came that night just as I was closing. She thought I was Martin, she had been too young to remember his brother who also was her mother's lover. She told me she had spent years tracing me and threatened me with the police. I could not explain her mistake without exposing Martin."

"Still protecting your brother."

"*Oui,* M'selle. At last she talks of money. For five thousand she will keep still and she said that was letting me off easy. I agreed to give it to her, but told her I had not that much cash. She said a check would do and she followed me to my office in the back of the dining rooms.

"There was a bottle of brandy on the tabouret and she poured a drink and took a chair with her back to the door. She sipped the brandy and talked as I got out my check book and began to pay her the first of her blood money. I knew it would not end with one check. I had just blotted the check when I heard a strange, gurgling sound and I turned to see Martin tightening the garrote cord about her throat."

"My God! And you sat there and watched him kill her?"

"I was like one paralyzed. I tried to call out, to move, but I could not do either. When I could—it was too late. She was dead. I could feel no sorrow for her death, even I felt some relief, M'selle. Martin carried her outside, opened the gate with a screw driver, and hid the body under the burlap bags in the Pacellis' yard."

"And Christina saw him do it. So he tried to kill her."

"I expect so. But I knew nothing of this and nothing of De André's murder until you told me. It was when I learned of these things I knew I must tell the truth, that I could no longer protect my brother. I knew he had gone mad and to kill meant nothing to him."

He leaned back wearily and closed his eyes.

"That is all I know and all of the story. I suppose I am

guilty of hiding him from the police and, in some measure, of Annette's murder. I am ready to be arrested, M'sieu."

Tommy shook his head.

"This has been rough on you, Villiere. I know it can't be fun to find out your maître d'hôtel was a killer and then have him get shot in your café. You better take a vacation, go away somewhere for a couple of weeks."

Everyone gaped at the detective, open-mouthed. I gulped down a lump that had somehow found its way into my throat.

"You mean, M'sieu—?"

"Tommy, you're not going to—?"

"I'm not going to do anything." Tommy said flatly. "The case is closed. The man who did the killings is dead. It's just too bad he had to work here. It might make some unpleasant publicity for the café, but that's *all.*"

"You're a peach, Tommy," I said and put out my hand toward him. The movement sent a sharp pain shooting through my shoulder and I winced. "Damn, my shoulder hurts." I put my hand on my right shoulder and it came away sticky. I thought: My God! I've been shot!

For the second time that morning I did a pass out.

24. *Bowed—But Unbloody*

WHEN I came to I was on the floor again and someone had tossed a whole pitcher of water on me. The circle of faces was gazing at me again and I was resting in the circle of Morrow's arms. I smiled weakly.

"Did—did you call the ambulance? Am I—Am I bleeding much?"

"Bleeding?" Johnny sounded bewildered. "You aren't bleeding at all."

"I am so bleeding. I felt the blood on my shoulder. It, it was sticky."

"Sticky?" Morrow rubbed his hand on my right shoulder and stuck a finger in his mouth. Then he roared. I sat up and glared at him.

"What's so damned funny?"

"Blood!" He choked out the word. "That isn't blood, honey—it's HONEY!"

"HONEY?" I grabbed at my shoulder and then tasted my fingers. Then I sat on the floor while my pals, including Gaston, rocked with laughter.

"Well, don't stand around laughing like a pack of hyenas," I snapped. "Help me up, one of you."

Johnny got up, still howling and held out a hand.

"Not you," I said. "You get away from me."

He picked me up from the floor anyhow and I sat down on a chair.

"I don't care what you think, my shoulder hurts like hell." I glared around at the group. Every member of it was chuckling heartily I thought bitterly: My friends!

239

"The table fell on you when you dived for the floor," Tommy explained. "There was a pitcher of honey on it and it must have spilled on you. And you thought—" He went off into another gale of uncontrollable glee.

"Have your fun, have your fun," I said acidly. "Someday it will be my turn to laugh."

"Oh, come on, Margaret," Tommy wiped the tears from his face. "Be a sport and admit it's funny as hell."

I thought it over for a second and the next I was laughing louder than any of them.

"I 'ave sent home the kitchen help and closed for a time," Gaston said, "but I can still remember how to make Eggs Benedict and *Café Brûle*. Shall I go to make them for us all?"

I looked to see what Tommy was going to say and read agreement in his eyes. Gaston bustled out to the kitchen and soon came back with platters of eggs in sherry sauce and the Brûle bowl. We set to with appetites like starving people. That is, all of us did but Gaston. He sat and toyed with his food and sipped his coffee. Gaston looked completely beat. I leaned impulsively toward him.

"Come on and eat, Gaston," I said, softly. "You must try to forget what has happened and carry on."

The words were hardly out of my mouth when the doorbell rang. It was the men from the morgue who had come to take Martin's body away. Tommy had seen to its removal to the kitchen and until the men arrived I'd forgot about its still being there.

Gaston watched them dumbly as they went through with the big basket and returned carrying their grisly weight. Gaston made as if to rise from his seat, but Tommy, who was sitting on the other side of him, pressed him gently back into the chair.

"There is nothing for you to do now, Villiere," he said. "You can make arrangements to bury your maître d'hôtel later, if you wish."

"Ah, yes. My maître d'hôtel," Gaston said quietly and tonelessly.

The business of the basket had spoiled my appetite and I pushed my plate away. As I shoved at it I caught a glimpse of my watch. It said nine-five. I groaned and Johnny looked at me inquiringly.

"What's the matter? Does your shoulder hurt that bad?"

"It's not my shoulder this time. It's my conscience. Do you know what time it is? Dennis will scalp me." I showed him my watch.

"Cripes! I'll get scalped too." He jumped from the chair. "I'll go with you as far as my sheet. Come on."

"We're beating it," I told Tommy.

"Okay, kids, behave yourselves. I've been hearing things about you two."

I turned brick red. "Don't believe everything you hear," I flung the words back at him as we moved toward the door.

I climbed in my car and Johnny got in beside me. As we pulled away from the curb he asked, softly, "Why not stop fighting me, honey?"

"I'm not fighting with you," I answered.

"You know what I mean. You're my girl and you may as well own up to it and start acting sensibly."

"I'm not your girl. I'm not going to be either. You can't run my life and tell me what kind of stories to cover. I'm a reporter and I mean to remain one."

"I only want you to stop putting yourself in danger, that's all. You could have been killed this morning. My God! It gives me the willies just to think about it."

I went all soft inside, but I kept my mouth firmly shut.

"As soon as you pulled out of the press room I went down to get Tommy," he told me. "I knew you were headed for trouble and I'd heard enough of your conversation with Rosa to know where you were going. I caught Tommy just as he was clinching things and getting ready to leave. We waited outside for you and when you got in your car we followed. We went around to the kitchen entrance and got in through a window. Then we hid. When Martin came down the back stairs from his room above, he passed so close to us we could have touched him."

"Why didn't you take him then? Why give him a chance to kill again?"

"Oh, he was covered from the minute we saw him. Both Gross and Beton had the drop on him. Tommy wanted to hear what he had to say. We sure got an earfull, but you were under protection all the time."

"Protection my eye! He certainly shot at me."

"I know—and thank God you had sense enough to dive for the floor. That bullet entered the wall just even with where your chest had been a moment before. Tommy fired right after he took that shot at you and then Beton started shooting too. He almost winged Gaston."

"Which would have been typical of that dumb flatfoot."

"He could have hit you too. Any of those wild shots could have killed you. If that had happened I—"

We had reached the street where Morrow worked. I braked the car and pulled in to the curb.

"This is where you get out. And stop worrying about me. I like murder stories. I even read murder mysteries."

"Yeah, I know. But Morgan is back on the job now and I hope Elison stays angry with you and Dennis has sense enough to keep you off the police beat."

"Elison isn't going to be angry with me much longer," I said with large assurance. "I mean to go see him today and apologize and tell him I have found out how wrong I was and that I'm sure he is a much better chief than Gross and much more co-operative."

Morrow groaned. "Of course you know he laps that stuff up on a saucer. Well, I guess you'll be around from time to time, then. At that, I do sort of miss you when you stay out of the press room for too long a stretch. But I wish you just came to see me."

"Do you, really? That's fine. Now scram. I've got to beat it."

He opened the car door and climbed out. "Okay, but remember you have a date with me at noon."

"Says you."

"Says me. You've got to collect that dough you won. I'll be waiting for you—in the back booth."

I started the car and drove off toward the paper, but a sudden thought of Tina turned me in the direction of the hospital. I went in and found out in what room the child was quartered and went up to it. The nurse was sitting by the bed and came to the door. I told her what had happened and she said she would tell the doctor at once. Tina was sleeping, she told me, and the doctor would take care of everything.

I drove from the hospital to headquarters and went looking for Elison. He glowered at me when I first walked in his office but, as Johnny had said, he lapped up my flattery and I soon had him purring like a contented cat. Then I went to the press room and called Dennis.

"Where the devil are you?" he shouted. "You get over here and fast. I just want to fire you, that's all." The receiver clicked in my ear.

I shrugged and went back to my car. I knew that as soon as Dennis heard the story he wouldn't fire me at all. When I strolled up to his desk he just looked at me.

"Now just keep your pants on until I finish telling you why I'm so late and why I didn't call before now," I said, pleadingly. "If you'll just listen—"

"I'm listening." He couldn't have been terser.

I told him the tale and I wasn't well under way before he began to show interest. When I finished, he leaned back and grinned at me.

"That's a good yarn, Maggie. It had to be good too, for darned if I wasn't set to fire you this time. And this time I meant it to stick."

"It wouldn't have stuck," I said blandly. "And Dennis, please don't pay any attention to anything Gross or Morrow says to you about keeping me off police."

"Why not? What are they going to say?"

"Oh, they're getting some crazy ideas about having to protect me—or something."

"Gross had to rescue you this morning, didn't he?"

"Well, yes. But you know I'm a darn good police reporter and I like to cover the beat when I can. Elison isn't sore at me anymore. I just fixed that nicely."

"Oh, you did, eh? And now that you've solved another murder, I guess your head will be so swelled no one can stand you around here."

I gazed at him blankly.

"Since I did what? Why, I didn't solve this murder. I thought Gaston had done it and it was Martin all the time. I was completely surprised when I found that out."

Too late I realized I'd spoken too hastily. Half-hour later derisive laughter was still ringing in my ears and every time I looked at Dennis he broke out with a whoop. I looked just then and he started roaring again.

"Miss Sherlock! Brother, this *is* a treat!"

"Oh, shut up and let me get this work done," I snapped. "I've a long feature to do. What do you want for thirty-five bucks a week—a detective as well as a reporter? Now stop riding me. I have a date at noon—in the back booth of Nick's. A date to hear silver bells."